CHASING THE SUN

CARRIE ELKS

Pushing open his office door with one hand, Jackson Lewis used the other to loosen his perfectly knotted tie. He sighed with relief as it came unraveled and he unfastened the top button of his white shirt, enjoying the freedom it gave him to finally breathe.

He hated wearing suits. Or any formal wear. He felt so much more at home in the jeans and t-shirts he usually wore in the office. But as the owner of Lewis Security Systems, when it came to visiting clients he had no choice. They wanted to know the company they paid to manage their cyber security was led by somebody serious. If it took a suit and tie to persuade them, then that's what he'd do.

His assistant, Lisa looked up from her desk, shaking her head as he undid the rest of his buttons and shrugged off his shirt.

"What did I say about stripping in the office?" she asked, her mouth lifting into a grin. "I don't want to see that kind of thing."

"I'm wearing a t-shirt underneath." Jackson threw his shirt onto the hook by the door. He stopped by her desk and ran his hand through his thick, dark hair. "Did I miss anything while I was out?"

"About a thousand phone calls and a million emails. The usual. I've marked anything urgent in your inbox." Lisa had been working for him for five years. Previously, she'd worked at Newton Pharmaceuticals, the main employer in their small California beach town of Angel Sands. He'd poached her from Newtons at the same time he'd left the pharmaceutical company to start up his own business, knowing despite her penchant for mothering him, he couldn't run this office without her. "Have you had a chance to look at those résumés I sent you?"

"What résumés?" he asked, walking over to the coffee machine. "You want one?" he asked, as he grabbed a mug.

"The résumés I sent you last week." Shaking her head, she pushed her desk chair back on its wheels and stood. "And I'm supposed to be getting *you* coffee. You have this whole boss-employee thing backward."

He ignored her and poured a second cup, passing it to her. "Consider it an apology for not reviewing the résumés."

"You really need some more staff. We can't go on like this." Lisa sighed, following him to his desk. "You're working seven days a week. I feel exhausted just watching you."

"I know. I get it. I just haven't had time to recruit and train anybody." He took a sip of his coffee, closing his eyes as the bitter liquid ran down his throat. "It's a catch-twenty-two situation."

Right now, Lewis Security Systems employed seven people. Jackson, Lisa, plus five programmers who mostly preferred to work from home, though they came into the office once a week for a team meeting. But even with everybody working every waking hour, they couldn't keep up with the demand for their services. In the past few years, he'd grown a reputation for creating unbeatable security systems.

Which was why he wasn't only wearing damn suits to meetings, but on the weekends he was in front of his laptop, programming like the rest of them.

It didn't give him a lot of time for anything else.

"If you give me a shortlist, I'll do the first interviews," Lisa suggested. "After that, I'll arrange for three of them to come and meet you. It'll take half a morning at the most. And think of all the time it'll save you in the long run. You need some free time. You're a man in his prime." She shrugged.

He grinned. "Thanks. I think."

"Seriously though, please look at them."

"I will." He promised. "Was there any other urgent calls?"

"Your mom." Lisa grimaced. "She wants you to call her back. I told her you were in meetings all day."

Jackson sighed. "Did she say what she wanted?" Not that he needed to ask. It was always about money. He had it and she needed it. Theirs was the ultimate transactional relationship. He wouldn't be surprised if she started demanding mortgage payments for the fact she'd rented him womb space thirty-three years ago.

"No, but I didn't ask either. I cut her off, to be honest. Sorry." Lisa wrinkled her nose.

"You don't need to apologize. She's my problem, not yours."

Lisa gave a huff. "Yeah well, mothers shouldn't be anybody's problem."

Maybe not. But Jackson's mom had been trouble since she'd walked out on him and his dad when he was ten years old. Since then, she'd flitted in and out of their lives whenever she was bored. Or whenever her bank balance dipped perilously low. It used to be his father that she'd targeted, but thankfully now it was Jackson. He could deal with her, he wasn't sure his dad could.

"I'll call her back some time." Probably not before she called him again. "Anything else I should know about?"

"Your friend Griff called. He sounded stressed, which is strange for him." She smiled dreamily. "He's always so laid back. And handsome."

Jackson swallowed a laugh. He'd been best friends with Griff since they'd started kindergarten. Along with their friends, Lucas and Breck, they'd formed a tight gang of four, spending their summers on the surf in Angel Sands, and their winters plotting how to get out of school and spend even more time on the waves.

Nowadays, Griff ran a whale watching company in Angel Sands and had recently become a father. Like Breck and Lucas, he was happily coupled-up, leaving Jackson the only one who was single.

And happy that way, he might add.

"Maybe the baby's keeping him awake," Jackson said, making a face at Lisa, who laughed. Griff and Autumn's baby, Skyler, was almost four months old now, but according to Griff she slept like a newborn. Jackson took his word for it. He had no idea about babies at all. Wasn't planning on learning any time soon, either. He lost enough sleep working, as it was.

Nope, being an almost-uncle to his friends' kids was enough for him. And now he was going to be a godfather, thanks to Griff and Autumn's request. He was still trying to work out why they'd chosen him.

Maybe some puzzles were better left unsolved.

"Thanks," he said, swallowing a mouthful of coffee. "I'll call him back now."

Placing his cup on his desk – and narrowly avoiding the dark liquid sloshing over onto some accounts he was supposed to approve last week – Jackson picked up his phone and clicked on Griff's contact.

"Hey," Griff's voice was larger than life, like the rest of him. "Thanks for calling back."

"You okay?" Jackson asked him. "Lisa said you sounded stressed."

Griff laughed. "I'm not stressed. I just have a favor to ask."

"Is it your laptop again? I keep telling you that thing belongs in a museum. I can get you a new one at a discount any time."

"Nah, the laptop's fine. I only use it for email anyway. Autumn does everything else on her computer." While Griff ran a whale watching company, Autumn owned the pier where it was based. She'd bought it sight unseen, and moved to Angel Sands from New York, surprising everybody, but most of all herself. And now she was part of the gang, and Jackson was delighted his friend had found someone so perfect to spend the rest of his life with.

"So it's not the laptop." Jackson grinned. "Please don't ask me to babysit. You know I'll end up hurting somebody."

Griff laughed. "Nope. You need to go through godfather boot camp before I let you loose with my kid. I was just wondering if you're free on Saturday. Autumn's sister's flying in from New York, but I've got a charter and Autumn's supposed to be meeting with the caterers for Skyler's naming day. I was hoping you could head over to the airport to pick Lydia up."

Griff and Autumn had decided on a naming celebration for their daughter, instead of a traditional christening. The ceremony on the pier would be a chance for all their friends and family to officially welcome Skyler into their fold. And of course, it was a great excuse for a party. Not that they usually needed an excuse.

"Lydia's coming early?" Jackson had only met Autumn's

sister twice, but she'd made a big impression. She was like a whirlwind, kicking up the dust of Angel Sands.

"She wants to spend time with Autumn and the baby. Says she's staying for just under two weeks. I'll believe it when I see it."

Another thing that fascinated him about Lydia. She never stayed anywhere for long. Blink and you'd miss her. She had a good excuse, being a travel consultant, but it didn't stop him from being intrigued.

"Well, I'm happy to pick her up." Jackson tried to push down all the thoughts of the programming he had to do this weekend. He'd just have to miss a night's sleep or something. "Message me the flight details and I'll be there."

"That's great." Griff exhaled loudly. "Autumn was panicking. She needs to be at the pier for this meeting. And I can't really turn down the charter, it's for a longstanding client."

Griff cleared his throat. The silence that followed made Jackson's brows lift up. "There's one other thing I want to ask you," Griff finally mumbled, as though he didn't want to ask.

"What?" Jackson grinned at his friend's reluctance.

"I know you wouldn't, but just in case you're thinking about it, please don't hit on her. She's important to Autumn, and like a sister to me. I know you have a thing for blondes, but not this one, okay?"

That's what you got for letting your friends think you were constantly playing the field. Like so many lies, it had started off as a truth. After coming out of a long – and frankly toxic – engagement, it'd felt natural to play the field and have a good time for a while. After a couple of years, when his friends started to settle down, one by one, it had become a good shield against their attempts to get him to do the same.

'Ember works with this great girl. She's single, you should meet her. Maybe we could double date.'

'My cousin's flying in from Atlanta next week. She saw a photo of you and is interested. Do you want her number?'

'You should really think about settling down with somebody. You're not getting any younger. Don't you want a family?'

Yeah, well settling down was fine for his friends. But Jackson knew how it ended. He'd had a ringside seat at the implosion of his parents' marriage. So he'd let his friends think he was a player. The kind they definitely *didn't* want to introduce to their sisters or cousins.

And now here it was, biting him on the butt.

"I'm not going to hit on Lydia," he promised, shaking his head. Lisa let out a laugh, and he glared at her. She lifted her hands and turned back to her laptop, but he could still see her shoulders shaking.

He'd deal with her later.

An image of Lydia flickered into Jackson's mind. He remembered the way she looked the last time he'd seen her when she'd flown in for Skyler's birth. He'd been working from six in the morning until ten at night that week, trying to put together a proposal for a total security system for a company in White City, and he'd only managed to see her briefly as he ran into the hospital to give Autumn and Griff a baby gift.

Lydia had been sitting next to Autumn, holding her tiny niece in her arms, her expression full of love as she stared down at the tiny bundle. She'd looked up and seen Jackson, and her lips had broken into a huge grin. In a different life, maybe he'd have flirted with her. Seen what was there.

But Griff was right. He wasn't dating material, and there was no way he was going to enrage his best friend.

Jackson wedged his phone between his shoulder and ear, switching on his laptop. "Send me the flight details and I'll be there," he promised, again.

"Thanks, man." Griff had the good grace to sound embarrassed. "I appreciate it."

After he ended the call, Jackson took a sip of coffee and opened up his emails, wincing when he saw a hundred of them awaiting his attention. He didn't have time to think about Lydia Paxton, or anything else for that matter. He had way too much work for that.

He'd pick her up from the airport, bring her home to Autumn and Griff, and forget all about her. Because sometimes life was simpler that way.

2

W alking toward the sliding double doors leading to the arrivals lounge, Lydia shifted a giant teddy bear in her arms, and pulled her oversized suitcase behind her, smiling when she saw the shafts of sunlight beaming through the glass wall of the airport.

This was the part of traveling she loved. Arriving in a city and soaking up the atmosphere. And if the sun was shining, all the better. She wrinkled her nose when she remembered one particular visit to London where it had rained for four-teen days. Not a shaft of sunlight at all. Thank goodness those Brits knew how to do museums.

The sun seemed to shine for ninety-nine percent of the time in California, and that was something she was thankful for. With only two weeks between jobs, this was her one chance this year at a break.

Which was wild, really, because her whole job revolved around vacations. Other people's vacations. She planned them, escorted them, and made sure they had the holiday of a lifetime. As much as she loved her career, it was exhausting, too.

Even Vacation Specialists needed time off.

The teddy bear's leg got caught on the doorjamb, and she had to tug hard to release his furry limb. He'd been a liability since she'd stepped into JFK that morning.

It was a good thing she loved her baby niece. Otherwise this bear might not make it to Angel Sands.

Her phone beeped. She pulled it from her pocket to see a message from her sister, Autumn. There were only a few years between them, but since they'd grown up without a mother, Autumn was definitely the caregiver in their relationship.

And now she was a mom to baby Skyler. Lydia beamed brightly. She couldn't wait to see her niece – the last time she visited Skyler had only been a few days old. How could she be nearly five months already? Time was passing too fast.

Hope you landed okay! Sorry I can't be there, but Jackson promised to drive safely. I'll see you at home. Can't wait! An xx

Lydia tapped out a quick reply and picked up her case and the teddy. She could barely see where she was going, thanks to the thick, soft furry animal who was obscuring her view. The sooner she gave him to Skyler, the better.

Somehow, she managed to maneuver her way through the baggage terminal, and through the sliding glass doors to the arrivals terminal without any catastrophes. She was just about to congratulate herself when the suitcase hit something, and her foot caught on a tile, sending her – and the teddy bear – flying onto the hard floor in front of her.

Except it wasn't hard. It was soft. *Too soft*. Her eyes widened in horror when she realized she'd barreled a young boy over with her.

"Oh my god, are you okay?" she asked him.

The little boy's lips wobbled. Her pulse raced as she realized he was about to cry.

"Let me help you up," she said, holding her hand out to

him. People were giving them a wide birth now, creating a pool of empty floor in the middle of the crowd.

"Does anything hurt? Your legs, your arms?" Where were his parents? She looked around for some responsible adults, because god knew she was anything but.

He started to sob, and her panic increased. She never could stand to make anybody cry. "Hey," she said. "Have you seen my teddy bear?" She waved the stuffed arm at the boy, hoping to divert him. "Isn't he cute?"

The boy nodded, swallowing his sob. "What's his name?"

The distraction was working. Lydia quickly searched in her mind. "Um, it's Freddie." She nodded. "Freddie the Teddy. He wants to know if you're hurting anywhere."

"It doesn't hurt." The boy sounded calmer, his eyes pinned to the teddy.

"He also wants to know where your parents are," Lydia confided, looking back at the stuffed toy.

"My dad's in New York. My mom's here." The little boy looked around. His lip started to wobble again. "She *was* here," he said, his voice lifting an octave. "Mom? Mom? MOM!!!"

Lydia looked around, her heart in her throat. "What does she look like?"

"She looks like my mom." A sob tore through his voice.

Of course she did. For the next five seconds, while scanning the crowd, Lydia could imagine herself on the front pages. *Travel Expert Causes Child to Lose Parent.*

"Charlie!" a panicked voice called out. "There you are. Oh sweetie, what happened?"

"That bear knocked me over," he said, his sobs making his chest shake. "He hurt me."

"It was me. I'm so sorry. I tripped and caught your son." Lydia looked up guiltily from where she was kneeling next to Charlie on the floor.

"You should look where you're going. He's only four," Charlie's mom said crossly. "Come here, sweetheart, are you hurt?"

He breathed in raggedly. "No," he whispered.

"No thanks to you," his mom said pointedly to Lydia.

"Is there a problem here?"

A pair of muscled, jean-clad legs appeared directly in Lydia's line of vision. She slowly looked up, trying to ignore the way the denim outlined its owner's thigh muscles, closing her eyes as she realized her gaze was threatening to stare right at his crotch.

"Oh!" Charlie's mom breathed, as if she didn't have a care in the world. "No, there's no problem. My son just fell over."

Lydia looked up to see Charlie's mom batting her eyelashes, a smile lighting up her face. She only knew a few men who had that effect on women. Her included, if she was being completely honest. And right now his sculpted thighs were firmly in her personal space.

She swallowed hard when her gaze met Jackson Lewis. Her future brother-in-law's best friend.

"You need some help there?" he asked, reaching his hand down. She took it and he lifted her to her feet.

A blue cap was pulled over what she knew was thick, dark hair. He hadn't shaved today, from the look of it, and the shadow of beard growth only emphasized the lines of his jaw. And she tried really hard not to stare at his lips, despite their perfect shape.

Was it her, or was it warm in here? Someone needed to turn up the air conditioning.

"Come on, Charlie." His mom huffed, sending Lydia one last dirty look. "Your granddad is waiting for us."

Charlie took her hand. "Bye, Freddie" he said, using his free hand to wave goodbye to the teddy.

"Bye," Lydia said gruffly, waving Freddie's stuffed arm at the departing boy.

Jackson sniggered, and she raised an eyebrow at him.

"How did you end up on the floor?" he asked, grabbing her suitcase in his hand.

"I was just, um, taking a rest," she lied. Not that he believed her. She could tell as much from his expression. "All this flying can take it out of you."

"Yeah, I get that." He nodded solemnly. "First thing I do when I get off a plane is sit down in the terminal. It's refreshing."

A laugh escaped from her mouth. "I knew you'd understand."

His fingers flexed on the handle of her case, drawing her eyes to his tanned forearms. A dusting of dark hair covered his warm, brown skin. She liked guys with a bit of hair. Maybe that's why she liked Europe so much. The men there were dark, tanned, and sexy.

Her gaze lifted to his t-shirt. Was there hair on his chest, too? When she looked up to his face, and her eyes met with his, a shot of warmth rushed through her.

"Hi," she said, smiling. "Maybe we can start again and pretend you didn't see me on the ground."

The corner of his lip curled up. "Sure." He let go of her suitcase and held out his hand. "Hi," he said. "I'm Jackson. I'll be your driver today."

She curled her fingers around his, smiling at the strength of his grasp. Why was everything about him so sexy? "Thank you for picking me up. I could have gotten an Uber."

"It's no problem. We're gonna be godparents, we have to stick together. Now you want to pick up your boyfriend? My car's in the short term parking."

"My boyfriend?" she repeated. "I don't have one of those."

"I meant the stuffed toy." He glanced at Freddie the Teddy. "I assume he's yours."

She grabbed Freddie, holding him with her left hand, and slid her other hand through Jackson's arm, curling her fingers around his elbow.

"Yes, he's mine, but hopefully not for too long. I'm hoping to fob him off on Skyler. He's a terrible boyfriend. Keeps flirting with other stuffed toys."

Jackson laughed. "A lothario teddy bear. Now I've seen it all." She felt his bicep flex beneath her fingers. His muscles were hard as steel. "Let's get him home before he causes any more embarrassment, like, you know, throwing himself on the floor."

"Good idea." Lydia nodded, her face straight. "Because that would be embarrassing."

———

Griff should never have told him Lydia was verboten. Because right now, with her wrapped around him like a monkey on a tree trunk, all Jackson could think about was how good she felt.

How amazing she smelled.

And how the hell he was going to stop himself from doing the one thing he'd promised not to.

His grip tightened on her suitcase as he took a deep breath to center himself. It was easy. He was way too busy to do anything but work anyway. He could bury himself in code and goddamn meetings for two weeks, then she'd be gone. That way he wouldn't piss Griff off, and that was a good thing.

He raised an eyebrow when he had to tug hard to pull her suitcase along. "What've you got in there?" he asked. "Dead bodies?"

"Just clothes. And toiletries, plus a few other essentials. After I leave here, I'm heading to Europe. From there to South America. I'll be away for a while, so I need a lot. Anyway, it's rude to mention how heavy a woman's suitcase is." She grinned at him.

He knew Lydia's job was all about traveling. Autumn had told him she was an independent travel consultant. And yeah, he might have occasionally checked her Instagram.

"It is?" Jackson frowned. "How did I miss that one in etiquette class?"

She laughed. "Stop it." Adjusting the ginormous stuffed toy she'd inexplicably brought with her, she curled her hand tighter around his bicep.

"You want me to take that for you?" he asked, inclining his head at the toy as they walked toward the exit doors.

"Nope, I've got him. Just." She wrinkled her nose. "He seemed a lot smaller in New York."

"Maybe he grew on the flight."

"It's all those beers I kept buying him," Lydia said, nodding as they made it to the sliding doors leading out to the concourse. "I'm gonna have to put him on a diet." Her warm eyes met his. "And take him out for bike rides."

He tried – and failed – to suppress a grin at the thought of her cycling with the stuffed toy around town. Walking with her felt like walking with a ray of sun, light and warm. He wanted to bathe in it.

Yeah, and then he'd get burned.

He sighed, and pulled his arm from her hold, pretending to root in his pocket for his keys. "I'm parked in that garage," he said, inclining his head to the left. "If you and your friend want to wait here, I'll go get the car and come pick you up."

"Oh. Sure." She smiled brightly. "But if it's too much trouble I can come with you. I'll even pull my case."

"It's no bother," he told her. He didn't add that he already needed the space from her. Not because she was bothering him, but because he was bothering himself. He only had one job. Take Lydia home to Autumn and Griff and get on with his damn work. It was simple, yet so damn difficult, because she made him think of things he knew he didn't want.

Of soft lips and warm breath. Of hands that caressed and a body that welcomed.

Damn it, this was all Griff's fault. He'd opened Pandora's Box. Made Jackson want things he knew he couldn't have. And even if he could, they weren't good for him.

Maybe it was him who needed to go on a diet. A Lydia Paxton diet.

J ackson was quiet on the drive, as though he had a lot on his mind. Lydia kept herself busy by scrolling through her phone, replying to email enquiries and responding to comments on her Instagram. This time in California was supposed to be a vacation from work. It was crazy, really, that she had to take a vacation from traveling, but that's how her life was. When she was in a foreign country, showing her clients around the sights they wouldn't normally see, it was non-stop. She barely got time to breathe. So she was excited about spending these few days with her sister and her family.

Sending the last email – setting up a video conference with a honeymooning couple she was taking to Rio – she slid her phone into her pocket and smiled up at Jackson.

"So, we're going to be godparents," she said, her voice light. "Isn't that funny?"

He lifted an eyebrow. "Yeah, I guess it is."

"Could they have picked two people less suited?" She smiled to let him know she was teasing. "Poor Skyler's going to grow up thinking we're normal."

Jackson lifted a brow. "I *am* normal."

Oh, she liked the way his voice was teasing. The heaviness that had been pushing down on him seemed to melt into the California air. "You think being a workaholic is normal?" she asked lightly. She'd heard Griff and Autumn talking about his business. All work and some play, but nothing in between.

"More normal than living life as a permanent vacation." His mouth quirked up, as he stared at the road through the windshield.

"I'll have you know vacationing is hard work." She crossed her arms over her chest in mock annoyance. "I haven't had a break in three months."

"So what do you plan to do while you're here?" he asked.

"Spend lots of time with Autumn and Skyler, I guess. And maybe lie on the beach and work on my tan."

"Doesn't look like it needs much work," he told her, glancing at her legs from the corner of his eye.

She bit down a smile. "I guess it's more about the lazing than the tanning." She couldn't wait for a few days of doing nothing. Running the tip of her tongue along her bottom lip, she looked over at him. The sun was shining through the driver's window, illuminating his face. No wonder Charlie's mom had lost all her bite when he'd asked if everything was okay.

Jackson Lewis must have that effect on a lot of people. God knew he was making her skin feel all tingly.

Autumn had told her he was a player. Not that it bothered her. She liked games, too. Especially when they involved a guy as good looking as him.

"Are you planning on doing any work?" he asked her, his eyes meeting hers again.

"I might do a little," she admitted. "I have to video conference with some clients who are honeymooning in June, and I need to finalize the itinerary for my trip to Barcelona next week."

"I guess I'm not the only workaholic around here," he murmured.

"Hopefully Skyler doesn't take after either of us."

He glanced at her again. She was getting used to the way he made her heart skip. "If she takes after either of us, I hope that it's you."

She wasn't sure what to say in response. Instead she looked over her shoulder, at Freddie the Teddy who was in the backseat of Jackson's car, a seat belt holding him in. "You hear that, Freddie?" she asked. "He wants Skyler to be like me."

Freddie stared back at her impassively.

Ten minutes later, Jackson was pulling off the highway, onto the winding road leading toward the shore and Angel Sands itself. She could see the glittering ocean through the windshield, as they drove past brush and fields, toward the distant houses.

That's when she saw it. Another bundle of fur. Not quite Freddie's size, but big enough.

"Stop!" she shouted out, craning her head to look over her shoulder. Was that what she thought it was?

"What?" Jackson frowned.

"You have to stop. Right now! Go back," she urged. "About a hundred yards. Please hurry."

He gave her a weird look, but did as instructed, bringing his Prius to a halt before making a U turn and slowly driving back up the hill.

"Here!" she shouted when she saw the ball of fur again, behind a rock twenty yards into the brush. "Stop right here."

"What's going on?" Jackson called out, as she opened the door and ran out of the car, leaving a dust cloud behind her as her sneakers pounded against the dry earth.

"A dog," she shouted back, her voice breathless. "I saw a dog."

He waited for her sudden bolt out of the car to lessen the attraction he felt toward her, because right now he'd take anything. But instead it made him want to pull open his own door and follow her across the road toward wherever she was running.

So he did just that, climbing out of the Prius, and thanking god the road to Angel Sands was quiet at this time of day. Lydia was already ten yards into the brush, her bare legs a blur as she ran.

A moment later, she came to a complete stop, and crouched down, reminding him of how he'd found her at the airport, on her knees in front of a stuffed toy.

But now she was leaning over something else, her voice low as she whispered. Damn, he hoped it really was a dog and not a wolf or a coyote.

Hearing him approach, Lydia turned, her eyes wide. "Don't scare him," she whispered. "He seems jittery."

She held her hand out to the dog. It looked fully grown, and of no particular breed that he could make out. If Jackson had to guess, there was some German Shepherd in him somewhere, but that had to be a generation or two back. "Is he hurt?" he asked, leaning over her to get a closer look.

"I don't think so. Just scared. He has no collar or tags." She reached out to stroke him, and the dog gave a throaty growl. "Hey, sweetie," she whispered. "It's okay. We'll find your mom and dad."

"Not out here we won't," Jackson said, looking around. There was nobody in sight. Wherever the dog came from, it hadn't escaped from any walkers around here.

"You're right. We should take him home."

"In my car?" Jackson blinked.

"Got any better ideas?"

He opened his mouth to tell her that any idea was better than taking some unknown dog in his car, but thought better of it. She was looking up at him, her brows arched, her hands firmly on her hips.

Stern Lydia. He kind of liked it.

"Okay, we'll take him in my car. My friend Brooke works as a vet tech in town. She can probably check if he's on the list of lost dogs or something."

Lydia beamed. "Great idea." She petted the dog again. "See, little buddy. We're going to take care of you."

"Hey, I said nothing about taking care of the dog."

"I know." She was still smiling. "But hopefully your friend will help us reunite him with his owner, and we can be on our way."

"Sure." He nodded. Glancing at his watch carefully, so Lydia didn't notice. It looked like he was going to be working through the next two nights at this rate. Lisa was going to be so pissed with him. "Are you carrying him over or am I?"

"You do it." Lydia nodded. "You're bigger than me. Throw me your keys and I'll open the car up."

"You want the good news or the bad news?" Brooke asked, as she walked into the waiting room where Lydia and Jackson were sitting. The veterinary technician was wearing green scrubs, her blonde hair pulled back from her pretty face.

"The good?" Lydia said, because who would take the bad first? She and Jackson had arrived at the Vet's Office half an hour earlier. Brooke had helped them carry the dog out of

Jackson's sparkling Prius, not even raising an eyelid when she noticed the giant teddy bear sitting in the back seat.

"There's nothing wrong with him. He's as fit as a fiddle. It looks like he's been taken care of."

"That's great." Lydia sighed. "So he has owners?"

"That's the bad news. If he has owners, I have no idea who they are. I've scanned him and there's no chip. And nothing on our database regarding a missing pup." Brooke pressed her lips together. "I've called other clinics and to some of our local groups and there's been no notification of a missing dog. So I can only suggest he goes to the shelter until we decide what to do with him."

Lydia blinked. "What do you mean decide what to do with him?" She wasn't sure she liked the sound of that.

"Well, either we find his owners or..." Brooke glanced at Jackson.

"Or?" Lydia asked, feeling alarmed. "Or *what?*"

"Or we put him up for adoption. But the list is short at the moment. The shelter had a huge influx of dogs after Christmas, and we're only just rehoming them all now. I hate the way people buy puppies for their kids, then get rid of them so fast." Brooke tickled the dog's ears. "The other option might be to find him a foster home."

"How long would it take for him to find a new home?" Lydia asked.

"A couple of months at the worst."

Lydia's eyes met Jackson's. "We can't let him be alone for two months. We should take him home."

He ran a finger along his jaw. "*We?*" he questioned, his brow dipping. "Who's we? You can't take him home, you're leaving in less than two weeks. And anyway, Griff and Autumn have a baby. We have no idea what this dog would be like with kids."

"We wouldn't advise that," Brooke agreed. "The shelter

prefers foster dogs to go to childless homes when possible. Dogs can be unpredictable."

Lydia's heart clenched. The pup was looking up at them, his melted chocolate eyes full of trust. "He's such a beauty," she whispered, running her fingers along his silky fur. It was stupid, but she felt responsible for him. She was the one who found him after all. But there was no way she could help. "I wish I could take him with me."

"I'll take him."

Jackson's deep voice took her and Brooke by surprise. They both looked up at him, their eyes wide.

"You'll take him?" Brooke said, cocking her head to the side. "Seriously? I don't mean to be rude, Jackson, but you can barely manage yourself. Ember told me the last time she was at your place your refrigerator was so barren it had sand in it."

"I'm an adult. I think I can take care of a dog."

"I can help while I'm here," Lydia said, still stroking the dog's warm fur. "I know a lot about dogs." She could feel a rumble in his chest, almost like he was purring. Maybe he knew he was going to be taken care of. "It would be amazing if you took him home." She ruffled the dog's ears and he nuzzled against her. "Look, he already knows we're going to take care of him."

"He's going to need a name." Jackson didn't sound so sure anymore.

"Eddie," she said quickly. "We'll call him Eddie."

Jackson glanced at her. "Why Eddie?"

"It rhymes with Freddie the Teddy," she said. Why were Brooke and Jackson looking at her as though she was from another planet? It made perfect sense, and was so easy to remember.

"If you want to take him home, I'll keep his details on file in case his family shows up," Brooke said, biting her lip. Her eyes were twinkling as she looked at Jackson. "And we can give you some food and the basics to start you off."

Jackson looked from Lydia to Brooke, and back to Lydia again. He swallowed hard and opened his mouth, buyer's remorse written all over his face. "Um..."

"That would be great, thank you so much," Lydia said quickly. Maybe Eddie would be good for him. If he was as much of a workaholic as Griff believed, having something to come home to might make him happy. "Thank you for checking him over," she said, giving Brooke a hug. "We owe you big time."

"You're welcome." Brooke laughed. "And I'll ask around about the owners. Who knows, you might only have to take care of him for one night."

Jackson nodded, looking almost relieved.

It took them five minutes to get Eddie back out to Jackson's car, and then coax him into the backseat, next to Freddie the Teddy. Brooke had given them a collar and leash, plus a box full of food, treats, and toys that made Jackson's mouth drop open. "Do you really think he needs all this stuff?" Jackson muttered as he stuffed the box into the trunk next to Lydia's suitcase.

"I guess so." Lydia shrugged, tickling Eddie beneath his chin before closing the back door. "I mean, I've never had a dog before, but I figure they need a lot of stuff."

"But you said you knew all about dogs." Jackson lifted his cap from his head, raking his hands through his hair. "That's what you said in there."

"A lot of my friends have dogs. And I really like them," Lydia said with a smile. "I mean, how difficult can they be?"

Jackson stared at her open mouthed, then slammed the trunk shut, shaking his head as he walked around to the driver's side. "One favor," he muttered. "That's what he said. One damn favor. Griff owes me."

Lydia felt bad for steamrolling him into this. But what choice did she have? The thought of Eddie all alone in a cage made her tremble. "I'm sorry," she said softly as she climbed into the passenger seat. "I'd take him with me if I could."

Jackson's jaw was tight. "It's okay," he managed. "As long as we find the owners fast. I haven't got time to take care of a dog and run a business."

Lydia reached out to touch his cheek, because he really looked like he could do with some human contact right now. "Oh, you have a scar," she said, noticing the shiny skin zig zagging along his jaw, between the dark shadow of hair. She traced it with her finger, and Jackson closed his eyes for a moment. "How did you get it?" she asked him.

"An accident when I was a kid."

"Surfing? Griff told me you were all daredevils."

"Scree skiing."

"Oh." She was still touching his jaw. It felt nice. Warm and bristly. "Sorry to hear that."

"It's fine." He sounded less tense now, thank goodness. Pressing his lips together, he blew out a mouthful of air. He had such a pretty mouth. On any other guy it might look out of place, but for him it fit perfectly. She'd wager a hundred dollars he was a really good kisser. It was impossible not to be with lips like those.

"So I should get you home now," Jackson said, his voice low. From the back of the car, Eddie let out a bark, as though he agreed.

She nodded in agreement. "I guess Griff and Autumn are wondering where I am."

"I already messaged them," Jackson told her, turning on the engine.

"You think of everything." She pulled her hand away from his jaw, so he actually had room to drive. "Thank you."

"Sure." His knuckles were bleached white where he gripped the steering wheel.

"I'm so glad it was you who picked me up today. Anybody else might have thought I was weird."

His jaw twitched as he pulled out of the parking space, and drove to the parking lot exit. "Thinking you're weird?" he managed to say. "Imagine that."

❧ 4 ❧

"You got a dog?" Ryan Lewis, Jackson's dad, asked, staring down at Eddie, and looked back at his son, his eyebrows raised. "Where the heck did he come from?"

"It's a long story." Jackson wasn't sure he had the energy to go through it all, and he definitely didn't have the patience to listen to his dad's laughter. "I'm just looking after him until his owner is found."

"But you've never had a pet."

"I know, Dad." He'd never wanted one, either. "And he's not mine. I'm babysitting him." He frowned. "Or dog sitting." *Whatever*.

Ryan ran his finger along his jaw, his eyes narrowing as he looked down at Eddie. "What kind of dog is he?"

Jackson shrugged. "Some kind of crossbreed, I guess."

"I hear they can be a handful."

"Yeah, well he's done nothing but eat and sleep since I brought him home. He's not exactly hyperactive." It had been two hours since Jackson dropped Lydia off at Griff and Autumn's house. With Eddie in the back of the car, he hadn't gone inside with her. Instead, he'd waved a hand and driven off, gritting his teeth together when he saw Eddie in his rear view mirror.

What the hell had he been thinking, agreeing to bring him home? Maybe he hadn't been thinking. That was the problem. He was too busy looking at Lydia and wanting to make her happy.

So he'd offered to take the dog home, and now he was regretting it, because dogs and his lifestyle didn't mix. Brooke hadn't been wrong about the inside of his refrigerator. It was like the Gobi Desert. He could barely feed himself, let alone a dog.

"He got a name?" his dad asked, leaning down to inspect Eddie closer.

"Eddie." When his dad started to laugh, Jackson put his hands up. "I didn't choose it."

"Who did?" Ryan tipped his head to the side.

"Just a friend."

"Hmmm."

Eddie lifted his head up to look at them both, and let out the most enormous fart.

"Damn!" Ryan said, screwing his nose up. "That'll teach me about getting too close."

"You want a beer?" Jackson asked him, inclining his head at the kitchen of his ranch house. For the past two years he'd lived on the cliff top overlooking Angel Sands. His house was small, but perfectly situated, with stairs carved into the rock leading down to the beach. On the rare occasion he got to spend any time here, he loved it.

"Sure." His dad followed him in, resting his arms on the granite countertop.

The whole place had been remodeled before Jackson bought it, including the kitchen he never used. He pulled open the doublewide refrigerator, and took two bottles from the lonely box of beer on the shelf. Popping the caps, he passed one to his dad, and lifted the other to his lips.

Eddie idled in, his tail down, and looked up at Jackson balefully.

"Sorry, man," he told the dog. "No beer for you."

"Does he have water?" his dad asked.

"Yes, he has water." Jackson pointed down at the bowl Brooke had so helpfully given him. "And he's eaten, too."

"No need to snap. I'm just asking." Ryan lifted a grey eyebrow and took a mouthful of beer.

"Sorry. It's been a hell of a day. And I've got work coming out of my ears. I have no idea how I'm gonna juggle this dog and my job."

"The same way anybody does." Ryan shrugged. "You'll muddle through."

Jackson eyed him carefully. "Maybe you can help," he said, his voice hopeful. "You're retired. You can take care of him for me."

"Oh no." His dad shook his head. "This one's all yours, son."

"Thanks," Jackson muttered, looking down at Eddie again. His eyes were so large and shiny, they looked like pebbles. He was still staring up at Jackson like he had all the answers.

Truth was, he didn't even know the questions.

"Maybe I can dog sit occasionally," his dad conceded. "As long as it's not during my chess games."

Jackson grinned at him. "Thanks, Dad."

"You heard from your mom lately?" his dad asked, his voice casual.

"She called the other day. I haven't had a chance to call her back yet." Jackson looked at his dad, taking him in. At the age of fifty-eight, Ryan Lewis kept up a good appearance, his grey hair perfectly trimmed, his body lean and tight. Before

Jackson was born, his dad had been a champion surfer, winning competitions both in the US and abroad. Once he settled down with Jackson's mom, and they'd had him, he'd gone to work at Newton Pharmaceuticals as a book keeper.

And that's where he'd stayed until he took early retirement last year. He'd worked through his marriage, and the breakup of it, when Jackson's mom had left without a backward glance. Now he spent most of his days hanging out at the beach with his friends, or playing chess at the coffee shop.

"It's okay. She needed a bit of help, I sorted it." Ryan waved his hand.

"You gave her money?" Jackson's chest tightened. "I thought we talked about this."

His dad looked down at his beer. "She was short on cash, I had some. That's all."

A wave of frustration washed through Jackson's body. This was so typical of his mom. She'd be silent for months, only contacting them when she needed money or some other kind of help.

It angered him that his dad fell for it every time.

"How much did she want?"

"That's between me and her, son. There's nothing to worry about. It's all sorted now. You just concentrate on working out how to look after that damn mutt."

"Why do you keep giving things to her?" Jackson asked. It was crazy. "She's the one who left, Dad. More than twenty years ago. She's not your problem anymore."

His dad exhaled heavily. "She's your mother. She gave me you. I owe her for that. And believe it or not, I loved her like crazy. She was this whirlwind twisting into my world and opening my eyes to what life could be like. You won't remember what she was like then, but everybody wanted to be close to her. And I was the lucky guy she chose."

"But then she left. And you never moved on. You haven't even dated since." As a kid, he'd loved that it was him and his dad. But now... he worried about him being lonely.

Yeah, he was the pot calling the kettle black.

"I tried dating. It didn't work." Ryan shrugged. "And excuse me if it's rude, but I don't need to take dating advice from you. It's not like you've held down a relationship."

"I was engaged once," Jackson reminded him.

"Yeah, about a hundred years ago. And you haven't had anything serious since." His dad caught his eye. "Try not to worry about me and your mom. We're old enough to take care of ourselves. And anyway, it's not as though I've got anything better to do with my money." He shrugged. "You're doing well enough to not need anything from me."

Jackson finished his beer, putting the bottle on the counter in front of him. "You're right. We're both big enough to take care of ourselves."

"Amen to that." His dad grinned.

"I'm not sure about taking care of a dog though," Jackson admitted, as Eddie started to sniff around his ankles. "You wanna walk him with me?"

"Yeah, okay." Ryan nodded. "As long as you're the one picking up his crap."

———

"Hurricane Lydia strikes again." Autumn couldn't stop laughing as Lydia recounted the story of finding Eddie in the brush above Angel Sands. "I bet Jackson didn't know what hit him."

"I can't believe Brooke let him take a dog home." Griff shook his head. "She knows better than that. Jackson can barely take care of himself."

. . .

31

Lydia rubbed her face with the palms of her hands. "I feel terrible," she admitted. "He looked like he'd been hit by a steamroller when we put Eddie in the car. I'm not sure he realized what he was getting himself into."

Autumn and Griff exchanged a glance. "Well, maybe it'll be good for him," Autumn said, lifting Skyler into a comfier position. "He's been living alone too long. The dog will keep him company. The responsibility might change him."

"This is Jackson Lewis we're talking about, right?" Griff asked Autumn. "Tall guy, dark hair, thinks he's good looking. Always stressed and running from one place to the next?"

"Well, he is quite good looking," Lydia offered. Autumn muffled a laugh behind Skyler's head.

"And he does run his own business." Autumn shrugged. "That's a responsibility in itself. We should know that." She glanced at Lydia and Griff. "Plus he's going to be Skyler's godfather. Taking care of a pet isn't much different to caring for a child. I think he's a good guy for volunteering."

Lydia grimaced. "I'm not sure he quite volunteered." Leaning forward, she took a sip of tea from the patterned china cup Autumn had given her. She loved this living room, with its soft cream leather sofas and hardwood floors. The walls were painted white, and the evening light bathed them in a warm orange glow. Since they'd moved in, Autumn and Griff had made this place feel like home.

It was probably the closest thing to a home Lydia had, too, since most of her belongings sat in storage while she traveled.

Autumn tilted her head to the side, interested. "So if he didn't volunteer, how did he end up with a dog?"

Lydia bit her lip. "I kind of got upset and he offered to make me feel better. I don't think he realized what he'd done until Eddie was in the backseat, ready to go home with him."

Griff's laughter was loud this time. He almost sounded

like he was choking.

"You know, I used to like you, Griff," Lydia told him. "You're my almost brother-in-law. You're supposed to be on my side."

"Oh honey, I'm on your side," he told her, walking over to give her a hug. He had big arms, and an even bigger chest. She loved how snuggly and lovely he was. "I just can't believe you got him to foster a dog. That's all. He can barely keep himself alive."

"Griff, come on." Autumn shook her head. "He's not that bad. He's a successful businessman. You have to be pretty good at organization for that. I'm sure he'll be the same with the dog. He can pay for sitters and walkers if he needs to."

"Hey, I'm not doing him dirty," Griff protested. "I'm just saying his track record isn't good. And yeah, he's great at business, because he's good at it. It never lets him down. And when he's knee deep in numbers and coding he doesn't have to think about anything else."

"Like what?" Lydia asked, intrigued. "What else should he be thinking about?"

Griff shrugged and looked out of the glass doors to the setting sun. Autumn squeezed his hand. There were words in their touches that Lydia couldn't quite understand. "It doesn't matter," Griff said softly. "You're both right. He'll be fine."

But Lydia felt terrible. She was the one who'd almost forced him to take Eddie home. She hadn't thought about how busy his life was, or how he'd find time to take care of a dog. "I did offer to help," she told them. "I'll go and walk him and keep him clean and give him lots of attention." She smiled at baby Skyler. "Just like I'm going to spoil my niece like crazy."

"Why don't you hold her for a moment?" Autumn stood and walked over to where Lydia was sitting. Gently, she laid her baby in Lydia's arms. Skyler snuffled against Lydia's chest, wriggling her body until she found a comfortable spot. Lydia dropped her head, feeling Skyler's downy hair against her lips.

"She smells so good," Lydia whispered, her eyes filling with tears. Skyler looked up, her deep blue eyes staring directly into Lydia's. She blinked, her thick eyelashes sweeping down. "You're such a beautiful girl," she whispered. "You probably get that from me. I'm your Aunt Lydia, by the way. Your favorite aunt. I know your mom and dad will tell you that I'm your only aunt, but that doesn't make it any less true. I'm going to be your godmother, too, and I take that very seriously. It's my job to show you all the wonderful things life has to offer. I'll teach you things like always having your passport ready, and a travel bag packed in case the mood to travel takes over you. And we can talk about boys and things, all the stuff your mom and dad won't want to hear."

"You're not talking to her about boys," Griff told her. "She's never going to meet any."

"She's already met about ten of them at baby class," Autumn pointed out.

"Yeah, well she can be friends with them until she's thirteen. After that she's going to a nunnery."

Lydia started to laugh. "Oh boy, Skyler. You're going to have to run away from home. I'll help you. I know all the best flights out of here."

Griff raised an eyebrow. "You're going to be a bad influence." From the sound of his voice, he wasn't looking forward to that.

"Yep." Lydia grinned. "I'm planning on it."

Skyler started to fuss, pressing her head against Lydia's chest. Her little tiny face wrinkled up, as though she was frustrated, and her bottom lip started to tremble.

"Oh god, I've made her cry," Lydia said, feeling her heart speed up. She really had to get over this fear of children crying.

"She's just hungry, that's all." Autumn was completely calm as she walked over. "I'll feed her and get her ready for bed. We'll eat a little later, if that's okay?"

"Of course. Is there anything I can do to help?"

"I'm ordering takeout," Griff told her. "You can set the table before it comes. But apart from that, I think we have it handled."

"You should go and unpack," Autumn suggested. "We put you in the back guest room."

"Okay." Lydia beamed. "Oh, and I need to put Freddie the Teddy in Skyler's room. Do you think she'll like him?"

"She'll love him," Autumn said, taking Skyler from Lydia's arms, as she kissed her sister softly on the cheek. "And she already loves you. Look how much she doesn't want me to take her."

Lydia nodded and blew a kiss at her niece. "Like I said, I'm her favorite aunt."

How's Eddie? Do you need some help with him tomorrow? I can walk him or whatever you need. Thanks for taking care of him. You're the best. - L. xx

Lydia read the message back to herself before pressing send. She was still feeling bad that Jackson took the dog. Not completely bad – it was still better than Eddie being lonely at the shelter – but enough that she wanted to help wherever she could.

It was just after ten. They'd finished their takeout an hour ago, and Lydia had insisted on cleaning up, taking extra care to make the surfaces shine. Autumn had gone to bed right after eating. Her poor sister was exhausted from all the night time feeds she was still doing.

Griff hadn't stayed up much later. He and Lydia had

talked a little about her upcoming trip to Spain, and he'd told her about his whale watching boat, but she could tell he was aching to join Autumn in bed. So she'd faked a yawn and stretched her arms over her head and said something about jetlag, even though she'd only flown in from New York.

Whatever. It had worked, and now they were asleep, while she was sitting in the queen size guest bed feeling wide awake.

She'd added a few photos to Instagram and answered some messages. Her profile was popular – she had just under a hundred thousand followers of her travel photos – and got a lot of requests for endorsements. But she rarely accepted them. Her income mostly came from her guided tours of different cities and countries.

It was funny how in demand her services had become. Her job had started as a favor to a friend of her father's, who'd asked her to show him around Barcelona, and let him see it the way locals do. He didn't want any of the usual tourist destinations – he wanted to eat, shop, and be entertained like any resident would be.

He'd been so bowled over by the experience, he'd told everybody he met about Lydia's knowledge of the different cities of the world. She hadn't even known she was the talk of the New York City dinner party circuit until she started getting phone calls asking how much she charged for a week's personalized tour of different cities.

At first she'd baulked at taking these offers. She traveled because she loved it, not to make money. But a glance at her ever-diminishing bank balance had told her not to look this gift horse in the mouth. Still, she'd quoted an exorbitant amount, fully expecting people to refuse, but the prices only seemed to add to her cachet.

She'd become the travel industry's equivalent of a rare diamond. People wanted to mention her when they came back from their vacations, as though she was an expensive trinket they'd picked up along the way. Not that she minded. She was being paid to travel, after all. Plus she got to share the joy with her friends – those running tavernas in Athens and selling goods at feiras in Rio. It felt good to be doing what she was doing.

Closing Instagram down, she laid back in her bed, and closed her eyes. But sleep didn't come. She was too busy thinking about her day. How weird it had been since she'd walked out of the baggage claim and had run that poor kid over, only to see the sexiest muscled thighs standing next to where they'd fallen.

She sighed. Jackson had barely said goodbye when she'd climbed out of the car, and only nodded when she thanked him for the ride. By the time Autumn had run out of the front door to greet her, he'd driven away. Was he annoyed with her for guilt tripping him into taking the dog?

Hopefully her offer of help would make it better.

Her phone pinged, alerting her to a reply. She looked down to see Jackson's name on the screen.

It's all good. I've got it covered, but thanks anyway. - Jackson.

There were no kisses. She was certain she'd sent him kisses. She scrolled up and saw she had. Yep, he was definitely annoyed with her.

Hmm. She needed to find a way to smooth things out. They were going to be Skyler's godparents, after all. It would be awkward as hell if they weren't at least civil to each other.

Maybe she'd ask Autumn for some advice tomorrow. She always knew how to make things better.

A cry cut through the silence of the room. Lydia sat up sharply, looking around. Baby Skyler was crying. She climbed out of bed and padded across the carpet, opening her door as quietly as she could.

Down the corridor, she could see Griff and Autumn standing in front of the nursery door, Autumn in a short nightgown, Griff in shorts and nothing else. Damn, she'd forgotten just how many muscles that man had. He should pay tax on them or something.

The country would never be in a deficit again.

"She's still asleep," Autumn whispered to Griff, not seeing Lydia at the end of the hall. "Must have had a bad dream."

Griff laced his arms around Autumn's waist, resting his chin on the top of her head as the two of them stared through the open door. "We'll just wait for a minute, make sure she's okay."

"Good idea." Autumn stroked his cheek.

He dropped his head to kiss her hair, and slid his lips down to her neck. "After that, I'm going to take you to bed and show you exactly how much I adore you."

Lydia's heart clenched. The way he was holding her sister was beautiful. They were a couple, a family, and the love radiating from them hit her right in the gut. She was so damn happy for Autumn. After her divorce, Autumn had moved to Angel Sands to run the pier, and she'd met Griff and found real love for the first time.

Autumn deserved all this happiness. She'd spent a lifetime taking care of everybody. Lydia, their father, even Josh, the asshole first husband who never deserved Autumn's love. And now here she was, all settled and happy.

How would it feel to be loved that way?

She shook her head. That kind of settling down wasn't for her. She'd go crazy being in one place for too long, everybody knew that.

Silently, she turned and padded back to bed, the ache in her chest still strong. There was only one way she knew how to get rid of it. She opened her purse and pulled an old, fraying envelope out of the pocket. Slipping the letter out, she carefully opened it up.

Dear Lydia,

The throb in her chest lessened as she read her mom's beautifully slanted script. She'd written this letter a few days before she died, when Lydia was still a baby. She'd been eighteen when their father had given the sealed envelope to her, and ever since she'd kept it close, ready to re-read whenever she felt sad or lonely.

There was one paragraph she especially loved. It made everything feel better.

Sweetheart, you're a light in the darkness. A smile when frowns are all around. You eat up life like it's a gourmet buffet and I adore that about you. Don't let that light ever be dimmed. Never stop searching for what makes you happy. Travel, meet new people, discover things you never thought you'd experience. Don't let yourself be tied down by the world's expectations because you are so much more than that.

Don't let the world change you – change the world instead.

She re-read the words, sealing each one of them in her heart. Her mom had wanted her to travel, and if moms didn't know what was best for you, who did? She folded the letter back up, carefully stowing it away so it would be there next time she needed it.

Yes, Autumn and Griff had something special. And she was so happy for them. But she needed to travel and keep searching for whatever filled her soul.

Otherwise, who was she?

$\text{❧}\quad 5 \quad \text{❧}$

S he. Needed. Coffee.

Lydia half-walked, half-crawled across the carpeted guest bedroom floor, her hair askew, her eyes open to slits, her hand sweeping away the air in front of her until her fingers curled around the cool door knob.

When she finally made it to the kitchen, she had to lean on the counter to fully wake up.

She wasn't a fan of mornings. Or any time she had to get out of bed. She could completely understand why Skyler wailed every time her eyes opened in the crib. It was frustrating, especially when you were in the middle of a very nice dream.

One, for instance, that contained chocolate from Brazil, red wine from Spain, and a very naked Jackson Lewis.

Whew.

What was she in the kitchen for? Oh yeah, *coffee*. Needed it now. She pulled open every cupboard until she found the jar full of grounds, and promptly walked into an open cupboard door.

"Ow!" Rubbing her head with one hand, she reached out

for the glass filter carafe with the other, her eyes still squeezed closed thanks to the pain throbbing in her brow.

The glass carafe smashed against the black tiled floor, making Lydia's eyes fly open. She jumped back to avoid the sea of shards surrounding her. Who knew a glass jug could make so much mess? She frowned again. Why didn't Griff and Autumn have a Nespresso machine like everybody else? It was like they were living in the stone ages.

Though Griff would make a great caveman. She bit down a smile at the thought.

Though it was a Sunday, he and Autumn were both at work. It was his second busiest day of the week, even during off-season. Between charters and tourist cruises, he rarely took a weekend off. And Autumn had modeled her own working week around his, doing admin work in her little office on the pier on Sundays, while Skyler sat contentedly in her little baby chair, staring out at the ocean.

Autumn had apologized profusely last night for not being there that morning, but Lydia had waved her off. "It's fine, I'm no fun in the morning anyway. I'll chill and maybe take a walk. We can catch up later."

And to be honest, she was kind of liking the silence in here right now. Skyler had woken up three times last night, and even though it wasn't Lydia who'd gotten out of bed, she'd still winced at how loud the screams were.

Seeing how tired Autumn was, she'd half-heartedly offered to look after Skyler for her today. Autumn and Griff had both laughed.

"Thanks for the offer," Autumn had said. "But let's not shoot for the moon too soon."

Lydia would have taken offense, but her sister was right. She'd never looked after a baby in her life. But how hard could it be? Skyler only slept, ate, and pooped. Yeah, she'd

41

definitely babysit for them this week and show them how easy it was.

In the meantime, she had a mess to clean up. But first she really needed that coffee. And now she'd have no choice but to go down to Autumn's favorite coffee shop, Déjà Brew. After that she'd work out how to get rid of this mess and secure a new coffee pot.

The sun was warm against her skin as she made her way down the boardwalk toward the main strip of Angel Sands. People were out on their skates, bicycles, and walking dogs. She wondered if Jackson had walked Eddie that morning.

Probably best not to message him and ask. He didn't need her fussing and assuming he couldn't cope with a dog. Enough people were doing that already.

She walked past Angel Ices, the ice cream parlor, smiling at a family who were sharing a huge bowl of ten scoops, and waved at the owner of the surf shop, who gave her a grizzled smile and waved back.

Oh, she did like it here. The all-year-around warm temperatures seemed to put everybody in a good mood. Next time she visited she'd bring her photography equipment and take some good shots for her Instagram page.

Déjà Brew, the local coffee shop, was buzzing as she pushed open the door and walked inside. Most of the tables were taken – with families and groups of friends, along with workers or students typing furiously on their laptops, and occasionally taking a break to sip their mochas or macchiatos.

Lydia inhaled deeply, the aroma of coffee making her mouth water. She could probably get high on this smell alone. Joining the order line, she found herself unable to stand still, her muscles as desperate for a caffeine fix as her mouth was.

"Hey you!" Ally, the coffee shop owner, said as Lydia reached the front of the line. Ally was one of Autumn and Griff's friends. Married to Nate, who co-owned the shop, she was tall and slim and ran along the beach every day without fail. And from the grin on her face she was happy to see Lydia.

Feeling exactly the same way, Lydia reached over the counter to hug her. "Hey. How are you?"

"Great." Ally grinned. "I didn't know you were here. You come early for Skyler's Naming Day?"

"Yep. I promised Autumn I'd be here in good time. Plus I get to have lots of cuddles with my gorgeous niece."

"I bet they're all happy to see you. When was the last time you were here?" Ally asked.

"When Skyler was born." Was it really *that* long? She'd spent most of December in Europe, at the ski resorts and taking tourists around the Christmas markets. And January and most of February she'd been in Mexico and Guatemala.

"Well I'm glad you're here now. What can I get you?"

"Just an Americano. Straight up, please." Lydia looked around the coffee shop. "I don't suppose you sell coffee carafes, do you?"

Ally shook her head and called out the order to the young kid behind the espresso machine. He looked up, his eyes widening as he saw Lydia standing there. She smiled and he grinned back.

"No we don't. We thought about selling some coffee machines, but why encourage people to drink coffee at home? We want them here." Ally tipped her head to the side. "Why do you need one?"

"I kind of broke Autumn's in my desperation for a caffeine fix." Lydia grimaced. "I need to get them a new one before they're home from work. Any ideas where I can find one around here?"

"I can't think of anywhere. Maybe Frank's hardware store?"

"Frank's closed today," Ally's husband, Nate, said, leaning over the counter to kiss Lydia's cheek. "And Hi. How're you doing?"

"I'm good." She beamed at Nate. "Or I will be until Autumn kills me for breaking her coffee pot. I guess I should just try the internet?"

"Why don't you head to the mall near Silver City?" Ally suggested, while Nate took the next order.

"How far is that?"

"About twenty miles. Just up the highway. You can find it easily."

Lydia ran her finger along her bottom lip. "I don't suppose there's a bus route heading that way?"

"Why do you need to take a bus?" a deep voice asked from behind her.

Lydia turned to see Jackson standing behind her, an alert Eddie at his feet. "Oh my god, look at you," she said, leaning down to ruffle Eddie's ears. "You look so happy. Has Jackson been treating you well?"

"Jack?" Ally said, sounding amused. "Is that dog yours?"

"I'm looking after him," Jackson told her.

Lydia stood and smiled as Eddie licked her hand. "He's fostering Eddie until his family is found. Brooke's on the case."

Ally nodded sagely. "I'll call her. I can't wait to hear her take on all this."

"Why do you need a bus?" Jackson asked again. "Where are you going?"

He was wearing dark jeans and a grey t-shirt, but no cap

this time. Lifting his hand, he raked his fingers through his thick, dark hair.

Lydia sighed. "I need to buy a coffee pot, and Ally says the mall's the best place." The barista brought her drink over and handed it across the counter. "Thanks." She smiled at him.

The barista blushed. "Enjoy." He stood and stared at Lydia for a moment. "I don't suppose I can get your number?"

"Um, no you can't, Ben," Ally said, frowning. "Stop hitting on our customers."

From the corner of her eye, Lydia noticed the smile slip from Jackson's lips. Had she done something to annoy him again?

"You can drive to the mall," Jackson suggested. "Take Griff's truck. I'm guessing he's out on the boat and doesn't need it."

Lydia pulled the corner of her lip between her teeth. "I... um... can't drive."

Everybody went silent. Lydia looked at Ally, Nate, and Jackson. They were all staring back at her with wide eyes.

"What?" Jackson was the first to talk. "But you're twenty something years old."

Top points for not saying her age. Lydia stored that little snippet away in her brain.

"And you've traveled all over the world," Jackson continued. "How can't you drive?"

"I never learned." She shrugged. "I grew up in Manhattan. Nobody drives there." She laughed. "Well *everybody* drives, but nobody sane, if you know what I mean. I used cabs or public transport. And wherever I travel there's either great connections or I hire people to take me places. I've just never needed to drive myself."

They were still staring at her. She shifted her feet. "Um, say something?"

"Okayyyy." Jackson ran a thumb along his jaw. "Like what?"

"Like you'll take her to the mall," Ally suggested helpfully. "You have your car here, don't you?"

His eyes shifted to Lydia. "Yeah, I have my car. I also have a dog and a mountain of work to do. I only came out to get some fresh air."

"It's fine," Lydia said quickly. She really didn't want to annoy him anymore. "I'll find a way there."

"How?" Jackson pressed his lips together.

"I'll take you," Ben, the barista, called out over the counter. "I get off in an hour and I've just gotten my license. My mom lets me borrow her car."

Lydia looked at his hopeful face. He was such a cutie. She hated to turn him down. But still, there was no way she was getting in a car with him. "That's so sweet—"

She didn't have a chance to say her 'but' before Jackson interjected. "I'll take you," he said, shooting a dark look at Ben. "Let me get a coffee, and I'll call my dad to ask if he can keep an eye on Eddie for a couple of hours."

"If he can't help, I know Riley would love to take care of your dog," Ally said, referring to her step-daughter. "She's at home, I can call her."

Lydia beamed at Jackson, then at Ally and Nate. "You're all so kind, thank you." She smiled over at Ben, because she hated leaving anybody out. "You, too."

Ben nodded and ambled back to the espresso machine, accepting defeat.

A minute later, Nate passed over Jackson's order. "It's on the house," he told Jackson. "Because I think you're going to need it."

Jackson's expression reminded her of her dad's, the day she told him she didn't need to go to college because she was planning on traveling the world. It was stoical. Almost long-suffering. Had she inadvertently steamrolled him again?

From the way he shifted his feet, she thought she had.

Jackson took the paper cup and tugged at Eddie's leash, before blowing out a mouthful of air. "Come on," he said to Lydia. "Let's go and get you to the mall before I change my mind."

Well this was going to be interesting.

He'd officially lost his mind. That was the only explanation. All those long days at the office, followed by late nights in front of a glowing screen had led to this. A complete breakdown.

Jackson had worked almost through the night, and had only taken a break to stretch his — and Eddie's — legs. But then he'd seen Lydia standing there, wearing denim cut offs and a sweater that clung to every delicious curve she had, and all thoughts of coding and clients and sitting in front of a computer had flown out of his mind.

And now here they were, driving down the highway toward Silver City Mall, the windows open, the radio blasting out, with Lydia singing along to Dua Lipa. Eddie was safe with Jackson's dad — who'd raised an eyebrow when he'd been introduced to Lydia, but said nothing else, though Jackson was almost certain he'd be getting the third degree later.

"I love this song so much," Lydia said, turning to smile at him. The breeze from the window lifted her hair, making tendrils dance around her shoulders. "How about you?"

"I don't think I've heard it before." Jackson shrugged. "But I like it."

"What kind of music do you listen to?" she asked, tipping

her head. The sun caught her blonde hair, reflecting into his eyes.

The music was interrupted by the shrill sound of his phone ringer through the Bluetooth speaker. Jackson looked at the dash – it was Alex, one of his programmers. He rejected the call, and looked over at Lydia.

"I guess I'm more of a rock guy. Soundgarden. Foo Fighters. That kind of thing."

"I love the Foo Fighters." Her eyes caught his, and damn if that didn't do something to him. "We should listen to them. *Best of You* is my favorite."

"It's mine, too," he murmured. *Who knew?*

She pulled out her phone, linking it with the speaker, and hit play. Tipping her head back, she sang the first line with a deep, throaty voice that made him grin.

She was dazzling. She'd only been here for two days, yet here he was, driving along the highway on a Sunday afternoon, listening to good music with a beautiful woman sitting next to him. Something other people did on a weekly basis, yet it felt almost alien to him.

And yet so damn good.

His phone started buzzing again, the ringtone interrupting Dave Grohl's lament.

"Boy, you get a lot of phone calls," Lydia said. "Doesn't that drive you crazy?"

"I usually work on Sundays." And every other day. "They're used to me answering all their problems."

"Who is it, a client?"

"Mostly my programmers. We bounce ideas off each other when we hit a block. They'll probably call another member of the team if they can't get ahold of me."

"Do you ever take a break?"

He gave her a half-grin. "I'm here, aren't I?"

"Yeah, but I can't help but feel it's my fault you are. I should have taken Ben up on his offer."

"You wanted to go to the mall with a teenage kid in his mom's minivan?" he asked archly.

She narrowed her eyes. "How do you know he drives a minivan?"

"I don't. But I'm trying to put you off."

"Oh." She looked down, smiling to herself. "Don't worry, I'm not interested in Ben."

Jackson stared out of the windshield, his hands a little tighter on the wheel.

"I'm really glad you brought me," Lydia said softly. "I like spending time with you."

He swallowed hard, a sudden image of Griff flashing into his thoughts. At six foot two, Jackson was taller than most guys he knew, but his best friend still towered over him. He had a mean right hook, too. Not that Jackson had ever been at the receiving end of it, but he remembered Griff using it a couple of times when they were younger.

And he definitely didn't want to rile his best friend up now.

The problem was, his body wasn't getting the message.

He gave an internal sigh of relief when he saw the Silver Sands Mall looming ahead. Pulling into the turn lane, he made a right into the main parking lot, sliding his car in between a F150 truck and a BMW.

Switching off the engine, he turned to Lydia. "Okay. You ready to hit the shops?"

🎇 6 🎇

J ackson needed cheering up, that was for sure. Lydia felt like Griff and Autumn had Jackson all wrong. He wasn't a player. He was a workaholic who had no time for meaningful relationships. And she might not have time to solve all his problems, but she could at least make him smile today.

They hit the department store first, heading for the appliance section. It was rammed full of shiny coffee machines that made her mouth water for another caffeine fix. She ended up buying a replacement glass carafe as well as a Nespresso machine, because if Autumn and Griff didn't crawl into the twenty-first coffee machine century soon, she wasn't sure she could stay with them again.

"Do *you* have a coffee machine?" Lydia asked Jackson when she'd paid at the counter.

"Uh, yeah. But I keep forgetting to order the pods." Jackson shrugged before adding, "Or buy milk."

He took the oversized shopping bag from her as she slipped her wallet into her purse. "You don't have to carry that for me," she told him.

"I know I don't. But I want to."

He was still in a strange mood. Had been since he'd returned a couple of calls while she looked around at the coffee machines. As they wandered out of the department store and back into the main mall, her brow dipped as she tried to think of a way to make him smile again.

That's when she saw it. The shop practically had their name on it.

"We should go in there," she said, pointing at the pink and grey signage.

"Doggie Couture?" Jackson shook his head. "Why on earth do we want to shop in that place?"

"Look! They have little four poster dog beds in the window." She laughed and pulled at his hand. "See? Imagine Eddie sleeping in one of those."

Jackson grinned in spite of himself. "Eddie doesn't look like the kind of dog who wants a four poster."

"What does he want then?"

Lydia liked the way he smiled. Maybe too much. It made his cheeks lift up and his eyes sparkle. She also noticed he had perfect teeth.

Lickable, even, if you were into that kind of thing.

Which she most certainly wasn't.

"A manly bed." Jackson nodded. "Just a cushion is all he needs. Wherever he lays his tail, that's his home."

"We should go in anyway." She hooked her arm through his. "Just to make sure he isn't missing out."

"If you say so." He let her pull him in, not even bothering to make a cursory protest.

As soon as they were inside the shop, the absurdity of some of the merchandise hit her. Not just the ornate dog beds, but the silver and gold plated feeding dishes, the hand embroidered pet carrier you could loop over your shoulder, not to mention tiny leather handbags you could attach to your dog's collar for all those doggy necessities.

"This is crazy," Jackson told her. "Eddie wouldn't be seen dead in any of this stuff."

Her eyes lit up at a clothes rack. "Hey," she said, dragging Jackson over. "They have little doggy leather jackets. How cute are they?" Searching through them, she found one in what looked like Eddie's size. Made of soft black leather, it had a sugar skull emblem sewn on the back, along with the logo 'Paws MC'.

"You are not putting my dog in a leather jacket," Jackson told her, his eyes crinkling as he took the hanger from her hands and replaced it on the rail. "Next thing I know you'll be buying him a bike."

She didn't mention the fact he'd called Eddie *his* dog. But she did store that fact away for later.

"Hi!" An assistant walked over, holding the leash of a chubby pug, who was wearing a Pink Ladies jacket. "Aren't these adorable? What kind of dog do you have?"

"Uh. He's a mix." Jackson looked at Lydia, as though he wanted to run away.

"He has some German Shepherd in him," Lydia added. "He's strong and butch, just like Jackson." She ran her hand up and down Jackson's arm. Damn, his muscles were hard. He had to work out.

"I like the sound of him." The assistant smiled. "Your boyfriend sounds like a wonderful dog owner."

Jackson blinked. "Boyfriend?" he mouthed. But he didn't protest.

Maybe they could have a bit of fun here. There was nothing like a game of pretend to make somebody laugh.

Lydia grinned at him, hoping he would go with it. "I was just telling my *boyfriend*," she said, emphasizing the word, "that Eddie would look amazing in these jackets."

Jackson bit down a smile and shook his head, but didn't correct her.

"And I was just telling my... girlfriend that Eddie doesn't need a jacket. God gave him a coat already."

She squeezed Jackson's hand. He was definitely going with it.

"I guess so," the assistant said. "But it's a way to show our furry babies how much we love them, isn't it? Look at Buffy here. She loves being dressed up. Every day she gets to choose a different outfit." She leaned down to ruffle the pug's fur. "But you know, if you're not ready for a full on outfit, why not start with a neckerchief? We have some great ones at the counter."

"Yes," Lydia said, smiling at Jackson. "We should get Eddie a neckerchief."

"I don't know how he's survived this far without one," Jackson agreed, deadpan.

She scanned his face. Yeah, he still looked like he was enjoying himself. Maybe it was time to take it up a notch. "Do you have matching daddy and doggy neckerchiefs?" Lydia asked, trying hard to keep a straight face. "Wouldn't that be perfect, sweetheart?"

Jackson narrowed his eyes at her, but his lips were still curled up. "How about a mommy and doggy matching set?"

She clapped her hands together. "Yes! We'll all get one. Won't that be wonderful?" She hugged him, pressing her face into his chest to hide her laughter. "You always have the best ideas."

"I live to make you happy," he said, raising an eyebrow.

She managed to keep the laughter down long enough for them to pay for three jaunty red neckerchiefs. But as soon as they were outside, she found herself bending over to stop from peeing herself.

Because Jackson's face was just so, so delicious.

"Remind me to never take you shopping again," he told her, putting the bag with the coffee machine down. "And also, you're wearing that scarf the next time you take Eddie out."

"Your face, oh my god, wasn't that fun?" she managed to splutter.

He blinked, as though it was a difficult question. "Yeah..." he finally said. "I guess it *was* fun."

She managed to stand, rolling onto the balls of her feet to press her lips against his cheek. He hadn't shaved again, and the roughness of his beard sent a shiver through her. "I owe you one," she told him.

"More than one. About a hundred. Why is it you create chaos wherever you go?"

She shrugged happily. "It's a gift."

"It sure is. And what was with calling me your boyfriend?"

"Sometimes it's fun to pretend to be somebody you're not. Like being a kid again, playing make believe." She eyed him carefully. "It's a way I stop thinking about all the things that worry me."

His mouth parted as he took in her words. Slowly, he ran the tip of his tongue along his plump bottom lip. Lydia didn't think she'd ever met a guy with such a perfect mouth. She wondered what it would feel like to press them against her...

Then his phone rang, chasing the thought from her head.

"Again?" she asked. She'd never met anybody who got more phone calls and messages than she did before.

Jackson pulled his phone from his pocket, sighing when he read the screen. "I gotta take this one," he said. "Give me a minute, okay?"

The way the light drained from his eyes made her feel sad. She'd almost got him there, dammit. "Sure. Take your time."

He slid his finger to accept the call, and lifted the device to his ear. "Mom?" He paused. "Yeah, I got your messages, I've been busy, that's all."

Jackson walked away to take the call so Lydia didn't have to hear the gory details. Exhaling heavily, he leaned on the tiled wall while his mom let out a stream of consciousness over the phone.

Same old story. Slightly different words. He managed to hmm and ahh at the right times, but really his attention was directed at the woman standing next to an oversize shopping bag, who was currently pulling a red neckerchief out and holding it in front of her face like she was doing the dance of the seven veils.

A mischievous grin pulled at her lips as she waved the neckerchief back and forth, her hips rolling sensually as she lifted it over her head and slowly turned in a circle, still gyrating and dancing to a beat nobody else could hear.

Everybody was staring at her, and either she didn't notice or didn't care. The latter, probably. She was having too much fun, twirling and waving and making him grin and shake his head.

"Jackson, did you hear me?"

"Sorry, Mom. I'm in the mall, it's loud. I can call you back later."

"No, please," His mom's voice was almost a shout. "I just need a little help, sweetie. A couple of thousand will do. I'll pay it back, just as soon as my friend gives me the money back."

Jackson realized he'd missed most of her story. Not that it mattered, he'd bet two thousand dollars it was all made up. "I spoke to Dad, he already gave you money."

Lydia slowly spun to a halt, and tied the scarf around her neck, then leaned forward and lifted her hands to her lips, blowing him an exaggerated Marilyn Monroe style kiss.

An old man sitting on a bench nearby started clapping.

"She's crazy, but she's hot," a younger guy said, walking by.

"This is for something else," his mom said. "And he promised not to tell you. I need it for something else."

"What?"

There was silence as she most certainly thought up an excuse. "My water heater is broken."

"So call the landlord."

"I have. And he's repairing it. But I can't live without hot water, Jackson. I need to move into a motel for a few days."

Damn, she was getting worse. This had to be the third time this year she'd called him for money, and it was only mid-March. And god only knew how often she'd called his dad. Everybody knew Ryan Lewis was a soft touch when it came to his ex-wife. *Especially* his ex-wife.

"I'm not giving you any money."

"What? But I'm your mom, sweetheart. I really need your help." She sounded almost panicked. "I promise I'll give it back. I will. Please, sweetie."

A man walked over and was talking to Lydia. He said something to her and she started to laugh. And damn if she didn't remind him of his mom in that moment.

Growing up, Jackson's mom had always been the life and soul of the party. He could remember how excited he'd get when she'd tell him he didn't have to go to school that day because they were going on an adventure. She'd take him to Disneyland without telling his dad where they were going, or on a whale watching tour when he should have been studying in second grade.

And then she'd left. Suddenly and painfully. He'd watched his dad wither beneath her loss, the same way Jackson had. As though the light had been sucked out of their life.

When the man walked away and Lydia smiled over at him again, Jackson didn't smile back. Because none of his thoughts were making sense.

"I'll think about it," he said, his voice almost robotic as he spoke to his mom.

"Oh thank you, darling. I knew you loved me really." She gave a little laugh.

"I have to go. I have work to do." His voice was dull.

"But I thought you were at the mall," she said. Realizing she'd gotten what she wanted, she quickly changed direction. "Never mind, maybe I misheard. I have to go, too, but I'll send you a text right now. Love you, baby."

"You, too." He ended the call and stuffed the phone back in his pocket, his mind still dazed by his sudden revelation about Lydia Paxton.

Though he knew part of it was untrue – she wasn't like his mom. She was too kind, too empathetic for that. But it didn't matter, because the protective shield he'd built up, the one that stopped him from feeling hurt or abandoned ever since his mom had left him, was slowly rising back up.

It only had one job. The same job it always had where relationships were concerned. To stop him from getting hurt.

❧ 7 ❧

"Can I ask you a question?" Lydia asked Autumn later that evening as they were walking along the boardwalk. Lydia was pushing Skyler in her blue stroller, as they headed toward Angel Ices for dessert.

Griff was still out on his charter, due back in to dock at nine, so the sisters had taken advantage of the time they had to spend together.

"Sure. Shoot." The boardwalk was empty, save for a lone jogger running up and down from the pier to the coffee shop. Lydia had no idea what kind of training he was doing, but he sure did look miserable doing it.

"What do you know about Jackson's mom?" she asked.

Autumn turned to look at Lydia. "Well, that wasn't the question I was expecting."

"What were you expecting?" Lydia pulled her jacket around herself a little tighter. A breeze had picked up, blowing in from the ocean, making the air smell salty. As the sun slid down the sky, the temperatures had dipped, turning the evening distinctly chilly.

"I have no idea," Autumn admitted. "That's the fun thing about you. Nothing you say is what I expect."

"So do you know anything about his mom?" Lydia asked again. She was still wondering why Jackson had been so silent on their journey home. She'd made a few silly jokes that had made him smile, but for the most part he'd been quiet, letting the music fill the silence that dominated the space between them. And when Lydia had asked him to come in to try the coffee machine out – a genuine, non-sexual offer, thank you very much – he'd declined, saying he had way too much work to do.

It was like he couldn't get rid of her fast enough. Though she'd still managed to shout at his retreating back that she'd be over tomorrow evening to walk Eddie. She owed him that much.

"Why do you want to know about her?" Autumn asked, leaning into the stroller to stroke Skyler's cheek. Skyler laughed and kicked at the blanket covering her chubby legs.

"He was really quiet on the way home from the mall," Lydia said. She'd already told Autumn about her accident and need to replace the coffee pot. "And I'm not sure if it was my fault, or if it had something to do with his mom. She called while we were there."

"Well, I don't know much about his family situation, but I know his mom left him and his dad when he was pretty small. For most of the time growing up it was the two of them."

"Oh. How sad." Lydia blinked. Poor Jackson.

Autumn shook her head. "You have way too much empathy, do you know that? You're feeling sorry for him, and his mom is still around, when ours died while you were a baby."

Lydia glanced down at Skyler. She was only a few months younger than Lydia had been when their mom died. "Yeah, but Mom didn't choose to leave us. It must be hard growing up knowing your mom's still alive but doesn't want you."

Autumn gave her a strange look. "I guess it is."

"At least he's got Eddie around now. So he won't be lonely."

"Jackson's never exactly wanting for company. He's always surrounded by women."

"That's what I don't get. He doesn't come off like a player." Lydia sighed. He was a still lake that ran deep. Strange how she wanted to dive beneath the surface and see what was there.

"I don't know what a player looks like." Autumn shrugged. "I know assholes, because I was married to one." She grimaced at the memory of her ex-husband. "But Jackson isn't like Josh. He's just... lonely, I guess."

"When was the last time he had a girlfriend?"

Autumn shrugged, as Lydia veered to the left to avoid a skater. "Not since I've known him. But he's a flirt. He could charm the tail off a donkey." She laughed. "He'd probably flirt with a plant if it gave him the eye."

"He doesn't flirt with me," Lydia said quietly. Not unless you counted the situation between them in Doggy Couture. But that was make believe. The rest of the time he treated her with kid gloves.

"Maybe because he knows better than to try that with you." They'd reached the ice cream parlor, and Lydia maneuvered the stroller over the front step.

"What does that mean?" Lydia asked, as they walked inside Angel Ices.

"He knows better than to mess with you since you're related to me. It's the bro code. Griff would probably kill him if he tried it with you. And anyway, you're out of his league."

Lydia shook her head. "But he's hot. I mean, really, *really* hot." She thought of the way his arm had felt beneath her touch. Warm, soft skin stretched over thick, knotted muscles. Did the rest of him feel that way?

"Oh no." Autumn shook her head. "No, no, no."

"What have I done now?" Lydia rocked the stroller back and forth as they waited in line. "Skyler, your mom has finally lost it."

"I haven't lost it, but I might if you do something I'll regret later." Autumn sighed. "You don't have to live here, but I do. And I'd be really grateful if you didn't mess with Jackson, or make Griff upset. I love you, Lydia, but you have this tornado effect. You leave devastation in your wake."

"I do not." Lydia frowned. "When have I ever left devastation?"

"How about when we went out to celebrate my divorce and you made me drink all that tequila?"

"Hey, I didn't force them down your throat," Lydia pointed out. "And you needed loosening up."

"I bought a pier while I was drunk," Autumn reminded her. "That's not loose, that's bat shit wild."

"And look at you now. Thanks to buying that pier, you moved here and met Griff." Lydia blew a kiss at Skyler. "This little chunk of gorgeous baby wouldn't exist if you hadn't been wasted. So before you say I leave devastation, maybe you should thank me."

"You're right." Autumn's voice was quiet. "I'm sorry. And thank you." She hugged her sister. "I just worry about you. And it sounds stupid, but I worry about Jackson, too. He's Griff's best friend. I just want him to be happy."

"I know." Lydia hugged her back. "I want him to be happy, too." The thought hit her like a fist to the chest. She really did want to make him happy. By the time she left Angel Sands, Jackson Lewis needed to be smiling a heck of a lot more.

She just needed to work out how to make it happen.

"Can I help you?" the woman at the counter asked, as they wheeled the stroller up to the counter.

"Hey, you're the new owner, right?" Autumn leaned over to offer her hand. "I'm Autumn Paxton, I own the pier. I've been meaning to come say hi. This is my sister, Lydia, and my daughter, Skyler."

"I'm so pleased to meet you. I'm Meghan Hart. And the little girl sitting in the office there," she said, pointing through the door behind her, "is my daughter Isla."

"Are you local?" Autumn asked her.

"No, we just moved here. And to be honest, everything's still a little weird." Meghan grimaced. "We were due to move into our apartment last week, but the upstairs neighbor flooded it, so we've been living in a motel until everything's repaired."

"So sorry to hear that," Lydia said, grimacing. "What a nightmare."

Autumn pulled out a business card. "If you need anything, call me. I remember what it's like to be new in town with nowhere to stay. And maybe I can introduce you and Isla around to some of my friends."

The woman took her card. "Thank you so much. That would be wonderful. Now what can I get you both?"

"I'll have a scoop of vanilla in a waffle cone please," Autumn said

"And I'll have three scoops," Lydia added. "Pistachio, lemon, and chocolate in a cup, please. With extra chocolate sauce and sprinkles on top."

"And now you see the difference between us." Autumn grinned. "Two sisters summed up by an ice cream order."

"You only live once," Lydia pointed out.

"You're right," Autumn agreed. "But I'd like to live without fifty extra pounds."

They ate their dessert while walking home. Lydia had chosen the pistachio first, and she closed her eyes as the cool nutty ice cream coated her tongue, and slid down her throat.

"Imagine," she said to Autumn. "Skyler hasn't tasted ice cream yet. She has no idea what an amazing life she has in front of her."

"I'm kind of dreading weaning her," Autumn admitted. "Right now all I have to do is flash the boob. It's so easy. And portable."

"Aww, but imagine her face when she gets to taste real things. Like chocolate and cake and candy."

"And carrots and peas and potatoes," Autumn added. "I want her to eat healthy."

"She's such a peach," Lydia said, as Skyler waved her hands in front of her, staring at them like they contained the answers to everything. "You seem so happy. Are you happy?"

Autumn smiled. "Yeah, I am. Moving here was the right thing to do. I can't believe I put up with living with Josh for so long."

"Griff is a dreamboat."

"Yeah." Autumn took a lick of her vanilla ice cream. "He's finding it tough getting through the night without sleep though. He has such a physical job. He needs rest."

"You should definitely let me babysit this week. You two deserve a break."

Autumn nodded. "I'll think about it." She looked over at the beach. "Hey, look, there's Riley. Ally's stepdaughter." She lifted a hand to greet her.

It was funny, but they could hardly walk a yard without Autumn seeing somebody she knew. Lydia knew a lot of people in a lot of cities, but her sister knew *everybody* in Angel Sands. It was a different kind of life.

And it made Autumn happy. There was something to be said for that.

———

Jackson woke in the middle of the night to find something hard and heavy on the mattress next to him. It took a moment, and a few blinks, to figure out that Eddie had managed to push open the bedroom door, and jumped up beside him at some point in the night. He was lying diagonally, his paws resting on Jackson's chest, snoring happily as Jackson winced at the smell of his dog breath.

He thought about waking him up and sending him back to his bed in the kitchen, but he didn't have the heart to move him. Eddie was clearly enjoying whatever dream he was having. His tail was twitching, and his tongue lolling over his teeth, as long heavy breaths escaped from his mouth.

Gently removing the paws from his chest, Jackson turned over to check his phone. Three a.m. *Great*. It was supposed to be his first full night of sleep for a week, and now he was wide awake. He unlocked the screen on his phone and scrolled down, his eye catching on Lydia's message

Thank you again for all your help at the mall today. I was wondering if I could repay the favor by taking care of Eddie tomorrow? – Lydia.

His first instinct had been to refuse her help. He didn't need any complications, and as much as she entertained him, she was one big complication with a capital 'C', wrapped up in a pretty package.

Jackson blew out a mouthful of air, looking over his shoulder at Eddie. His mouth was moving now, like he was eating something he couldn't get enough of. How easy it must be to be a dog. Nothing to worry about except eating and walking. But then he remembered how he'd been lost, and it had taken Lydia's eagle eyes to spot him in the brush. Yeah, maybe being a dog wasn't that much fun.

And that brought his thinking around to Lydia once more. It didn't surprise him – she'd been in his thoughts ever since he'd dropped her off at Griff's house after their shopping expedition. He'd tried to shoo away the thought of her with numbers and coding, as he leaned over his laptop with his reading glasses perched on the bridge of his nose, his eyes too tired to focus on the screen without them.

He really had to work. They wanted to run this new application next week, to test it and work out any bugs. Without his part of the coding, it wouldn't work.

Yet... every time he tried to concentrate, there she was. Just like she was now, when he should be asleep until his six a.m. alarm. Instead, he was thinking about the way she'd danced in the middle of the mall, just to make him smile.

Ah, smiling was overrated anyway. Let's face it, he had no time for things like that. Not when he had a business to run, and a dog to take care of.

As if he knew Jackson was thinking about him, Eddie let out a low growl and rested his muzzle on Jackson's shoulder. It was strange how comforting it felt.

Jackson quickly tapped out a reply on his phone, because he knew himself well enough that he'd forget to reply by morning.

I'm taking Eddie to the office, but if you want to take him for a walk in the evening, he'll be waiting for you at seven. - Jackson

And if that meant Jackson had to wait with him? Well, wasn't that what good dog owners did?

"Oh my god, what's that?" Lisa asked the next morning, as she walked into the office to find Eddie curled up at Jackson's feet.

"It's a banana," Jackson replied, looking up from his laptop. He'd been here for almost an hour, having arrived after taking Eddie for a long stroll on the beach. And of course, Eddie had run into the ocean, making himself wet and sandy, which meant an impromptu shower in the office bathroom.

"Shut up, it's a dog," Lisa said, her face lighting up as Eddie slowly stretched and stood, then padded over to her and started sniffing her legs. "Aren't you a gorgeous thing," she said softly, ruffling his ears. "But who are you and what are you doing here?"

There was silence. Jackson shook his head and looked back down at his laptop screen, as Lisa fussed over Eddie, making cooing noises as she cupped his furry face.

"So why have you got a dog?" she asked, her voice a little louder this time.

Jackson sighed. "He's a stray. We found him in the brush and I agreed to take care of him."

Lisa snorted. "*You're* taking care of a dog?" She looked down at Eddie again. "You poor little baby," she said in a cooing voice. "Has he even fed you?"

"Yes, I've fed him," Jackson said, swallowing down a sigh. "And I've walked him, washed him, and now he was trying to sleep until you walked in."

Eddie's tail started to wag like a metronome, hitting the trashcan and almost knocking it over. "Sit!" Lisa called out.

Much to her – and Jackson's – astonishment, Eddie did exactly as he was told, slamming his behind on the tiled office floor as he looked at Lisa with a pleased expression.

"Oh wow. I'm good, right?" She grinned. "Let's try another. Lay down."

On cue, Eddie folded his front legs, and rested his chin on the tile.

"He's well trained," Lisa said, looking up at Jackson. "Somebody must be missing him."

"I guess. We've put in feelers at the vets and the animal shelter. If they find the owners, they'll let me know."

"You should put an advertisement up," she said. "Maybe post in the community Facebook page. Somebody has to know who he is. I bet his owners are missing him." She stroked Eddie's head. "Because you're a gorgeous little thing, aren't you? Especially with that cute neckerchief." She pulled at it. "Was he wearing this when you found him?"

Jackson swallowed hard. "No."

She grinned. "So you bought it for him?"

"Kind of. It's a long story." One he didn't intend to share with his assistant. If she ever found out he had a matching neckerchief in his bottom drawer at home, he'd never live it down. "Hey, why don't you take his photo and post it wherever you suggested. And while you're at it, I took a look at those résumés you gave me. There's three I think are worth an interview. I spoke to Derrick, and he said he'd be happy to ask the technical questions when you interview them."

Lisa slowly looked up, her eyes wide. "You looked at the résumés?" she asked, her voice lifting with surprise.

"Yeah. You asked me to, so I did."

"But you never do anything I ask."

Jackson shrugged. "Maybe you asked nicely this time."

"And maybe you're some kind of cyborg that Jackson created so he can toy with my emotions." Her brows knit together as she walked over and tapped him on the head with her knuckles.

"Ow, that hurts." He shot her a dirty look. "What was that for?"

"You can't fool me. I've seen *Ex Machina*. In fact, I think I saw it at your house when we had that team building session. How do I know you are who you say you are and not a robot version of yourself?"

"Because I'm the only one who can drive you crazy like this. A cyborg couldn't do that. And anyway, if I was a robot, wouldn't Eddie notice? Dogs always bark at robots in the movies."

"Hmm." She narrowed her eyes. "Maybe. But I'm keeping my eyes on you, Jackson Lewis. Just in case."

"I wouldn't have it any other way." He shook his head. But Lisa was too busy angling her phone and sweet talking Eddie again as she snapped photos of the dog, ready to upload to the community social media page.

And that was a good thing, wasn't it? Jackson didn't need any ties. Not when he had a business to run. Lisa made kissy sounds at Eddie, who wasn't having any of it, refusing to look up at her no matter how sweet she tried to talk to him.

After she finally gave up and just took some shots, Eddie gave a little growl and ambled back to Jackson, lifting his soulful eyes up to look at his almost-kind-of master, before resting his chin on Jackson's thighs.

Damn, it was hard to resist him. Jackson stroked Eddie's brow, unable to hide his grin when Eddie almost purred like a cat with contentment.

"Okay, I've uploaded them," Lisa said. "I put the office phone in for the contact details, since you barely ever answer your phone."

Eddie's eyes drooped, even though he was still standing, his head resting on Jackson. "Thanks," Jackson said, patting him with one hand, while typing with the other.

"No problem. But when I find his real home I expect a bonus."

Weird how that made Jackson's stomach contract. Maybe he was worried for Lydia. She liked Eddie so much she made them purchase matching neckerchiefs, after all.

Yeah, well Lydia's only here until next week. The ache in his guts increased, making Jackson blink as he read the email in front of him.

Soon, Lydia would be flying off to Europe, and Eddie would more than likely be reunited with his owners. That would leave Jackson alone again. And that was exactly the way he liked things.

Wasn't it?

❧ 8 ❧

L ydia felt like she'd been walking for days, even though
her watch told her it had been just over an hour and a
half. When she'd set out, the sun had been high in the sky, a
huge golden disc reflecting yellow ripples across the ocean.
Now it was burnished, slipping down the horizon, shading
everything orange and pink.

She'd spent today with Autumn at the pier, playing with
Skyler while her sister had meeting after meeting in her
pretty office overlooking the ocean. Lydia and her niece had
explored the pier, then they'd visited with the lovely shop
owners on the boardwalk, which meant lots of cuddles and
kisses for Skyler, and a lot of questions for Lydia.

Frank Megassey had wanted to look at her Instagram and
asked for advice on where he should take his wife for their
Ruby wedding anniversary. Lydia had asked him a few questions about the kind of things they liked to do during the day
while they were on vacation, and what his wife's favorite food
was. They'd settled on a trip to Italy – visiting Rome and
Venice in the fall, once the worst of the heat had dissipated,
but before the cold arrived. She'd written down his email

address so she could send him some places to visit – the 'off the beaten track' restaurants and galleries that would make him look like a hero in his wife's eyes.

After she had left Frank's hardware store, with a toy rattle he'd gifted to Skyler, they'd headed to the book store to look at baby books. It was owned by Deenie Russell, the mom of one of Griff's best friends. As soon as Lydia wheeled Skyler's stroller through the door, she'd run over to give the baby a kiss on the cheek.

"She's so big. And look at her goofy smile. Doesn't she take after Griff?" Deenie had asked.

Lydia had laughingly agreed, though the rest of Skyler's features looked astonishingly like Autumn's.

She'd spent an hour at the book store, reading to Skyler, who promptly fell asleep in the middle of Dr. Seuss' *Oh, The Places You'll Go*. While she slept, Lydia had helped Deenie set up an Instagram page for the bookstore, and they'd taken a lot of photos for her to feature over the next few days.

"Remember, lots of hashtags, and you need to interact," Lydia told her. "And post regularly. Once a day if you can. You have enough books here to take photos for years."

After the bookstore, Lydia had wheeled Skyler to Déjà Brew for a chat with Ally and Nate, before they headed back to the pier. Griff's whale watching boat had just docked, and his customers were spilling off the metal gangplank and onto the pier – a group of children from the local school who were talking excitedly to each other.

Lydia had waited for them all to leave before she wheeled Skyler up to the boat. She was wide awake by that point, and as soon as she spotted her daddy standing on the pier she'd let out a squeal.

Griff had looked equally pleased to see his daughter, walking over and scooping her out of her stroller, before lifting her high and peppering her cheeks with kisses. Skyler had squealed, her arms flying as she tried to grab his hair in her chubby fists. Damn if seeing the two of them didn't do something to Lydia's ovaries. She'd grinned insanely as her soon to be brother-in-law rubbed his beard against Skyler's face, making the baby giggle loudly.

It was only when the four of them – Autumn, Griff, Skyler, and Lydia – had made it back to their beachside ranch house that Lydia announced she was going out again.

"Where?" Griff had asked. "You don't know anybody here, do you?"

Autumn had bitten down a grin. "Sweetheart, Lydia's been here for more than a day. She knows literally everybody. Do you know how many people have called to tell me what a darling my sister is?"

"People have called you?" Lydia asked.

"Who?" Griff had added, his brows knitting together as he looked from his fiancée to her sister.

"Well first of all, Frank called and told me she'd solved his anniversary dilemma. After that, Deenie called to rave about what a tech wizard she is." Autumn smiled fondly at her sister. "Then Lorne Daniels called to tell me that if he was fifty years younger, he'd be asking her out on a date."

"Lorne, the surf shop guy?" Lydia verified.

Autumn nodded. "The very same."

Autumn and Griff turned to look at Lydia, who shrugged. "I just like talking to people, that's all. And so did Skyler."

"So where are you going?" Griff asked her.

"I promised Jackson I'd take Eddie out for a walk," she told them. "He's kind of half my dog, too."

"He's not yours or Jackson's," Griff pointed out. "He belongs to somebody else. Jackson is just taking care of him."

"I know." Lydia's voice was bright. "But since I'm the one who found Eddie, it's only fair I do some of the work."

"Is Jackson picking you up?" Autumn asked, cradling Skyler against her chest. "Or would you like a ride over?"

"I can walk. It's a lovely evening."

"Jackson lives five miles up the coast," Autumn had pointed out. "It's not exactly a short stroll."

"It can't be *that* far," Lydia argued. "I can practically see his house from here. It's on that cliff, isn't it?"

She noticed Autumn and Griff exchange a glance.

"Yep," Griff said. "That's the one."

And now she was walking up the cliff steps toward Jackson's house, having taken the route Griff had shown her, along the boardwalk, then past the bigger houses until she reached open sand, walking along the coastal path until the cliff curved around. That's when she'd seen the steps he'd described. They looked as though they'd been carved out of the cliff face a hundred years ago, their once sharp edges worn down, and damn if they didn't make her legs ache as they twisted and turned to the top.

She was breathless when she made it to the grassy lawn leading to Jackson's house. There was a fence containing his backyard, and she pulled on the gate to open it, stepping inside.

Jackson and Eddie were in the yard, play-wrestling. Jackson was on his back, his denim-clad legs bent at the knee, his bare feet planted in the grass. He was wearing a black henley, and his biceps bulged beneath the dark cotton as he held Eddie's thick trunk, while Eddie yapped and barked and jumped all over him.

When Jackson tried to sit up, Eddie pushed him down with his paws, making him laugh loudly. Eddie jumped back, enough for Jackson to scoot away, before Eddie leapt on him and the wrestling started all over again.

"Okay, okay, you win!" Jackson said, laughing, as Eddie finally stopped jumping. "Now sit."

Much to her surprise, Eddie did exactly as he was told, gracefully planting his haunches on the grass and his paws in front of him, as he looked up at Jackson.

"Good boy," Jackson murmured, ruffling the pup's hair. Eddie looked as pleased as punch.

"Have you been training him?" Lydia asked. Their two heads swept around in tandem to look at her. Eddie cocked his head to the side, while Jackson blinked at her sudden appearance.

"Where did you come from?" he asked, a smile curling at his lips. "Is it seven already?"

"A quarter after." Lydia had the good grace to look apologetic. "I'm late. It took longer than I'd expected to get here. Especially with all those steps."

He stood and brushed the grass from his top. She tried really hard not to look at the sliver of skin between the hem and his jeans. "Didn't you get a ride?" he asked her.

"I decided to walk. It's a lovely evening."

"So you walked five miles here, to take Eddie for a walk, and later you'll walk five miles back?"

"I guess." She honestly hadn't thought about the journey home. But that would be okay.

"You really need to learn how to drive."

"Then teach me," she joked.

"Okay."

Her mouth dropped open. "I was just kidding. You don't have to do that. I'd drive you crazy. *Literally*. The only time I've ever been behind a wheel I almost drove into a wall."

Jackson nodded. "Noted. We won't go near any walls."

"You're serious."

"I am. You can't live the next seventy years of your life not being able to drive. I can at least show you the basics. Then when you're ready you will be prepared to eventually take lessons."

The thought of Jackson taking her out to drive his car made her feel fluttery inside. It was those damn biceps. Every time they flexed her heart missed a beat. And if he was teaching her to drive, they'd have to flex *a lot*. And maybe reach across her, to show her how to turn the wheel properly.

"You really don't have to. I've survived this long without learning."

"It's fine. We'll start tonight after you've taken Eddie for a walk. I'll drive you home and explain all the basics. Then tomorrow, I'll pick you up and you can do some driving."

She nodded. "It's a deal." And one that she would benefit the most out of. She made a mental note to herself to do something – *anything* – to make his life easier. Something that didn't involve him looking after a dog or teaching a wild woman to drive.

"Okay." He didn't look perturbed at all. If anything, he looked amused. "I'll go grab Eddie's leash, and you can take him down to the beach while I finish up some work."

Jackson sighed and pushed his laptop away. He wasn't getting any work done. He was too busy looking beyond the screen to the beach below his cliff house. When he'd first looked at this place, it had been the view that had drawn him. The ocean had been part of his life for as long as he could remember. First with his dad's career as a professional surfer, and when he gave that up for a steadier, more local job, it was Jackson who'd surfed more.

The ocean was choppy tonight. He smiled as he watched Lydia and Eddie run alongside the foaming waves as they crashed against the beach. The sun was halfway beneath the horizon, casting a low, orange glow across the surface of the water. Part of him wanted to be down there, running with them. But he was already too far gone. He liked her. More than he wanted to. She made him smile in a way he hadn't for a long time. She made him want things he had no place wanting. Things like soft touches and knowing grins. Warm, welcoming lips and soft tender thighs.

He groaned, shifting in his chair. She was leaving in ten days. He had to get through them, and he'd be okay. He was used to people leaving – he'd watched his mom do it too many times over the years. Just keep that protective armor over his heart and everything would be okay.

Eddie jumped at Lydia, shaking his wet body all over her. Most girls he knew would have screamed at that, but he could see Lydia laughing while shaking her hair back at Eddie, who barked with delight.

He'd never met anybody quite like her. Never felt the kind of pull he did every time she was near. It felt out of his control, and he didn't like that.

Nah. That wasn't true. He liked it too much. Like an addict drawn to their next fix.

The way his dad was always drawn to his mom, no matter how many times she walked away.

In the distance he could see a big swell moving steadily toward the breaking point. The kind of swell that would make his heart race if he was on a board right now. He'd paddle toward it, his eyes transfixed on the shape, working out exactly the right spot to ride the giant wave into shore.

Lydia had her back to the ocean, leaning down toward the sand as though she was searching for something to throw. She was close to the breaking waves, enough that her bare feet were covered with salt water every time they hit the shore.

Jacksons stood, walking toward the edge of his yard, and called out her name. Lydia looked up, smiling, and waved at him. He shook his head, pointing at the wave that was now lifting and foaming in readiness to break. From the shrug on her shoulders she had no idea what he was trying to say. Not until the roar of the rolling water hit her ears, and she looked over her shoulder at the oncoming surge.

Eddie chose that moment to jump at her again, knocking her over right as the wave broke. It poured over them both, obscuring them completely as the white water rushed up the beach.

By the time it receded, Eddie was happily swimming back with it, while Lydia was coughing and spluttering in an attempt to stand.

Shit.

Jackson ran down the cliff steps as fast as he could, his leg muscles lengthening and contracting rhythmically as he made it to the sand. She was bent over – damn, was she hurt? He sprinted toward her, his heart pummeling against his ribcage.

She looked up. Her hair was drenched and matted with sand and salt. Black mascara ran from her eyes and down her cheeks, like dark viscous teardrops. Her shorts and white t-shirt clung to her body like they never wanted to let go. He swallowed hard, trying to drag his eyes away from her soft, beautiful curves.

Lydia laughed. Not just a giggle, but a full-on roar. Her eyes crinkled, her body bent over, her hair cascading over her shoulders.

"You okay?" he asked, reaching out a hand to help her up. She curled her fingers around his, climbing to her feet, her body still shaking with laughter.

"Did you see that?" she asked. "Eddie got me good."

"Yeah, I saw it." *Eyes on her face, man.* "Did you swallow any water?"

"About a gallon." She looked down at her wet clothes and up again. "I think I've got more water in my stomach than there's left out there."

Eddie suddenly noticed Jackson standing there, and let

77

out a happy bark, bounding toward them both. "Sit!" Jackson shouted, not expecting it to work at all. But he did it, his tongue lolling out, his fur wet with brine.

The sun had almost disappeared. The air around them felt fresh, breezy. "You should take a shower," Jackson told Lydia. He was still holding her hand. Funny how he felt in no hurry to let it go. "I've got some old clothes you can wear."

"But I haven't taken Eddie for a walk. We were too busy playing on the beach."

Jackson glanced at the dog. He was panting, his eyes shining as he looked adoringly at Lydia. He knew how he felt. "He looks happy enough. And if he's still full of energy later, I'll take him then."

She sighed. "I was supposed to be doing you a favor. Now I feel like I've given you more work to do."

He grinned. "You've made me laugh, which is favor enough. And I think you've made Eddie's day, too. It's getting cool. Come up and get showered, then I'll drive you home."

9

Jackson handed Lydia a towel from his heated linen cupboard in the hallway, and pushed open the bathroom door. The interior was masculine and calm, with black tiled walls and a grey tiled floor, the chrome fittings so shiny she could see a rounded reflection of her face in them.

"Wow, this is clean," she said, holding the warm towel against her drenched skin.

"You sound surprised."

She bit her lip. "Most guys' bathrooms I've seen are grubby. I wasn't expecting it to be so... nice."

"I don't know whether to be offended by your assumptions, or curious about how many guys' bathrooms you've seen." He winked at her, and damn if it didn't make her heart skip a beat. "But instead, I'll admit that the cleaner came today. And this is the guest bathroom. Mine is messy and full of crap."

"In a weird way that makes me feel better." She smiled. He was so damn easy going. And tall. She hadn't realized how tall until she was in her bare feet beside him. It wasn't her fault that her eye line was almost exactly at his chest. Well, it was if she lowered her gaze just a bit. And that action was worth it, because the black henley he was wearing was tight enough for her to see the outline of his chest through it.

His strong, defined chest. She curled her hands tightly around the fluffy towel in case they decided to go rogue and reach out to trace the outline of his pectorals. She couldn't trust her damn fingers around him.

"Okay. I'll go shower." She smiled brightly at him. "Anything I need to know? Does it run cold? If you flush the toilet am I gonna get scalded?"

He laughed. "Not that I know of. And I promise not to flush the toilet. I'm going to make you some hot coffee though. I'll leave it outside the door, okay?"

"I can come down and get it."

He looked directly at her. "I know you can. But I want you to get warm, so I'll bring it up."

"You're kind of hot when you're masterful, you know that?" She turned and walked into the bathroom, a grin on her lips.

"Get in the shower, Lydia."

"See?" She looked over her shoulder. He was shaking his head. "Hot."

He closed the door behind her, and she could hear him muttering something, though his voice was far too low for her to make out. Hanging the towel on the gleaming heated rail next to the shower, she pulled her shorts down and lifted her t-shirt over her head.

That's when she caught a glimpse of herself in the mirror. Her eyes widened as she took in her wild, matted hair. Dear god, had he really seen her like this and not laughed? He was sweeter than she'd thought for not saying anything.

Five minutes later, she was happily singing in the steaming hot shower as she massaged Jackson's shampoo into her hair. It smelled like him, all woody and mellow. She took a look at the name on the black plastic bottle. Maybe she'd treat herself to some.

Not because she wanted to smell of him. Just because it was good. That was all.

Once she'd rinsed and conditioned, she turned off the spray and stepped out of the oversized cubicle, reaching for the towel. The room was full of steam, though the vent was doing its best to remove it. She walked over to the mirrored cabinet, pulling it open, wondering if he had a spare hairbrush in there. Sadly it was empty. She did her best to rake her fingers through her slippery locks before wrapping them in the towel.

"Your coffee's out here," Jackson called through the door.

"Thank you." She looked around until she saw her wet clothes in a bundle on the floor. Picking up her soaked panties, she grimaced. "Um, do you have those clothes you said I could borrow?"

"Sorry?" he called out, his voice muffled.

"I need some dry clothes," she shouted again. "Do you have any?"

"You need what?"

Sighing, she wrenched the door open. "Do you have a t-shirt or something?" she asked him. "My clothes are soaking."

It was only when his mouth dropped open that she remembered she was as naked as the day she was born.

Jackson froze long enough for his wide eyes to take in her perfectly curved body. When he finally looked away his body pulsed with heat, and his voice was thick and low.

"You have a tattoo."

Lydia looked down at the cherry blossom curling around her left hip. He was struck again by how different she was.

Any other woman he knew would have screamed and either covered herself up or slammed the door in his face. But not Lydia. Instead, she was looking back up at him, her eyes soft.

"Cherry blossoms were my mom's favorite. She went to the festival in Washington every year. I got it on my twenty-first birthday while in Japan." She slowly untwisted the towel on her head, the movement lifting the perfect swell of her breasts. When she pulled the towel around to cover her body, he wasn't sure whether to be disappointed or grateful.

"It's pretty." He hardly recognized his voice. He really needed to stop looking at her like this. She was a guest in his house. Autumn's sister. Verboten. "I have one, too."

"A cherry blossom?" She tucked the end of the towel in over her breasts. Even covered up, her body made his blood feel thick and heavy.

"No. An eagle."

She laughed. "Let me see."

"Now?" He lifted an eyebrow.

"Yeah, now. You saw mine."

It was only fair. He pulled his top over his head and threw it on the floor, looking right at her. She could see the eagle, wings spread, covering the top of his right arm. Her gaze dipped, taking in his bare chest.

The air between them was so thick he could feel it pressing against him. Their eyes met again, and he felt it in his gut. Blood rushed straight to the part of him that didn't care he wasn't supposed to be here doing this.

Standing half naked in his home with Lydia Paxton, who was completely naked under her towel.

"Can I touch it?" she murmured, her voice low.

"If I can touch yours." He was all about quid pro quo tonight.

Her lips curled. "I was banking on it." She reached out, tracing the outline of the eagle's wings. "Why did you get this?" She moved her hand to his chest, tracing the outline of his pectoral.

"Because I was young, foolish, and drunk."

Her finger brushed against his hard nipple. "How young?" She stepped closer. Until he could feel the warmth of her skin radiating from her.

"Lydia..." It was a warning. This aching desire felt inevitable. As though everything before this was leading to them standing here, half naked, in his hallway. He'd tried to fight it. Tried to ignore it. Tried to push it away. But he was tired of fighting. "I was eighteen."

The attraction was winning out.

She moistened her bottom lip with the tip of her pink tongue, and it made him ache harder. "Do you regret it?" she asked him.

His head was fuzzy. He couldn't think straight. "Regret what?"

"The tattoo."

How could he regret it when it had somehow led to this? To her standing in front of him, her body less than an inch from his. "Regrets are useless," he told her, his voice thick as molasses. "I don't have time for them."

"Me either." She looked up at him through thick eyelashes. "Now it's your turn to touch mine."

She opened the towel until he could see the twisting stem of the cherry blossom. Jackson swallowed hard and reached out, his finger feathering her taut skin as it traced the tattoo.

She moved, parting her thighs just enough that he could tell it was an invitation. "You want me to?" he asked, his voice thick.

Lydia swallowed. "Please. That's exactly what I want."

"Damn, Lydia." He lowered his head until his brow was touching hers. Could feel the wetness of her skin against his. "What are you doing to me?"

"The same thing you're doing to me." Her breath was soft against his lips.

There was an edge to her voice that sounded as needy as he felt. Her chest was lifting and falling rapidly, the towel brushing against his bare abdomen every time she exhaled. One pull, and her breasts would be against him. His dick swelled at the thought of it.

With his free hand he cupped her jaw, angling her face until her deep green eyes were staring straight at his. She swallowed hard, and her lips parted, and he knew this would be the best first kiss he'd ever have.

Because it was with her.

"You're beautiful," he murmured, tangling his fingers into her wet hair. His other hand curled around her bare hip, pulling her closer, until there was no air between them.

"So are you."

The drumming in his ears reached a crescendo, matching his racing heart. He ran his thumb along her jaw, adjusting her face until their lips brushed. She moaned softly against his mouth, making him so damn hard it was painful. He was full of her. Her touch, her smell, the way she looked as she stared back at him. There was no space for conscious thought or rational decisions. He was her and she was him.

He slid his hand down her stomach, swallowing hard at the thought of touching her there. Once he did, he wasn't sure he'd be able to stop.

"Are you sure?" he asked.

"I'm sure."

He opened his mouth to tell her she was beautiful, but Eddie started barking, the gruff sound echoing through the hallway.

Jackson pulled away, his brows knitting as Eddie let out another howling bark. Releasing her hold from his neck,

Lydia pulled the towel tightly around her, looking over her shoulder in concern.

"Is he okay?"

"Jackson?" another voice called out.

They both blinked at the unexpected interloper. Unlike Lydia, he knew exactly who it belonged to.

"Where are you?" the masculine shout echoed through the house. The dog started barking happily, as though he was being stroked. "Hey Eddie. Is my boy upstairs?"

"Your dad?" Lydia asked, looking down at the small towel wrapped around her, and at Jackson's bare chest.

"Yeah." He exhaled, stepping back to have some air between them. His skin protested at the sudden cold against it. "That's my dad."

Tiptoeing downstairs, Lydia tried not to trip over the grey sweatpants Jackson had given her. She'd rolled them up to make them fit. Her hair was brushed away from her face and the old, soft t-shirt she'd knotted across her waist smelled so much of him it made her chest feel tight.

Her skin felt overheated. A combination of the shower and Jackson Lewis. She let out a sigh, remembering how good it had felt to be touched by him. His soft fingers, his warm lips, and that almost-kiss.

"She fell in the ocean and that's why she had to take a shower?" Jackson's dad was laughing in the kitchen. "Sure. That's exactly what happened, son."

There was a bang, as though Jackson was brewing more coffee. How much did he drink in the evening? No wonder he couldn't sleep. Maybe she should introduce him to green tea.

"Will you cut it out?" Jackson said. She lingered on the bottom step, not wanting them to know she was listening.

"She came to walk the dog, got submerged by a wave, and needed a shower. End of story."

"You have a beautiful woman in your house and nothing happened?" Ryan sighed. "Why not? Are you blind or something?"

"She's Autumn's sister," Jackson said as though it explained everything. "And she's leaving soon."

Lydia sat on the step, resting her chin on her hand. It was wrong to listen, she knew that. And yet she couldn't help herself.

Anyway, she was still trying to calm down. She'd rather not let Jackson's dad see her all flushed and excited. That would really contradict Jackson's story about nothing happening.

"So she's leaving. Doesn't mean you can't see where things go. I think she likes you."

"Can we shut up about this now?" Jackson asked. There was a loud bang, as though he was closing a cupboard with force. "What did you want anyway?"

"I just wanted to check on Eddie. Make sure you're taking care of him."

Hearing his name, Eddie gave a bark.

"Eddie's fine. And so am I. Now I'm going to finish my coffee, give Lydia a ride home, and get on with some work."

"I'm worried about how hard you're working." Ryan's voice was low. "You need to let go. You're still young. Life doesn't get any easier once you settle down and have a family. You should be enjoying it now, letting loose, having fun."

"Like you did?"

"If you'd like," Ryan agreed. "I got to travel the world, follow my dreams, and achieve everything I wanted."

"And then you met mom and everything went crazy." Jackson sounded sad. Lydia shifted on the step, her brows knitting together.

"I've never regretted meeting your mom. She gave me you," Ryan said softly. "The best kind of prize a man can get."

There was silence for a moment. Lydia's heart clenched at the emotion in Ryan's words. She had to blink to stop tears from forming. How sweet was he? Was that where Jackson got it from? Because despite his hard exterior, she knew he could be sweet, too.

"Dad..."

"It's okay."

"It's not okay. I'm not like you. You gave your life up for mom and me. She walked out and left you alone to raise a kid. I saw how hard it was for you. How hard I made it for you sometimes. And I know you don't regret it, but maybe I wanted more for you."

"That's not the way it works, son. We take what we get and make the best of it."

Jackson sighed. "Yeah, and that's what I'm doing. Building my business, making sure we're both set for life. That's all I have time for right now."

"And if Hayley hadn't left? Would you have chosen something different then?"

Who was Hayley? Lydia leaned forward, shaking her head at herself. This had went from listening to a father and son conversation to something more. Something she wasn't supposed to overhear. She stood and cleared her throat, padding across the cool tile floor from the stairs to the kitchen. "Hey!" she said, painting a smile on her face. "What do you guys think of my outfit?"

Ryan grinned as soon as she walked in. "Looks better on you than Jackson."

She gave him a little curtsey. "Thank you kindly, sir."

Jackson was on the other side of the breakfast bar, his bare elbows leaning on the Corian counter, his hands curled around a grey coffee mug. Their eyes met, and she felt it again. That slam in her chest which made her heart skip a beat.

His eyes were dark. Narrow. His lips pressed together. He swallowed hard as he scanned her from head to foot, taking in his clothes knotted and rolled on her small body.

"You warm enough?" he asked, his voice graveled.

"Yeah. You have a toasty shower. And thank you for the coffee."

"Shower's even warmer with two." Ryan coughed behind his hand.

Lydia bit down a grin. "You offering?"

"If I was twenty years younger, I'd be begging, sweetheart." He winked at her. "But I have a feeling you're too much woman for me."

From the corner of her eye she could see Jackson watching them intently, a rhythmic tic to his jaw.

"I think you could cope." She shrugged. "I hear you taught Jackson, Griff, and Lucas how to surf. If you can wrangle those three you can do anything."

"Do *you* surf?" Ryan asked, tipping his head to the side. He was a handsome man, the same square jaw as Jackson, but unlike his son he was freshly shaven. His silver hair brushed back from his face.

"I've tried it a few times on my travels. In Hawaii, of course. And Bondi Beach. And did you know they surf in England? In the west of the country. I tried it there once."

"I was in a competition in Newquay once."

"Fistral Beach?" Lydia asked.

Ryan grinned. "That's the one. Those English guys are unbelievable. And that water is damn cold. I swear I had goosebumps on top of my goosebumps."

Jackson cleared his throat. "If you two are finished with the travelogue, I need to take Lydia home. I got a hell of a lot of work to do tonight."

"Oh. Of course." Lydia nodded at him. "Sorry for delaying you."

"It's fine." He grabbed his keys from the counter. "You okay to look after Eddie for a minute?" he asked his dad.

"Sure."

"Then let's go."

The air in his car crackled and buzzed between them as Jackson drove down the cliff road toward the beach. Griff and Autumn had a ranch house on the other side of town that they'd bought before they had Skyler, complete with ocean views.

"Do you mind if we take a raincheck on the driving lesson tonight?" Jackson asked her. The thought of being in the car with her any longer than necessary was putting him on edge. It was hard enough knowing she was sitting next to him in his clothes. His dad was right, they did look better on her.

They'd look even better in a heap on the floor of his bedroom, while he ran his lips along that tattoo on her hip.

He gritted his teeth to chase away the thought.

"That's fine by me." Her voice was light. "I've taken up way too much of your time already."

"You're not mad?" he clarified. He wasn't sure why that made his chest tighten.

"Why would I be? It was a nice offer, but we can do it another time." She shrugged. "Or not at all."

"No, we will," he said quickly. "I'll call you and we can arrange something."

She smiled at him. "Sounds good."

The lights were red as he drove along the main street in town. Jackson took the opportunity to look at her as she stared out of the car window at the bookshop. Her jaw had the perfect curve to it. Delicate, yet defined. He wasn't sure he'd ever noticed a woman's jaw before, let alone felt drawn to it. He had to tightly grip his hands around the steering wheel to stop himself from tracing a line across her soft, tender skin.

Yeah, sure, a driving lesson would be great. Well done, Jackson.

"I really like your dad," she said, turning back to him. "He's a sweetie."

"Yeah, well he likes you, too." Jackson pulled his gaze away from her jaw. Didn't stop him from wanting to touch her, though. Every time he inhaled he could smell the aroma of her freshly washed skin. It made him feel weird inside to smell the woody notes of his soap on her.

"He does?" She looked strangely gratified at that.

"Of course he does. Who doesn't like you? You're... very likeable."

Lydia laughed. "I can be too much for people." Her voice dipped. "I know I make you angry sometimes."

"You don't make me angry." He glanced at her, frowning. "What makes you think that?"

Her lips twitched. "I guess it's the way you look at me. Exactly the way you are right now."

How was he looking? Jackson took stock of his expression. Brows knitted together, lips turned down. Eyes narrowed to a slit. She thought he was angry at her? Dammit. He was angry at himself, not her.

Angry because he wanted her even though it was wrong. Angry that he couldn't have a normal life like Griff and Lucas and their families. That he couldn't seem to get it together the way his friends had. And that he spent way too long thinking about this stuff.

"I'm not angry with you," he said, his voice soft. "Not at all." He steered the car onto Griff and Autumn's road. The sky was completely black now, with pinpricks of stars shining down. Their reflections lit up the dark ocean, dancing with the waves. Jackson turned into the driveway and brought his car to a stop.

"You're not?"

He shook his head slowly. "I'm not." He switched the ignition off. Silence filled the car. "And what happened back at my place? Outside the bathroom? I'm sorry."

Lydia blinked, her lips parting. "Okay." She nodded. "In that case, I should be sorry too." Unclipping her seatbelt, she reached for the door knob. "And thanks for the clothes, I'll get them back to you once I've washed them."

"No rush. And no need to clean them." Because he was a dog, and wanted to smell her on them.

"Goodnight." Lydia gave him the smallest of smiles. "Don't work too hard tonight. You need sleep, too."

The corner of his lip quirked up. "I'll try not to."

She cracked opened the door and froze. As if on impulse, she turned and leaned across the car, cupping his jaw with her hand and planting a huge kiss on his cheek. "By the way, I'm not sorry at all about what happened outside your bathroom."

Before he could reply, she was hopping out of the car and closing the door behind her, carrying her wet clothes in the bag he'd given her, as she sashayed along the driveway to Griff and Autumn's house.

Jackson laughed to himself, because what else was he supposed to do?

The truth was, he wasn't sorry, either.

❧ 10 ❧

Lydia was the last to get up the next morning. By the time she climbed out of bed at nine, Griff was long gone, and Autumn was flying out of the house, Skyler in her stroller. "I'm in meetings this morning," she told Lydia. "And this afternoon I have the decorators coming to nail down the plans for the ceremony. But tonight is girls' night. Ally's invited us all over for cocktails." She wiggled her eyebrows. "You up for that? We can go somewhere just the two of us if you prefer."

"Girls' night sounds good," Lydia said, smiling. She liked Autumn's friends. After last night's heated exchange with Jackson, maybe a room full of estrogen was what she needed.

And anyway, they had the info on Jackson. And Hayley, whoever she was. Fun and facts – that was the kind of night she liked.

Lydia pressed a kiss to Skyler's smooth brow. The baby grabbed her hair and held on tight, making Lydia laugh.

"You sure you'll be okay alone today?" Autumn grimaced. "You can come to the pier again if you'd like?"

"It's good. I have a video conference this morning with

some clients. After that, I'll walk to the boardwalk to do a little shopping. I want to check on Deenie's Instagram, and I promised to set Lorne Michaels up, too."

"You know more people than I do here," Autumn teased.

"Hardly. But they're nice and I like helping them." Lydia shrugged. "So please don't worry. I won't get bored."

"You never do," Autumn agreed. "That's one of the things I admire about you."

That made Lydia's skin glow. Her older sister wasn't big on compliments. So when they came, they really meant something. "You sure I can't look after Skyler for you while you're working?" she asked Autumn.

"That's so sweet of you, but I want to spend a bit of time with her between meetings." Autumn gave her a quick hug. "You have the spare keys to the house, right?"

"Sure do." Lydia grinned.

"Okay. I'll see you this evening. Be ready for girls' night." She pulled open the front door and wheeled Skyler out to her car, lifting her from the stroller to her car seat. Lydia blew a kiss at them both and closed the door.

After pouring herself a coffee, and silently congratulating herself for not breaking anything, Lydia placed her laptop on the kitchen table, and grabbed her pad, quickly scanning through her notes.

Serena Blake had booked Lydia's services last year, the day after she'd gotten engaged to her fiancé, a successful investment banker in New York. When Lydia had told her she wasn't available for more than twelve months, Serena had taken it in her stride.

"That's fine," she said. "We can plan the wedding around your availability." She wasn't even joking.

Now it was only three months until they were due to go

to Rio for their honeymoon, and Lydia had sent over their itinerary last week. Wherever possible, she always tried to follow it up with a meeting or video call to make sure things were to their liking. It was important her clients were happy.

Clicking on the icon to start the call, Lydia waited for it to connect, and smiled when she saw Serena and Damon appear on the screen.

"Hi," she said. "How are you?"

"Great," Serena said. Damon nodded and said nothing. From the set of his eyes, Lydia was certain he was scrolling through his phone.

Behind them, Lydia could see the elegant lines of their expensive living room furniture, and a window overlooking Central Park, the trees swaying softly in the spring breeze.

"Thanks for agreeing to do this virtually. I'm sorry we can't meet in person," Lydia told them.

"No no, it's fine." Serena leaned forward, her baby blue cashmere sweater pulling down to reveal a tiny silver locket nestling at the dip in her throat. "We're just grateful you have time to meet with us. We know how exclusive you are." She took Damon's hand and squeezed it. He looked up from his phone, eyes widening as though he didn't expect to be looking at a computer screen filled with a woman in California.

"Isn't that right, honey? We're very lucky Lydia could fit us in."

"Yeah." He gave an absent nod and looked back at his phone.

"Have you taken a look at the itinerary?" Lydia asked. "Since you're honeymooning in June, it'll be winter in Brazil. Which is perfect, because the weather ranges between seventy and eighty degrees." Lydia smiled at the camera. "That should mean we can see a lot of things without getting overheated."

"I have and I love it." Serena nodded. "But there's one issue. You haven't included the Christ the Redeemer statue. We really want to visit it, don't we, Damon?"

He looked up with those same wide eyes. "Yeah." He nodded, though it was clear he had no idea what he'd been asked. "Sounds good."

"I put two free days into your schedule. I won't be charging for those," Lydia told them. "I figure you can use those to do the usual touristy things, or to rest if you prefer. There's no point in paying me to take you to Christ the Redeemer. You can easily get there yourself."

"Oh." The woman blinked. "I thought you'd be with us the whole time."

Lydia bit down a smile. "But it's your honeymoon. Won't you want some time together alone?" She glanced at Damon. He'd given up any pretense at listening and was typing furiously on his phone screen, his lips pressed together so hard they were white.

Serena shifted in her chair. "Um, I guess."

"I can always write a few things into the free days with directions on how to get there," Lydia told her. "I could arrange a spa visit, or have a driver take you to the beach. We have a couple of months to get the fine details arranged." She smiled widely. "You must be excited about the wedding."

"The wedding?" Serena's eyes widened. "Oh that. Yes, of course. Very excited. Aren't we, darling?"

"Sorry. Work email." Damon flashed a smile, and put his phone down. "What did you say?"

Those two really needed some quality time together. Maybe she'd take them up to The Maze one night. It was a nightclub at the top of the hill of one of the favelas, full of beautiful, sensual people and music that made you lose your inhibitions.

Perhaps she'd also somehow get Damon to lose his phone.

The thought of him traveling around Rio without paying attention to his new wife, or the beautiful city, made her stomach turn. She'd have to think about it. One thing was for sure, she'd make it a perfect vacation for them.

"If there's anything else you need, let me know," Lydia told her. "I'll be traveling for the next couple of months, but I can be contacted by email or messenger."

"Where are you going?" the woman asked, her eyes lighting up with interest.

Lydia laughed, because she could talk about her travels all day. "Right now, I'm in California for my baby niece's naming day. Then I'm off to Spain and Europe for a month."

Serena clapped her hands together and turned to her fiancé. "Hey, aren't the Bartons going to Spain?" She glanced back at Lydia. "Ella Barton. Is that who you're taking?"

"I can't tell you." Lydia shrugged apologetically. "Client confidentiality."

The woman pursed her lips. "Oh, don't worry. I'll find out another way."

I bet you will. "Do you have any other questions about the itinerary?"

"Not that I can think of. As long as we also get to see the statue, I'm happy."

"Great." Lydia smiled at them. "But drop me an email if you think of anything. I'll answer as soon as I can. Either way we will be in contact before June, but the plan is to meet at Galeão International Airport, and that's where your tour will begin."

"Thank you so much." Serena smiled widely. "Oh! And can we take a selfie with you? Just so we can show our friends we've been video calling with you? I'm a big fan of your Instagram page."

"She's a stalker," the man said, finally putting his phone down. "Like your number one fan."

"Sure. Of course."

Serena turned her back to the screen and made Damon do the same, holding her phone up high to take a photo of the three of them. "There," she said. "That's perfect. I'll tag you."

"Great." Lydia smiled. "Thanks."

She didn't really mind. This was what they paid her for, after all. Not just a chance to see the real cities of the world, but also the opportunity to brag about it to their friends. She wasn't part of that world, no matter how much her father would have liked her to be. She preferred airplanes to dinner knives, fiestas to cocktail bars. As long as she was traveling, she felt like she was living.

Not simply existing, the way so many people seemed to do in New York. And if a few selfies and Instagram tags made her clients happy, then she was happy, too.

"Thank you." Serena smiled. It genuinely lit up her face. Lydia made a mental note to make her smile a lot when they were in Rio.

"Any time."

"And congratulations on your niece. I hope the naming day goes well."

"Thank you." Lydia grinned warmly. "And good luck with your wedding preparations. I can't wait to hear all about it in Rio."

"Be good," Griff said, kissing Autumn on the cheek. She leaned down to kiss Skyler before hugging him hard.

"We will. It's just girls' night."

"I know what happens at girls' night." He lifted an eyebrow. "I've already sent Nate my commiserations. I can't believe he agreed to host."

"Nate loves being surrounded by women," Autumn

pointed out. "Anyway, just be thankful we're not all coming here. This way you get to cuddle with Skyler and watch whatever you'd like on the television."

"And you don't have to listen to girl talk all night," Lydia teased. "That's a double win."

"I like girl talk." Griff tapped her with his elbow. "You know that."

"Don't worry. We'll fill you in on all the gossip when we're back. Unless you're asleep."

They waved goodbye to Griff, and Lydia couldn't help but smile at the difference between his giant body, and the tiny form of Skyler. She was snuggled against his chest, a contented smile lifting her chubby cheeks.

A glance at Autumn's expression told Lydia she was as captivated with Griff as her daughter. Her bottom lip wobbled, as though she didn't want to leave them.

"Come on," Lydia said, sliding her arm through her sister's. "We'll only be gone a few hours. And you can message Griff while we're gone."

"I might not answer though," Griff told them. "I'm kind of sleepy."

"You'd better." Autumn lifted a brow. "And I want photos, too."

"The naked kind?" Griff waggled his eyebrows.

"Eeugh. Can you guys cut it out?" Lydia pleaded. Though her thoughts weren't on Griff and Autumn at all. Instead, she was thinking about Jackson and the way his finger trailed along her hip last night. How his lips had felt warm and soft as they'd brushed against hers. She swallowed hard at the memory of the rush of blood to her skin as he curled his fingers around her hip, pulling her closer.

And then it had ended abruptly, with the arrival of his dad.

In just a few days, he'd come to dominate her thoughts,

and she had no idea what to do about it. All she knew was that she wanted to know him. To feel him. To touch him.

And she also wanted to know who Hayley was.

Tonight, she was going to find out. All of Jackson's friends – of the female variety – would be at Ally's house for cocktails. They'd have to know about Hayley and Jackson, and why he kept blowing hot and cold.

"When I asked for photos, I mean of Skyler, you goof." Autumn shook her head at Griff, and allowed Lydia to lead her to the waiting car.

Griff winked and blew her a kiss. Autumn blew him one right back.

"Come on, let's go," Lydia said, pulling open the door. It was time to kick back, have some fun, and maybe get some answers about Jackson.

***

"It's seven o'clock," Lisa pointed out. "You should go home."

Jackson looked up from the screen, his eyes blinking as they adjusted to the darkening office. "Seven? Seriously? Last time I looked it was four."

Lisa shook her head. "I've fed Eddie, but he needs a walk." She leaned down to tickle Eddie's chin. His tongue lolled out with pleasure. "And you need to get some fresh air. You've been in here for twelve hours."

"What are you still doing here anyway?" Jackson asked her. "You finish at six, don't you?"

Lisa nodded. "Usually. But I worked an extra hour tonight because I have an appointment tomorrow, remember?"

No, he didn't. But he was always flexible with his staff's hours. Two of his programmers were pathologically allergic to early mornings, so they didn't start work until eleven. They usually finished at eight, but sometimes worked through the night like Jackson.

As long as they got the job done, he really didn't care what hours they worked. He was the one who needed to be here during office hours, in case of problems with their clients.

Being in the office had one added bonus. He didn't keep walking past the bathroom to remember that damn hot almost-kiss he and Lydia had shared last night.

Who was he kidding? He didn't need to be there to remember it. Each slide of his finger and hitch of her breath was etched into his brain. That's why he'd tried to bury himself in his work, so he didn't keep wondering what would have happened if his dad hadn't arrived.

His lips curled up as he remembered her parting words. That she wasn't at all sorry about what happened. He wasn't either. He was just sorry it had ended so abruptly.

Yeah, so why haven't you called her?

Truth was, he'd thought about it all day. But he had this damn program to sort out before somebody figured out how to get through the hole in his client's defenses. But now the job was almost done – ten minutes and he'd run some tests. After that?

The night was his.

He lifted his hand as Lisa wished him a goodnight. Seeing his pal leaving, Eddie padded over to Jackson and lay his head down on Jackson's thighs, looking wistfully up at him.

"I'll take you for a walk in half an hour, buddy," Jackson told him. "Promise."

Eddie let out a little whimper.

"I'll even take you on the beach. And I won't complain if you get wet."

Satisfied, Eddie curled up on the floor by the chair, while Jackson started to run the program.

As the data scrolled across his screen, he picked up his

phone and scrolled until he hit Lydia's number. Before he could think better of it, he hit the call button, his jaw ticking as he waited for it to connect.

"Hey," Lydia answered, her voice breathless. "How are you?"

She sounded pleased to hear from him. It was strangely gratifying.

"I'm good. Still in the office, about to head out and walk Eddie." The dog opened one eye at the sound of his name, before closing it again when he realized he was being talked about, not to. "And I was thinking after that we could head out for your driving lesson. If you're still up for it."

"Oh." Lydia's voice fell. "I can't. I'm on my way out right now. I assumed you were busy."

It was on the tip of his tongue to ask her where she was going, but he swallowed that question down. It was none of his damn business.

"It's girls' night," Lydia added, as though he'd asked the question out loud. "Autumn and I are heading over to Ally's. We're having cocktails."

His shoulders relaxed. "In that case, let's take a raincheck."

"I'm free tomorrow," she suggested. "I could come over and take Eddie for a walk, and after we could go for a drive."

"Sounds good." He was glad Lisa wasn't there to see his smile.

"I promise I'll stay dry this time."

He chuckled. "I don't care if you get wet." And damn if that didn't make him think about a different kind of activity altogether. One that involved finding exactly where her cherry blossom tattoo ended.

Over the phone he could hear the car door slam.

"Jackson?"

"Yeah?"

"I've got to go." She sounded reluctant. "We've just got to Ally's and she's already handing Autumn a cocktail. She's not even reached the doorstep yet." Her voice lowered. "Last time I saw her drinking cocktails she ended up buying a pier. I need to keep an eye on her."

"Why do I think it's the other way around?" Jackson asked her, his voice teasing. "I'm pretty sure you're the one who needs keeping an eye on."

"Is that an offer?" she asked lightly.

"It's whatever you want to take from it." The corner of his lip quirked. "I'll pick you up tomorrow. Seven okay?"

"Seven's perfect. Oh and Jackson?"

"Yeah?" He was getting used to her parting shots. They made his muscles feel tight and full.

"Maybe tomorrow I'll show you the other tattoo I have. The one on my ass."

❧ 11 ❧

Jackson didn't bother to drive all the way home to walk Eddie on the beach. Instead, he steered his car to the central boardwalk, parking outside of the coffee shop. Seeing the shutters down reminded him where Lydia was right now. At Nate and Ally's house, no doubt entertaining the rest of them with stories of her travels. She had a way of talking that made everybody listen. She wasn't a show off, not at all. But she was interesting.

Intriguing, even. He was damn certain she wasn't like anybody he'd ever met.

When he opened the back door of his car Eddie leapt out, his tail wagging so hard Jackson could hear the swoosh it made in the air. His furry body was almost trembling with excitement as he looked from the ocean then up at Jackson, waiting for the command that would let him run to the water.

"Okay, go."

Eddie gave a yelp and barreled toward the empty beach, not stopping he careened across the golden sands. He'd made it to the ocean's edge before Jackson had a chance to lock up his car, lolloping into the water with a howl of delight.

Stuffing a ball in one pocket and Eddie's leash in the other, Jackson ambled onto the sand. Eddie was swimming in the shallows, his paws digging at the foamy water as he turned and looked at Jackson expectantly. Pulling the tennis ball from his pocket, Jackson lobbed it into the waves in front of Eddie, who splashed and crashed until he reached it, securing it in his jaws. He swam to the shore, running toward Jackson, spray flying everywhere until he came to a stop and dropped the ball at Jackson's feet.

There was an expression of utter bliss on Eddie's face. For him, life didn't get any better than an evening swim and a ball being thrown a hundred times.

"Hey!" a deep voice called from the boardwalk. Jackson turned to see Lucas Russell standing on the concrete path, an ice cream cone in one hand, a stroller in the other. His son, Arthur, was sitting in the stroller, his legs swinging as he gripped a waffle cone so tightly it was sagging in the middle

"Unc Jack!" Arthur called when he spotted Jackson. "Daddy, Unc Jack there."

"Hey buddy, you enjoying that ice cream?" Jackson called out. Arthur strained at the straps of his stroller to get out.

Lucas unclipped his son and gently lifted him out of the stroller, steadying his treat when it threatened to tumble to the ground. Jackson walked over, keeping one eye on Eddie who was still happily playing with the ball, and ruffled Arthur's hair.

"You don't stop growing, kid," Jackson told him. "I think you're gonna be bigger than Griff."

Not that Lucas was small. The town's fire chief was over six feet, with the kind of muscles you only got from hard, constant work. His hair was closely cropped, revealing a warm California tan.

"I hope not. He's already bankrupting us with new shoes

every month," Lucas said dryly. "And you should see how much he eats."

Arthur took a mouthful of ice cream, as if to underline his dad's point.

Noticing he wasn't the center of attention anymore, Eddie ran out of the ocean to where they were standing.

"Look! Dog!" Arthur flung his arm out to point. Eddie gave him a curious look, and shook his body, water droplets flying through the air. They showered the little boy, and Arthur screamed with laughter and held his ice cream out to the dog.

"Ah no, buddy. Dogs can't eat ice cream," Lucas said, gently moving the cone away from Eddie. Looking up at Jackson, he lifted his brows. "I heard you got a dog. Didn't believe it, though."

"It's only temporary." Jackson took the ball back from Eddie and threw it into the ocean. Arthur clapped his hands as Eddie careened across the sand, following the line of Jackson's throw. "I'm taking care of him until his owners are found."

"That's what Ember said. I thought she was joking." Lucas looked over at Eddie, who'd just reached the ball. "I gotta say, you're a natural. Wouldn't have believed that either."

"We swim, too?" Arthur asked Lucas, pointing at Eddie doggy paddling in the ocean.

"Not tonight, pal. Your mom would kill us."

Jackson laughed. "Has she gone over to Ally's for girls' night?"

"Yeah. How did you know about that?" Lucas took a napkin from his pocket and wiped a trail of ice cream and drool from Arthur's chin.

"Lydia told me. Autumn's sister," Jackson told him. When Lucas raised an eyebrow he added, "Don't look at me like that. She's helping with Eddie. It's kind of her fault I have him."

"I wasn't looking like anything." Lucas laughed. "I was just thinking about the dog. He looks good on you. You seem, I don't know, more relaxed than I've seen you in a while."

Yeah, maybe that had something to do with Eddie. Or perhaps it was more due to Lydia. Whatever it was, Jackson definitely felt happier. As though he was able to breathe a little easier. Live a little more. Lydia had only been here for a few days, and she'd already turned everything upside down.

"You okay?" Lucas asked. "You seem a hundred miles away."

It was on the tip of Jackson's tongue to say he was fine. And really, he was. But he also wanted to talk to someone. To one of his friends. And he knew for damn sure he couldn't talk to Griff.

"I was just thinking," Jackson murmured, as Eddie ran back again. This time he stopped in front of Arthur, dropping the ball at the boy's feet.

"About what?" Lucas scooted down next to his son, cupping his small hand in his own, and helped him to throw the ball back into the ocean. Eddie turned, spray flying from his body, as he raced back to catch it.

"About Lydia."

"Ah." Lucas nodded. "I thought you might be."

"You did? Why?" Jackson blinked.

"Because she's the first woman I've heard you mention by name in months."

That wasn't a big surprise. Despite his friends' opinions on his love life, he really hadn't had time for anything but work for the longest time.

"Yeah, well I won't be mentioning her in front of Griff. He's already warned me off."

Lucas looked shocked. "He what? Why would he do that?"

"Because he thinks I'm gonna screw her around." Jackson shrugged, though the words stuck in his throat.

Arthur handed Lucas the soggy end of his cone, wiping his hands on the napkin he was given.

"You want the end of this?" Lucas asked Jackson.

"Nah. It's all yours."

Lucas laughed, and wrapped it in the napkin, holding it in his hands.

"We sit?" Arthur asked, looking at the edge of the boardwalk.

"Sure." Lucas lifted him to sit on the end of the boardwalk, his short legs ending a foot from the sand. Lucas sat next to him and Jackson took the spot beside his friend, all three of them looking out to the water.

"So, *are* you going to screw her around?" Lucas asked Jackson, returning to their conversation.

"No." Jackson was vehement. "I know you guys think I'm some kind of asshole playboy, but I'm not."

"You went a little wild there after Hayley left," Lucas pointed out.

Jackson sighed. "I was hurt and wanted to forget about her for a while. I wanted to go out and have a good time, so I did. But I never messed with anybody's heart. Never made promises. And to be honest, those women had a lucky escape, because I wasn't in any shape to have a relationship."

Lucas nodded. Next to him, Arthur was singing a song, something about a shark.

"But you're in shape for a relationship now?" Lucas clarified.

"I don't know. Maybe I would be. But even if I was, Lydia isn't looking for something like that. She's too busy traveling to settle down."

"Have you asked her that?" Lucas asked him.

"No. But since she's leaving for Europe next week, it's pretty obvious."

"But you like her, right?" Lucas asked.

"I do." Jackson kicked the sand with his sneaker. "A lot." Eddie was back on shore, the ball firmly wedged in his mouth as he dug at the sand. Another dog was running around him, trying to get his attention.

"Do you think she likes you, too?" Lucas asked.

Lydia's cherry blossom tattoo flashed into Jackson's mind. Followed by her wide eyed gaze as his lips brushed against his.

I'm not sorry at all about what happened outside your bathroom.

His lips curled at the memory of her words last night. "Yeah, I think she does." And wasn't that making him feel all heated up and needy?

"Well man, I guess it's up to you. Usually I'd say take it slow, see where it goes, but you don't have that luxury. If she's leaving soon, there's no time to waste."

"So what do I do?" Jackson asked, more to himself than Lucas. "And how the heck is Griff going to feel when he finds out I've been hanging with Autumn's sister."

Lucas laughed out loud. "You're scared of Griff?"

"I don't want to hurt him," Jackson admitted. "He's our friend after all."

"Yeah, he is," Lucas agreed. "And like me he wants you to be happy. I guess if he knew you had feelings for her..."

"I didn't say I had feelings."

"You said you liked her," Lucas pointed out. Arthur slithered down the edge of the sidewalk to the sand, sitting and drawing circles with his finger.

"I do."

"Well that's a feeling."

Jackson froze. He didn't like that thought at all. Because if you had feelings, you could get hurt. "Yeah, but it's a *like*-like, you know? We have fun together. She makes me smile." He chuckled. "She's kind of wild, and that's really damn attractive."

Lucas said nothing. He was looking at Jackson with narrowed eyes, as though he was trying to figure something out.

"What?" Jackson asked.

"I didn't say anything. I was just thinking." Lucas ran his finger along his jaw. "I'm wondering whether regretting what you never had is worse than losing what you did." He smiled as he watched Arthur dig his hands into the sand. "If I lost Ember tomorrow, I'd be devastated," he murmured. "But I'd never regret meeting her. Never regret falling in love and having Arthur. Because it's made me who I am."

"But that's different. You two are married."

Lucas nodded. "Yeah, but even if we'd only ever had one date, I wouldn't have regretted that either. She changed me with one kiss."

"Kiss?" Arthur said, standing and lifting his face. Lucas jumped off the boardwalk and kissed his son, hugging him tight. Arthur hooked his arms around Lucas' neck, leaning his head on his shoulder.

"I should get this guy home. It's his bedtime."

"Not tired," Arthur said sleepily as Lucas lifted him into his arms and stepped onto the boardwalk, putting his son in his stroller.

"Yeah, I need to get Eddie home." Jackson nodded, trying not to smile at the fact he had his own responsibilities now. For so long he'd been different to his friends, as they paired off one by one. Having relationships, buying houses together, making families.

And that still wasn't in his future, but maybe *something* was. Lydia was here for a few days, not a lifetime, but that didn't mean he had to ignore the crazy attraction between them.

If she got on that plane without him spending time with her, he'd regret it. That he knew for sure.

They could have a good time while she was here, and then say their goodbyes. All they had to do was go into it with open eyes. That way nobody would get hurt.

———

"We should play spin the bottle," Ally said, carrying a tray full of cocktails into her spacious living room. Lydia was sitting between Autumn and her friend, Ember, on the cream leather couches, facing the floor-to-ceiling glass doors overlooking the ocean. Ally passed the cocktails out, and sat down on the ottoman opposite.

There were seven of them there altogether. Lydia, Autumn, and Ally, along with Ember and Brooke – Ally's best friends – and Caitie, Ember's sister-in-law, and her friend, Harper.

The girls had spent the evening gossiping about their partners. All of them apart from Lydia were in relationships, and nearly all of them had children. Ally had put them all in fits of giggles telling them about her stepdaughter, Riley, who brought a boyfriend home from college to meet her dad the previous week, and how Nate almost had a heart attack when she asked if they could share a bedroom.

"I mean, she's twenty. Almost twenty-one. I asked Nate if he remembered being that age," Ally said. "But that made him go beet red and tell Riley she wasn't allowed to date until she was thirty."

Lydia took a sip of her margarita. The lime stung her tongue in the best way. It was funny how the cocktails were affecting them all in different ways. Autumn was already slurring a little. Harper was half-asleep and Ally was hyperactive, talking non-stop.

Ally put an empty champagne bottle on its side and twirled it on the coffee table. "Okay, who's going first?" she asked them.

"Don't we need guys here to play spin the bottle?" Ember asked in response to Ally's suggestion. "I love you all, but I don't want to kiss any of you."

Ally grimaced. "Oh yeah. Let's play truth or dare instead."

"No way." Their friend Brooke shook her head, and winked at Lydia. "I've played that with you guys before. I ended up having to call Frank Megassey to tell him I loved him."

"We were seventeen," Ally pointed out. "And it was funny as hell."

"How about never have I ever?" Lydia suggested. "I say something like 'never have I ever kissed a girl,' and if you've actually done that, you drink."

"Have you kissed a girl?" Autumn asked, tilting her head to stare at Lydia. Her eyes were as fuzzy as her speech.

Lydia bit down a smile at how drunk her sister was. "Yep." She grinned. "But only once and there were no tongues."

"Okay," Ally said, picking her glass up. "I'll start. Never have I ever had a threesome."

Everybody's glasses stayed down. Ally wrinkled her nose. "You guys are boring." She looked over at Lydia. "And I'm disappointed with you. I thought you were the adventurous sister."

Lydia laughed. "What can I say? I like all the attention on me."

"Ah, me too," Harper said with a sigh. "James doesn't get to touch anybody but this girl." She poked herself in the chest and winced. "Ouch."

They all laughed.

"You go next," Ally suggested to Lydia, shaking her head. "And make it exciting. We need some of that in Angel Sands."

"Okay." Lydia bit down a smile and lifted her drink. Here went nothing. "Never have I ever kissed Jackson Lewis." She took a big swig of her cocktail.

They were all staring at her. Autumn was the first to break the silence. "You kissed Jackson?"

"Kind of." Lydia shrugged. "I mean, our lips touched. But his dad interrupted us."

Autumn put her drink down. "I need to know more. When? How? What else has been going on that I don't know about?"

The girls all leaned forward, their eyes wide.

"I'll tell you, if you promise to answer me something," Lydia said, her voice serious.

"What?" Ally asked.

"Who's Hayley?" Lydia put her glass on the driftwood coffee table in front of her. "I heard his dad mention her name. And say that she hurt Jackson."

Ally glanced at Ember. "Hayley was Jackson's fiancée."

"*Was?*" Lydia asked. "What happened to her?"

Ally sighed. "I don't know all the details. It was before we hung around with them much."

"I know," Caitie said, scooting forward in her seat. "I kind of grew up with Griff and Jackson, since they're Lucas' best friends." She grimaced in the way only a little sister could. "Jackson and Hayley met at college, and after they graduated, they came back here to live. He was working at Newton's and she was a dental assistant. They got engaged after a few years, and were in the middle of planning their wedding when she got pregnant."

Lydia's mouth dropped open. She wasn't expecting *that*.

Caitie grimaced and added, "Only the baby wasn't Jackson's."

"Oh my god." Lydia's mouth dropped open. "Whose was it?"

"Her boss'. She'd been doing the dirty with him."

"I guess teeth weren't the only things getting drilled at the dental practice," Ally murmured. Ember coughed into her cocktail glass.

"That's awful," Lydia said. "Poor Jackson."

"Yeah, well after that he more than made up for it. Started screwing every willing woman this side of LA." Caitie shrugged. "I guess it made him feel a bit better."

Lydia took another sip of her cocktail, trying to take it all in. She'd had a few failed relationships – none that lasted very long – but she'd never had someone rip her heart out. That kind of betrayal stung. She knew that from everything Autumn had been through in New York. And from talking to people as she traveled.

It was amazing how many people flew to different countries to get over broken hearts. And a lot of them hired her to show them the cities while they were there.

"Okay, so we answered your question. Now spill. What happened with you and Jackson?" Ally asked, leaning forward to prop her chin on her hand.

Lydia ran her finger around the rim of her cocktail glass. "Well," she said, kind of enjoying the attention. "It all started when I took Eddie for a walk." As she told them about the wave and Jackson trying to save her from it, the girls all leaned in, rapt with attention. "But Eddie started going wild," she said, bringing them up to date. "And the next thing I knew, Jackson's dad was there."

"What a cock block." Ally sighed. "And I'm never going to look at Jackson the same way again."

"Oh, I always suspected he had moves." Caitie sat back on the sofa. "He has that little lost boy, bad boy combination women can't resist. Women want to save him and ravage him at the same time."

"So what are you going to do about it?" Autumn asked Lydia, concern etching her voice. "There's no future, is there? Not with you leaving soon."

"I don't think there would be any future anyway," Caitie said, giving Lydia a small smile. "He's the love 'em and leave 'em type."

Lydia shrugged, putting her glass down on the table. "I'm not looking for anything serious," she said, though the little tug in her gut made her wish it was different. "I'm too busy. Maybe a little flirting with Jackson is just what I need."

And if it went further than flirting? She was okay with that. She was a woman of the world. She knew there was an attraction between them that made her heart pound and her breath quicken. Maybe in another life, if she and Jackson were other kinds of people, that would lead to the kind of commitment Autumn and all her friends had with their partners.

She had a little over a week. Maybe it was time to have fun before she headed off again to throw herself into travel and work.

And perhaps she could stop her heart from wanting more than it could get.

"If you're planning on seeing more of Jackson, you'll have to deal with Griff," Autumn murmured, leaning back on the sofa. "He's gonna bust a blood vessel."

"Come on guys, let's get back to this game," Ally said loudly, all heads turning to her. "Brooke, how about you?"

Brooke shrugged, a blush stealing across her high cheekbones. "Here goes nothing," she muttered, holding up her glass. "Never have I ever had sex on the beach."

Everybody lifted their glasses to take a drink and they all started laughing. Because when you lived in a beach town, some things were a given.

12

Jackson pulled into Griff and Autumn's driveway, parking his car next to Griff's old truck and climbed out, locking the door and shoving the keys in his pocket.

He'd managed to make it home for a shower between leaving the office and coming here, and his hair was still damp. He ran his fingers through it in an attempt to get it under control.

When he pushed the doorbell, it occurred to him that even though he'd been here a hundred times before, this time felt completely different. He wasn't here to share a meal with Autumn and Griff or watch Sunday afternoon football with burgers on the grill.

He was here to see Autumn's sister. The beautiful blonde who haunted his dreams.

The door swung open and Lydia's face split into a grin as she saw him, reaching for his hand and pulling him inside. "Hey!" she said, pressing her lips to his cheek. "I just need to grab a jacket. Can you wait for me?" She ran down the hallway toward the guest bedroom, and he followed her with his eyes, admiring the way her short dress flared out around her thighs.

Damn, she was gorgeous.

The corner of his lip quirked up, but he felt a prickle on his neck. The kind you get when somebody's watching you and you don't quite know it.

From the corner of his eye he saw Griff standing in the kitchen, his arms folded across his chest. Jackson sighed. So Griff was still unhappy about the situation.

"Hey man," Jackson called out, lifting an eyebrow.

Griff nodded, and grunted out a hello.

Damn it, this was crazy. They were best friends. "Listen, can we have a quick word outside?" Jackson asked him. He wasn't going to let his friend spoil the night. But he also didn't want to lose his friend.

Lydia came out of the bedroom, pulling on a cropped denim jacket and flicking her long blonde hair over the collar.

"What's going on?"

"I'm just going to have a quick chat with Griff before we go," Jackson told her. "Won't take long."

Lydia bit down a smile and walked over to him. "Okay," she nodded, looking almost excited.

"Let's go to the deck," Griff said, inclining his head at the kitchen door. He walked outside and Jackson followed. When he glanced over his shoulder, Lydia was still grinning. Damn if he didn't want to kiss that smile off her face.

"Are you staying?" Jackson asked as she leaned on the door frame.

Lydia tipped her head to the side. "I figure you're gonna be talking about me, and I want to hear what you say. And if you start fighting, I need to video it for my Instagram."

Jackson laughed. "I live to give you social media content."

Pursing her lips together, she blew him a kiss. "I'll make it worth your while."

He shook his head. Damn, she made him smile like nobody else could.

Griff was sitting on a wicker chair, his arms still folded across his chest as he stared out at the ocean. Even though the chair was substantial, he still looked too big for it, his denim clad legs stretching out from the seat.

Jackson walked over to his friend and took the seat next to him. "You been out on the boat today?"

"Nah." Griff shook his head. "No bookings today so we did some maintenance. Got to surf this morning."

"The waves looked good."

"It was fine." Griff turned to look at him, a neutral expression on his face. "You and Lydia, huh?"

So they were getting straight to that. Maybe he should be thankful. He didn't want to waste the evening on small talk when he could be driving into the mountains with her. "We're just going out," Jackson told him. "Nothing to worry about."

"She's practically my sister. Of course I'm worried about her. Remember how Lucas was when Breck started dating Caitie?"

Yeah, Jackson remembered. It led to a black eye for Breck on Christmas Day, courtesy of Lucas's right fist. "That all ended up fine in the end," he pointed out.

Griff huffed. "Because they made a commitment and live together. I'm guessing that's not what's happening between you and Lydia."

Jackson caught his eye. "How long have we been friends?"

"You know how long." Griff grunted. "Since Kindergarten."

"And I'd never do anything to jeopardize that. You've been with me through thick and thin, man. We've been there for each other. I'm not going to do anything stupid."

Griff looked away, his knuckles bleached as he grasped his beer bottle tightly. "I don't like it."

"You don't have to. You just have to let it go. Lydia and I are adults. We know what we're doing."

"She's too young for you."

"I'm twenty-seven," Lydia called out from the kitchen door. "There's only six years difference."

"She's also a big pain in the ass." Griff shook his head at her then turned back to Jackson. "Are you sure you know what you're letting yourself in for?"

Lydia walked out of the kitchen, and over to where Griff and Jackson were sitting. She leaned down to give Griff a hug. "I love you to death, Griff, but you're acting like an idiot. Now we're leaving to have a good time, and maybe I'll even drive his car. That's it. He won't make me cry, or knock me up, or give me a STD, will you, Jackson?"

She caught his eye, and he could see it there. The attraction that pulsed back and forth between them.

"I wasn't planning on it," he said, managing to keep his face straight.

"Griff, can you read to Skyler?" Autumn called from the kitchen. "And maybe leave these two alone?" She flashed Jackson an awkward smile. "Hey Jackson."

He winked back at her to let her know it was all fine. Contrary to Lydia's suggestion, there would be no fighting here. He just wanted his friend to stop being so damn overbearing.

"Griff?" Autumn said. "You coming inside?"

Griff looked back at Jackson as though he was waiting for something. Catching his eye, Jackson gave him a nod.

I won't hurt her.

He didn't say it, but he meant it. And maybe somewhere deep inside Griff heard it, too. Because he nodded and turned to walk back into the kitchen, lifting a hand to wave them goodbye.

"So you're twenty-seven," he murmured.

"Is that a problem?" she asked lightly.

"No." Maybe it should be. A few years ago it would have

been. But since he'd picked her up from the airport, he hadn't once thought about her age. As he'd told Griff, they were adults, and thirty-three wasn't that far away from twenty-seven.

And it didn't matter anyway, because in just over a week she'd be gone, and their relative ages would mean nothing at all.

She slid her hand into his. "That was kind of hot," she told him. "I've never had a guy go through something like that before just to take me on a date."

"You never took anybody home to meet your dad when you were in New York?" His brow crinkled. He could still remember *the talk* he had with Hayley's dad when they started getting serious. When he'd promised to never hurt her.

And wasn't that ironic, since she was the one who did all the hurting?

"The kind of guys I dated back then weren't the sort you take home to meet your family." She wrinkled her nose. "And the ones I've dated since have been in different countries. So I guess I've never had this opportunity before." She smiled again, and he couldn't help but smile back, because she was so damn infectious.

"Well, I hope you enjoyed me battling for your virtue." He shook his head.

She clutched her hands over her chest. "I really did. You're my hero."

She rolled onto her tiptoes and pressed her lips against the corner of his mouth. He curled his hand around her hip, feeling the warmth of her skin through the thin fabric of her dress. Her breath caught in her throat, making her lips fall open, and it took every ounce of restraint he had to stop himself from kissing her hard and fast.

"Thank you," she murmured. "For being so kind to Griff. He means well, really."

"Yeah, I know." He wasn't sure what was biting Griff's ass about him and Lydia, but whatever it was, he hoped he got over it soon. "Come on, let's head out before it gets dark," he said. This time he curled his hand around her waist, pulling her against him. Her body fit perfectly against his.

"Good idea." She rested her head against his shoulder and he tried not to like that too much. "Lead on, handsome."

"You need to release the parking brake, first," Jackson said, pointing at the lever in the footwell of the car. "Then ease your foot on the gas pedal, and pull out into the road." He'd driven to the hills, where he knew the roads were quieter, especially at this time of evening. They'd only passed one truck and a guy struggling uphill on a bike. It was the perfect location for Lydia's first lesson.

Lydia nodded. She was leaning forward in the driver's seat, her hands tight on the wheel, her brows pinching together in concentration as she tried to do what he instructed. It was easier than the one time she'd tried to drive a stick shift, but she was pretty sure brain surgery was easier than that.

Lydia pulled the released the parking brake, then pushed her foot onto the gas pedal. The car lurched forward. "Shit!" she said, taking her hand off the wheel to cover her mouth, which made the car veer to the left.

Jackson leaned over her to steady the wheel, his arm brushing hers. "It's okay. Feel free to swear all you'd like. Just keep your hands where I can see them."

She grinned. "You're the first guy who's ever made that request. Are you sure you want to do this?" The car had stopped moving. "What if I drive us off the edge of the road?"

"Then we'll die." He shrugged, his voice deadpan. "No pressure."

"They might not ever find our bodies," she mused. "Maybe not for years. We'll be like that couple they found in Pompeii, their petrified cadavers curled around each other."

"Or maybe Griff will remember I've taken you for a driving lesson and he'll come looking for us when you don't meet your curfew."

She laughed. "I prefer the Pompeii scenario."

"Let's try again." He hit the brake release. "Steady now," he murmured, as she tapped her toe against the gas pedal. The movement was smoother this time, and she took a deep breath, staring out of the window to make sure she kept on the right side of the white lines down the middle of the road.

"You can speed up a little," Jackson suggested. Lydia nodded, getting used to the feel of the car in her hands. There was something instinctual about driving that she hadn't anticipated. Like her hands were just the tool, connecting the car to her brain.

"In fifty yards, you're going to take a left," Jackson told her.

"I don't know how to take a left," she pointed out. "I'll end up on the sidewalk."

"We're in the hills, there aren't any sidewalks. You can take it as slow as you'd like." She liked the way he sounded so calm. It made her feel calm, too. Was this how Eddie felt every time he told the dog to sit?

"Move your foot from the gas to the brake."

Of course she hit it too hard, and they both lurched forward as the car came to a premature stop.

"Next time do it a little smoother."

"Next time you're driving." She let out a grunt of annoyance. "I'm terrible at this."

"No you're not. You're doing fine. When you were driving you almost looked happy."

"The driving I can do. The stopping, turning, and everything else are awful. It's so much easier to put my hand out and hail a cab."

He laughed. "But imagine the freedom of being able to drive wherever you want. Not everywhere you visit must have good public transport. I bet there are places you'd like to go but haven't visited because you can't drive there."

"I'd hire a driver. There really isn't a problem." She bit her lip, because he was being so nice, and she felt like a brat. "Sorry. I hate not being good at things."

"I can understand that. I hate it, too. But driving is one of those things you have to practice to get good at."

She nodded. "Like sex."

He coughed out a laugh. "Yeah, I guess it is. At first it kind of feels good, but you don't know what you're doing. Then you work out what moves you forward and what doesn't."

"And you always have to think about the passenger." She gave him a side glance. "Whether they're having a good time, too."

He looked at her for a moment, taking in her profile. He tucked her hair behind her ear, his finger leaving a trail of heat across her skin. "I'm having a good time," he told her.

"Yeah." She nodded. "So am I." Despite the way the car lurched every time she tried to accelerate or stop. And despite the way her heart hammered against her ribcage when she looked at the edge of the road. Somehow she wouldn't want to be anywhere else but here.

With him.

An hour later, she was getting the hang of taking lefts and rights, and had even managed to make a three-point-turn, though it had turned out to be more of a ten point, not that she was counting.

"Okay, I think you're ready for the next step," Jackson said, as she pulled onto the mountain road again.

"What's that?"

"Let's head to Captain Burger. It has a drive-thru. Let's see if you can steer the car around that."

"Oh no, buddy." She shook her head firmly. "I'll drive to the burger place, but I'm not going through the drive thru. That's all on you."

"You sure?"

"Yep." She blew out a breath. Pleased, because she hadn't made a complete idiot out of herself – and wasn't that a novel thing – but also because she was ready to stop driving this damn car around the hills. She hadn't been able to look at him. She was too busy staring out of the windshield for that. And that made her sad, because she really liked looking at Jackson Lewis.

Especially when he was wearing a t-shirt that stretched across his broad shoulders, and revealed just a hint of the muscles she knew were beneath the fabric.

"Okay. Let the lesson end," he agreed.

She caught his eye. "And let the fun begin."

13

True to her word, Lydia drove to Captain Burger, though she started to panic when she realized she had to pull into the crowded lot.

He'd smiled gently, and suggested she stop in the entrance and they'd swap seats.

When they picked up their order of burgers and fries from the window, he'd driven them along the cliff road overlooking the Silver Sands Resort, parking on the deserted grassy knoll.

"I don't want to give you the wrong impression," he said, grabbing the bags of food and climbing out of the car. "But when I was a kid this was the popular make out spot." He looked around. "Not that you'd know it now," he said, surprised at how deserted the place was. "I wonder where all the teenagers make out nowadays."

"They probably do it online. Maybe they make avatars and do it on Fortnite."

He laughed and opened her door. "That's a shame. Because it has an amazing view." They walked over to the cliff edge. Lydia's eyes widened as she saw the Silver Sands Resort sprawled beneath them, and to the left the twinkling lights of Angel Sands itself. "Over there was where we used to go cliff jumping," he said, pointing at a piece of the cliff jutting into the ocean. "When we were young and foolish."

"Last year then?" She lifted a brow, following the direction of his finger.

"Something like that." He inclined his head at the cliff edge. "We can eat there, unless you don't like heights."

"Are you kidding? I love heights. They always give you the best views." She grabbed his free hand and started walking. "The ocean is so pretty at night. And quiet, too," she added as they sat on the grass. "You could almost believe we're all alone out here. Views like this always take my breath away."

"What's your favorite view?"

She pressed her lips together, thinking. "I don't know. I mean, the Grand Canyon's pretty spectacular, but who hasn't seen that? And it's hard to beat the Victoria Falls. They're a bit like Niagara on Viagra." She waggled her eyebrows and he bit down a grin at her pun.

"I guess my favorite has to be Preikestolen in Norway. It's like this big rugged cliff that juts out into the fjord. When you stand there looking out at the mountains and rocks surrounding it, and at the mist rising up from the water, you could almost be back in prehistoric times." She reached for a blade of grass, pulling it from the ground and twisting it between her fingers. "If a dinosaur had walked along at that moment, I wouldn't have been surprised."

"You make it sound amazing," Jackson said softly. "I'd love to see it."

She lifted her gaze. There was something lazily seductive about the way he was staring at her.

"I'd like to take you," she admitted. He'd make the perfect travel companion. Easy, fun, and so damn good to look at.

He handed her one of the wrapped burgers, his fingers

brushing hers. A delicious pulse of electricity shot up her arm.

Suddenly she didn't feel hungry at all. Not for food, anyway.

For a moment neither of them said a word. Her mouth felt dry, her chest tight, and she couldn't pull her gaze away even if she wanted to.

"You should eat," Jackson said, his voice thick.

Lydia nodded, unwrapping the burger. The bun was thick and soft, lettuce and tomato at the top. She lifted it to her mouth, managing a nibble before her stomach contracted in mutiny.

She put the burger back in its wrapper. "I'm sorry. I'm just not hungry."

Jackson tipped his head. "I should have asked what you wanted to eat, instead of assuming. I guess burgers taste pretty average when you've eaten all over the world."

"You wouldn't believe how many times I've longed for a real burger while I've been traveling," Lydia admitted. "I love trying new food, and eating what the locals eat, but sometimes the lure of a patty can't be ignored."

"So why can't you eat it now?" he asked. Even his voice sent a shiver down her spine. What the hell was wrong with her? She felt like some kind of giddy teenager, something she'd never been even when she was younger. Yet sitting here with Jackson Lewis was sending her body into a spin.

It was a delicious, exhilarating, nauseating ride.

She looked up at him through thick eyelashes. "It's your fault," she admitted. "You're making my stomach flip."

He stared at her curiously and put down his burger, gesturing for her to come closer. She scooted over, and he pulled her onto his lap, her back against his chest.

Flipping her hair over one shoulder, he brushed his lips against her neck. "Does that help?" he murmured softly.

That brief touch made her shiver. "Not really."

He chuckled against her skin, kissing his way up to below her ear, his breath hot against her sensitive flesh. "How about this?" he asked, sliding his mouth to her jaw.

She wanted to turn, to capture his lips with hers, but he was holding her too tightly.

"Or this?" He ran his fingers through her thick hair, his gaze catching hers. His eyes were dark, needy, and sent a shot of electricity through her veins. Pushing the straps of her dress down past her shoulders, his fingers teased her skin as he pressed his warm lips against hers. He took his time as he kissed her, his movements slow and sure.

Excitement flooded through her veins. Making her nipples taut and her thighs ache. He lifted his hand to cup her chin, angling her head as he deepened the kiss. Her body felt boneless and hot, as though she was melting into him. His hand was tracing circles against her abdomen.

She could feel his excitement, too. Pressing against her as he moved his hands up her body, his fingers lightly brushing against her chest, making her nipples tighten and ache until she almost couldn't stand it.

"Touch me," she whispered.

"Where?"

"Everywhere." She couldn't get enough of him. Of his lips, his touch, the sensations his fingers were creating everywhere they moved. Twisting in his arms, she turned until she was facing him, her bare thighs straddling his denim-clad legs. He slid his hands beneath her behind, pulling her closer, until she could feel him *there*, right where she needed him. So hard and hot and perfect.

"God, you're beautiful," he said, sliding his hand up her back until his fingers were wrapped around her hair, tugging gently until she exposed her neck to his kisses again.

Every touch, every kiss, felt like fire against her skin. She wrapped her arms around his neck, her fingers brushing the short hair on the back of his head. God, he was a good kisser. Firm, yet soft and warm at the same time. And every time his tongue swept against hers, she moved against him, the pulse inside her strong and rhythmic.

He slid his hands beneath her dress, tracing circles on her bare back. His eyes met hers, and she could see the question in the depths. Nodding, she rotated her hips, encouraging his fingers as they slid beneath her panties.

It was crazy how excited she was, when they were both still fully clothed. Yet she could feel the pleasure coil inside her, growing every time their bodies touched.

"You're wet," he whispered in her ear, as his fingers feathered against her core.

"It's your fault," she gasped, and he laughed softly.

Sliding the soft pad of his finger inside, he found the sensitive part of her, circling until she let out a loud gasp. He smiled against her neck and circled again, making her almost buck off his lap.

"Does it feel good?" he asked.

"So good," she gasped, barely able to form the words. Her world had shrunk to a pinpoint, focused only on his lips and his fingers, and that oh-so-hard part of him she couldn't help but grind against.

Gently, he pushed his finger inside of her, and her toes curled with delight. She was on the edge, a heartbeat away from falling, as he pushed a second finger in, and her whole body exploded against him.

He captured her cries with his lips, one hand holding her steady as the other prolonged her pleasure, twisting and stroking inside her as she slowly came down from her high. When she opened her eyes, he was staring right at her, his expression a mixture of gratification and excitement.

"You okay?" he asked.

She nodded. "More than okay." She traced her hand down his chest and ran her finger along the seam of his jeans, tracing the outline of his steel-like hardness. "Unlike you, by the feel of it." She pressed a kiss against his lips. "I can help with that."

"Later." His eyes caught hers. "Not here. When we have sex, I don't want it to be in the open where anybody can find us. I want to take my time with you. Strip you naked. Make you come until you can't breathe anymore."

Reluctantly, she pulled her hand away. Damn, she really wanted to see what he had going on down there. From the outline she could see, there was quite a lot.

Her stomach rumbled loudly, making them both laugh. Any tension left between them dissolved into the air.

He grinned at her, his eyes sparkling. "I guess now you're ready to eat."

———

As they drove back to Jackson's house, the evening air rushed through the open car windows, lifting Lydia's hair until it danced around her face. She was staring out at the ocean, the setting sun making her skin glow, making her look almost other-worldly.

Though his hard-on had thankfully abated, the memory of Lydia's coming apart hadn't. If he'd thought she was beautiful before, that was nothing compared to seeing her in mid-orgasm, her lips parted, her breath coming in pants, her body undulating against his until he'd coaxed every last ounce of pleasure from her.

"You sure you're okay to come back to mine?" he asked, as he turned onto the main road into Angel Sands. "You don't have to." He didn't tell her she didn't owe him anything, but it was implicit in his words. Of course he wanted her – what red blooded man wouldn't – but he didn't want her to feel any pressure just because he'd made her come. It was completely up to her.

"Of course I want to come back to yours. After what you promised..." her voice trailed off. She gave him a dirty smile that sent his pulse rating. "And anyway, I want to see Eddie.

"Eddie," he repeated. "Shit. I'm supposed to pick him up from my dad's."

"I love your dad. He's fun."

"Do you mind if we stop at his on the way? It'll only take a minute."

"Sure," she agreed readily. "Let's do it."

Ryan Lewis still lived in Jackson's childhood home, on the edge of Angel Sands. He'd bought the bungalow soon after he'd started working at Newton Pharmaceuticals. Back then, Jackson's mom had been a homemaker, though his abiding memory of her was sitting out in the yard with a cigarette in her hand as she dangled her toes into their small swimming pool.

More often than not, it had been Ryan who cooked dinner when he got home from work. And Ryan who would sit with Jackson when he did his homework, or when they would watch sports together on the television.

Parking on the sidewalk outside of his dad's bungalow, Jackson walked around to the passenger side, opening the door for Lydia. He took her hand in his, and walked with her up the pathway.

Before they even made it to the steps, Ryan opened the door, his brows lifting as he glanced at their clasped hands.

He opened his mouth to say something, but Eddie came bounding out, leaping at Lydia, his tail wagging with excitement.

"Eddie, come here," Ryan shouted. Eddie ignored him

completely, jumping up and down, and doing a little dance at Lydia's knees.

"Eddie, sit," Jackson said firmly. When Eddie went to jump again, Jackson repeated himself, and Eddie dropped his rear to the ground, his eyes rolling at Jackson.

"Can you talk to me like that later?" Lydia whispered to him. Jackson laughed.

"Did you two lovebirds have a good evening?" Ryan asked.

"It was perfect," Lydia said, smiling warmly at Jackson's dad. "Jackson taught me to drive, and then we went to Captain Burgers and up to the cliff at Silver Cove."

"The hot and heavy make out spot?" Ryan's eyes crinkled as he looked at Jackson. "Surely you have better moves than that, son?"

"It wasn't a move," Jackson told him. "It has a good view."

"Sure." Ryan nodded. "And people only watch porn for the storyline."

"People?" Jackson snorted. "Or you?"

"Hey, I don't watch that kind of thing." Ryan held his hands up. "And I don't take pretty ladies to the cliff to make out either."

"Who said we made out?" Jackson asked.

"Oh, we definitely made out," Lydia said, as though she was enjoying the banter between father and son. "I like it up there. I'd go again."

Ryan chuckled. "Jackson, you gotta keep ahold of this one. I like her."

Jackson swallowed hard, because there was no way to keep ahold of her.

"We should go," he said to Lydia. "It's getting late."

"You sure you two don't want to come inside?" Ryan asked.

"Maybe next time," Jackson said, certain he didn't want to be anywhere except at his own house. With her.

"I'd love that." Lydia smiled at his dad, who grinned back at her. It was weird how them liking each other made his body feel warm.

"Well, you two kids have fun. And be good."

Once they'd gotten Eddie into the backseat, Lydia and Jackson climbed into the car for the short drive up to his cliff-side home. The pleasure he'd felt from watching his dad and Lydia interact was still lingering, making his lips curl up into a permanent smile.

"Can I ask you something?" Lydia said, as they drove back up into the hills.

"Sure. Shoot."

"Has your dad dated since your mom left?" Her voice was soft, as though she wasn't sure whether to ask or not.

"No." Jackson blew out a mouthful of air. His dad's lack of moving on had long been a source of contention for them both. "I think he's still holding a candle for my mom after all these years."

She looked thoughtful. "My dad's the same. Since mom died he hasn't dated anybody. Not publically anyway. I mean, he has to have been seeing somebody, you can't go twenty years without sex, can you?"

Jackson wrinkled his nose. "I don't know. And I guess I don't want to know what my dad gets up to."

Lydia laughed. "He's definitely had sex before. Where do you think you came from?"

"I know where I came from." Jackson shook his head at the amusement in her voice. "But I don't really want to think about it. Those kind of mind movies can get stuck in your head, and I'm not ready to deal with that."

"I bet your dad's good in bed."

"Lydia!" His eyes widened. "Where the hell did that come from?"

"Hear me out. He's a nice guy. Wants to make people

happy." She bit her lips to stop herself from grinning. "Kind of like his son. And since I know you have all the skills, maybe he does, too."

"You think I'm nice?" Jackson winced at the word.

Her eyes narrowed as she took him in. "Hmm. I guess I think you *can* be nice. You were nice to me this evening. Took me driving and bought me dinner."

"For ten dollars. You weren't exactly an expensive date." He rolled his eyes.

"But other times you're not so nice. You were short with me when you drove me home from the airport on Saturday. I thought I'd done something wrong."

He shook his head. "I was fighting the attraction. Trying to do what Griff asked me."

Lydia sighed. "Let's hope he's stopped trying to interfere with my love life." She ran her finger over her bottom lip, and it made him want to kiss her again. "So you're not nice when you're fighting the attraction to me, but you are nice when you give in to it. Do I have that right?"

He snorted. "Pretty much."

She clapped her hands together. "That's simple. Stop fighting it. Be nice to me." Reaching out, she traced the seam of his jeans along his inner thigh. Damn, her touch felt good. "The way you were nice to me when we were kissing on the cliff."

"Nice is a weak word." Her finger moved up further. He was torn between wanting her to carry on and wanting to keep his concentration on the road. Good thing they were almost home.

"Tell me a better one," she whispered.

He swallowed, turning onto the road leading to his house. "I desired you. Needed you. Wanted to make you feel things you hadn't felt before. I wanted to see you come apart in my arms, and hold you until you could breathe again. I wanted to kiss you until our lips hurt, until we had to pull apart because we need air like we need each other." He turned left into his driveway, parking in the usual spot. Switching the engine off, he turned to her, a half-smile on his face. "How's that?"

She swallowed hard, her cheeks flushed. "Yeah," she said, her voice ragged. "That'll work." She looked from the house and back to him. "Let's go in. I'm ready for you to show me exactly how un-nice you can be."

❧ 14 ❧

Jackson filled a bowl with water and threw a treat into Eddie's waiting mouth. "You need to stay down here, boy," he told him, when Eddie barked indignantly at Jackson walking out of the kitchen. "This is adult business."

Eddie buried his head in the water bowl, but let his tail hang down so Jackson knew he was pissed. It was okay, Jackson would make it up to him. Maybe take him for an extra long walk in the morning. They could both go for a swim.

He'd think about it later, when his brain was working properly, and not full of the gorgeous woman waiting for him.

"Is he okay?" Lydia asked when Jackson walked back into the hallway. She was leaning against the wall, her hands clasped behind her. She'd kicked off her shoes, and he noticed her toes were painted the same color as the cherry blossom on her tattoo.

"He's fine. Sulking because he wants to play."

Her eyes twinkled. "He needs a girl dog."

"No, he really doesn't." Jackson shook his head. "A litter of baby Eddies is the last thing we need."

She laughed. "Well, I guess he'll have to sulk for a minute."

"A minute?" Jackson frowned. "What do you take me for?"

She smiled coyly. "I was just checking." And flirting. Damn, was she good at it. He'd never been one for banter before. Or for spending hours talking to a woman. But with her, it felt so natural.

He liked it almost as much as he liked touching her.

He walked over to where she was standing, until there was just a breath of air between them. She looked up, her green eyes dark, her lips parted.

He was already hard. From the closeness of her and the memory of her on the cliff, when she'd rode his fingers as he'd brought her to climax. "I should take your jacket," he said. She nodded and he reached for the denim, lifting it from her shoulders. Her silky hair brushed against his hands as he took it from her, hanging it from the hook on the other side of the wall.

"Come here," he said, his voice thick. She stepped away from the wall, her wide eyes still on his. Curling his palm around her neck, he caressed her skin with his fingers, making her swallow hard.

"Jackson?"

"Yes?"

"I haven't done this in a while." She looked uncharacteristically nervous. "Just so you know."

His expression turned serious. "Neither have I."

"You haven't?" Her voice rose up. "I thought you were *Jackson, the ladies' man*. The player."

His heart was hammering. He didn't want her to see him that way. "I'm mostly Jackson, the overworked company owner nowadays," he told her, threading his fingers into her hair. He massaged her scalp, and she let out a sigh.

"That sounds stressful," she murmured, as he slid his hand down to the small of her back, gathering her into his arms.

"It is." He lowered his face to hers. "So stressful..."

She was watching him intently. "You must need some relief."

Reaching up, she cupped his jaw, her fingers splayed out across his cheek. His hands explored the hollows of her back, wanting to commit every dip and curve to memory. She pressed her body against his, making him ache and pulse against her.

"I'm not a player," he said again. For some reason it was important for her to know that. To know him, the *real* him. Not the shield he put on for other people.

"I know," she whispered, her eyes fluttering as he pressed his lips to hers, reclaiming her mouth as he crushed her to him.

She let out a gasp as he slid his hands over the smooth curve of her behind, hitching her into his arms, her legs wrapping around him. She curled her hands around his neck, her mouth warm, demanding, her fingers caressing his skin in teasing circles.

Need for her coursed through his veins, making him rock her against his body as they plundered each other's mouths. She slid her hands down to his shoulders, her fingers dancing against his corded muscles. "This needs to come off," she said against his lips. "Right now."

Putting her down, he lifted the t-shirt over his head, throwing it onto the floor. She made no attempt to hide the fact she was ogling him, her breath hitching as she took in his chest, his abdomen, and the thick v of his hips as they disappeared into the waistband of his jeans.

"Upstairs?" he asked her.

"Yeah." She breathed. "Upstairs."

By the time they reached the bedroom, they were in a state of disarray. Jackson had slid Lydia's dress from her shoulders when they'd started kissing on the stairs, unable to make it up three risers without touching each other again. The rapid thump of her pulse echoed in her ears as his mouth hungrily took hers. She slid her hands down the planes of his chest and the taut skin of his abdomen, before unbuckling his belt.

He closed his bedroom door and leaned against it as his eyes raked over her body. There was a hot ache inside her, coiling and dancing deep down, as she shucked her dress off and stepped out of it. She loved the way he was looking at her. As though she was everything he never knew he wanted.

"Turn around. Show me your other tattoo."

She'd forgotten about teasing him. With a lazy grin, she turned around, pulling her panties down enough so he could see the butterfly on her behind. Its wings were unfurling, as though it had just escaped from the chrysalis.

Glancing over her shoulder, her eyes caught his. They were dark. Needy.

"What does it stand for?" he asked, his gaze dropping to her behind again.

"It's me, when I first started traveling. Like I'd been in a cocoon for most of my life, waiting for it to begin." She ran her tongue along her bottom lip. "Do you like it?"

His voice was thick. "Yeah, I like it.

With his eyes set on hers, he slowly unbuttoned his jeans, until he was wearing shorts and nothing else. She turned to watch him, her heart hammering against her chest.

She was on fire just from looking at him. Wide shoulders, muscled chest, thighs that looked like they wouldn't be out of place on a Greek sculpture. And in the center of it all, straining against his dark boxers, was the one thing her body needed.

Without a word, she stepped toward him and dropped to her knees, pulling his hard length from his shorts and wrapping her lips around it.

Jackson muttered a low oath, his head falling back as she took him in. *All of him.* Every smooth, hot, masculine inch.

Coiling his fingers around her hair, he murmured words she couldn't quite make out as she moved her mouth up and down, loving the way his legs were almost buckling. She slid her fingers up his thighs and around to his muscled ass, digging into the taut flesh as she brought him as high as he'd brought her.

He pulled away, his eyes flashing, his mouth open. She looked up, her brows knitting together as she wondered if she'd done something wrong.

"I want to be inside of you when I come," he told her with a graveled voice, as he took her hands and pulled her up. "Get on the bed."

Her lips curled, because there was something damn sexy about being told what to do in the bedroom. Stepping back until she felt the softness of his bedcovers against her legs, she sat down on the edge of the mattress, looking up at him expectantly.

"Take your bra off."

She did as she was told, unclasping it at the back and sliding the straps down her arms. He swallowed hard as he took her in.

"And my panties?" she asked breathily.

"Keep them on. They're mine to take off." He pushed her gently down on the bed and kneeled in front of her, running his fingers up her inner thighs, making her muscles tremble as he reached her aching center. Pulling her panties aside, he slid a finger against her.

"Still wet," he murmured, pulling her panties down her legs and sliding them from her feet. "So damn ready for me."

"Always."

Her breath caught in her throat, because he was kissing her *there*, his lips tugging at her, his tongue caressing.

She heard a rip of a condom wrapper. He slid it on and braced himself over her, cupping her jaw with his hand as he kissed her again. She could taste herself on him, sweet and tangy, but then he pushed his hardness against her and all thoughts flew out of her mind.

Her mouth fell open as he pushed inside her, his eyes catching hers to make sure she was okay. She nodded, and he pushed more, until he filled her to the hilt. She took a deep breath to get used to the thick, full sensation.

"Too much?" he asked.

"No," she gasped. "I'm good. Don't stop." Hooking her legs around his hips, she encouraged him against her, feeling that familiar, hot electric need as he slowly began to move.

A moan escaped from her lips every time their bodies ground against each other. She was so aware of every part of him. His lips against hers, his hands caressing her breasts, his hardness moving and teasing and making her fly.

She was tightening around him, white hot ecstasy making her cry out his name as he groaned loudly, slowing his movements as she rode out the waves.

He stilled his breath hot and fast against her face, his low voice muttering her name as he shuddered with ecstasy.

She could feel his heart pounding against her skin, matching the rhythm of her own. Slowly, he pulled out, taking care of the condom before he looked at her with soft eyes.

"You okay?" he asked, brushing the hair from her face. He was smiling at her, and damn if it didn't make her heart do a crazy leap.

A wave of pure happiness washed over her. "I'm good."

She caught her lip between her teeth, staring up at this man who knew exactly what to do to make her feel good. The man who made her wish for things she'd never have. Things she knew were never meant for her.

"Come here," he said, helping her up the mattress until their heads were on the overstuffed pillows, his arm circling her as he pulled her against him. She dropped her chin on his chest with a sigh, pleasure still warming her skin and loosening her muscles.

"You're amazing," he whispered into her hair.

"So are you. Three times amazing." She smiled against his chest.

"Give me half an hour and we'll make it an even four."

She laughed softly. "I'm not sure I can take much more. And anyway, I should go back to Autumn's house soon. It's getting late."

"You could stay here."

"We probably shouldn't give Griff an aneurysm," she said, drawing circles with her fingers against his stomach. She liked the way it rippled every time she touched him. "Not until after the naming ceremony, anyway."

"I guess…" He sounded reluctant. And she liked that. Maybe too much. Laying here in his arms was so easy, so natural. But it wasn't real. None of this was. "Stay for ten more minutes," he suggested. "Just let me hold you for a while."

Snuggling against his chest, she nodded, letting out a sigh as he stroked his fingers through her hair.

"Ten minutes," she agreed. After that, she'd let herself get back to reality.

Closing the front door behind her as quietly as she could, Lydia tiptoed down the hallway toward her bedroom, holding her breath.

But all her ninja tactics were for nothing, because Griff and Autumn were in the nursery, calming a screaming Skyler as they tried to get her to nurse.

"Hey." Lydia smiled at them, because damn, she was feeling mighty fine. "You guys still up?"

Griff glanced at his watch, his brows lifting as he took in the time. It was past one in the morning, Lydia knew that because she'd seen it on Jackson's car clock before she'd climbed out.

"You're home late," Griff said, trying – and failing – to keep his voice light.

Autumn sighed at him.

He looked at her. "What?"

"I thought we talked about this. What Lydia and Jackson do is their own concern." Autumn adjusted Skyler against her chest. "Did you have a good evening?"

"It was great." Lydia grinned. "How about you guys?"

But Griff was having none of it. "I thought he was taking you for a driving lesson."

"He did," Lydia told him. "We drove all around the mountain roads."

"Until one o'clock?" His eyebrow arched.

"Still not her father," Autumn muttered to him.

"You both look tired," Lydia said, changing the subject. "How about I babysit for you tomorrow night? You can go out and have fun for a change."

"Are you trying to sweet talk me?" Griff asked. "Because it won't work."

"She doesn't need to sweet talk you, because whatever's going on between her and Jackson is none of your damn business." Autumn treated him to a fantastic glare. Lydia took note to avoid pissing her sister off.

"I'm worried about them," he muttered.

"I know." Autumn patted his arm with her free hand.

"And I love them both."

Lydia smiled at him. "We know that. But we're grown-ups. Imagine how you'd feel if someone had told you not to see Autumn. You'd have been annoyed as hell."

"That's different," Griff said, sitting on the loveseat next to his fiancée. "Autumn and I were serious."

"Not at first we weren't," Autumn protested. "You were all about never settling down."

He pressed a kiss against her brow. "And then I realized how amazing you were, and that I couldn't live without you." He glanced at Lydia. "Is that how you feel about Jackson?"

Her cheeks flushed. "I don't know. We're just having fun, I guess." She didn't want to think too deeply about it, because she was scared what she might find.

Autumn looked from Lydia and back to Griff. "You know, honey, we really could do with a night out. I can't remember the last time I ate using both hands."

Lydia sent her sister a silent wave of gratitude. She knew Autumn was worried about her and Jackson as well. She'd said as much when they went out for ice cream the other night. But her sister was soft hearted, and she believed in letting people do their own thing.

So did Griff, for the most part. And if she was honest, Lydia kind of liked his protectiveness. She was a free bird, but even free birds liked a safe place to nest sometimes.

From the way he was stroking Skyler's hair, Lydia could guess exactly where Griff's anxiety came from. He was a father now, and that made him constantly concerned for his daughter. His protectiveness over Lydia was just a reflection of that.

"Yeah," Griff agreed. "Maybe a night out without this monkey would do us both some good."

Lydia grinned, because she knew they both needed this. "I'll take good care of her, I promise. You'll have such a good time."

Autumn glanced slyly at Griff. "Maybe Jackson could come over to help. He's going to be Skyler's godfather, after all."

Griff's head shot up. "What?"

"Only if you want him to," Autumn told Lydia. "But as you can see, four arms are usually better than two. Especially when it comes to changing diapers."

"Jackson could probably do with the practice," Lydia agreed happily. "That way he can get comfortable and maybe he'll be able to babysit after I leave. Give you guys a break."

"If you think I'm leaving my only child with Jackson..." Griff trailed off when he saw Autumn's expression. "Okay," he conceded with a sigh. "He can come help Lydia. But he's not to be left alone with Skyler until he's more experienced with babies."

"I'll call him in the morning," Lydia said. "See if he's free. And you two should start planning your date." She raised an eyebrow at Griff. "You probably need to make it pretty special."

Griff huffed. "I'm getting that idea."

Autumn kissed him softly. "Anywhere is special with you."

"Yeah?" he breathed, cupping her cheek. The way he looked at his fiancée made Lydia's stomach contract. There was so much love there, but passion, too.

"Always." Autumn stared back at him, her eyes shining.

Lydia suddenly felt like an interloper. She ran her tongue along her dry lips and started to back down the hallway. "I'm beat," she told them. "Time for bed for this girl."

"Sleep tight," Autumn called out as Lydia opened the door to the guest bedroom.

Truth was, she'd never felt more awake in her life. After tonight, her whole body was buzzing, like an electric storm crackling in the night sky.

And as for her mind? Well, she had a lot to think about.

❧ 15 ❧

"Here are three shortlisted candidates I want you to meet," Lisa said, laying out three résumés on Jackson's desk. "They're all good. And this guy was in charge of a department at his last job." She pointed at the sheaf of paper at the top.

"Why did he leave?" Jackson asked her.

"The owner sold. New owner wanted his own people in place." Lisa shrugged. "There's nothing sinister about him. Meet him and you'll see. I already did the hard work and interviewed them. They're all good, I promise."

Jackson read the name at the top. Carl Rubens. He didn't know the guy, but he'd make a couple of calls to make sure he was as good as Lisa said. Not that he didn't trust her, but he was running a security business. Anybody he took on was a reflection of him. "Okay, arrange for me to meet with him early next week."

Lisa beamed. "I'll call him now. And the others?"

"I'll meet Carl first. If he's as good as you say he is, he can help recruit anybody else."

"Right you are." She patted Eddie, who was curled in his

usual spot at Jackson's feet. "Oh, and I haven't had any sensible replies about Eddie. Just a few stupid ones. And a dick pic. Why do people always send dick pics?"

Jackson frowned. "You got a dick pic? Maybe you should close the inquiry. I don't want you being harassed."

Lisa shrugged. "I can take it. We should leave it up. Somebody has to be missing this guy. He's too cute not to be loved."

"Yeah." Jackson nodded. "I guess he is."

"I'm gonna miss him being in the office if his family is found." Lisa blew Eddie a kiss.

"He's only been here for a few days," Jackson pointed out. "And you're forever complaining about his farts."

"Doesn't mean I don't think he's the cutest little schnookums ever," Lisa said in a cutesy voice, ruffling Eddie's head.

"Go call this Carl guy and leave me alone."

Lisa narrowed her eyes. "You're cute when you're upset because your dog could be leaving, you know that?"

Jackson shook his head and turned back to his computer, biting down a smile as Lisa stomped back to her desk.

"And don't think I haven't noticed what a good mood you're in today," Lisa called out, as she sat on her chair. "A little bird told me you had a date last night."

If she wasn't such a good assistant, he'd fire her. But he'd only be hurting himself by doing that. Any right minded business owner would snap Lisa up in an instant, and he'd be the one losing out.

"I'm putting my headphones in now," he told her. "So I can block out the annoying noise and concentrate."

She grinned and lifted her phone to her ear, tapping in numbers as she read them from the résumé.

Jackson grabbed his wireless headphones. He really did have tons of work to do, and listening to white noise always helped him concentrate. But right as he was pulling up his tried-and-tested playlist, his phone started to buzz. Before he could stop it, a smile curled his lips when he saw Lydia's name on the screen.

"Hey," he said, sending up a silent prayer that Lisa was too busy talking on the phone to notice his grin. "You doing okay this morning?"

"I am." Her voice was warm. "I've been doing some work at the coffee shop. The couple I'm taking to Rio wanted a few changes made to their itinerary, so I've been messing around with that."

"When do you go to Rio?" he asked. "I thought you were heading to Europe."

"I am. Rio isn't until June, but I like to plan everything out with as much notice as I can. Things can get booked up very quickly."

"How long are you in Europe again?"

"Almost two months. Barcelona then Madrid, and after that I'm heading to Paris. I've got a tentative booking for two sisters to go to the champagne region of France, though goodness knows why they need *me* to be there. Then it's Italy for the second half of May, and Rio in June."

So she'd be busy. Maybe too busy to come back here. He ignored the dryness in his throat. "When will you be coming back to visit Autumn?"

"I don't know," she said softly. "I hope it won't be too long. I'm growing fond of this place."

And he was growing fond of her. Maybe it was a good thing she was leaving soon, before he got in too deep.

"Anyway, that's not why I'm calling. I was wondering what your plans are for tonight."

His muscles relaxed. "No plans. Why, what are you up to?"

"Griff and Autumn are going out for the evening, and I'm babysitting. I wondered if you'd like to come help me." She cleared her throat. "I'm not exactly practiced with babies. I'll need all the support I can get."

"And you thought of me?" he asked, making sure his voice was light. "I know less about babies than you."

"Autumn suggested you come actually."

"And what does Griff think about that?" Jackson asked. Across the office, he could see Lisa had finished her call. She was pretending to read something on her computer screen, but he could tell by the way her back was ramrod straight that she was trying to listen in to his conversation.

He shook his head. She was nosy, but she was good at what she did. Nobody was perfect.

"Griff knows better than to contradict Autumn," Lydia said, her voice bright. "And I think he's genuinely scared about leaving me alone with Skyler. I got a lecture this morning about how to hold her head. She's four months old. She can hold her own head up perfectly. He's losing it, he really is."

"I'd love to come help you." He wanted all of her nights right now. "But I have Eddie. I can't ask my dad to watch him again. It's his chess night with the guys."

"Wait one moment." He heard muffled voices, as though Lydia was covering up the mouthpiece of the phone. A moment later, she came back on the line. "Autumn says Eddie can come if we keep him in the yard. Do you think that'll be okay?"

He glanced down at the dog sleeping at his feet. "Yeah, we can make that work."

"Great. Because I don't know if I've told you, but I'm horribly allergic to poopy diapers. So that'll be your job, okay?"

"Hey, I deal with Eddie's stuff. That's enough crap for me on a single day. The diapers are all yours."

She laughed. "Listen to us discussing who's cleaning up

after the dog and the baby. We sound like an old married couple."

"I guess I'd better get back to work. What time shall I come over?"

"They're leaving at seven. So maybe ten minutes before? That'll give us enough time to give Griff the heebie jeebies."

"I'll bring some takeout with me. We'll need fuel to look after the baby."

"Perfect. See you tonight, Mr. Nanny."

Shaking his head, Jackson hung up the phone.

Lydia opened Autumn's front door, a smile breaking out on her lips when she saw Jackson standing there, his hands stuffed into his jeans, Eddie's leash wrapped around his wrist. Eddie was sitting patiently next to him, but when he saw Lydia, his tail started to wag like crazy.

Jackson leaned forward and pressed a sweet kiss against her lips and she felt all giddy and warm. Damn, he smelled good. She wasn't sure what cologne he was wearing, but it made her leg muscles feel like mush. Would it be wrong for her to go through his bathroom cabinet the next time she was over and find out? Just for the sake of curiosity, of course.

"Hey," he said. "Shall I walk Eddie around the back?"

Autumn appeared behind Lydia, fastening an earring. "You can bring him through," she said, inclining her head at the hallway. "The kitchen door is open. I've put a few bean-bags out in case he wants somewhere soft to rest."

"I'll take him through." Lydia held out her hand for the leash. Jackson passed it to her, his fingers caressing hers.

She swallowed hard. He was so damn distracting.

"Let me see this dog," Griff said, as she walked him into the kitchen. Skyler was cradled in his right arm, her hair fluffy from her bath, wearing a fresh pink onesie covered in printed sheep. She lifted her hand from her drooly mouth and smiled as she looked at Eddie, her eyes full of interest as the dog stopped at Griff's feet.

"Sit, Eddie," Lydia said, willing him to obey her. She really wanted to spend tonight with Jackson, and if Eddie wasn't welcome here, he wouldn't stay.

Eddie took a calculating look at her and slowly sat, looking up at Griff, his tongue lolling out.

Griff touched the pup with his free hand, and Eddie gave what almost sounded like a purr.

"He likes you," Lydia said. "That's his contented sound."

"Does he always do what you tell him?" Griff asked her.

"It's Jackson he listens to the most." She turned her head to see Jackson and Autumn standing in the kitchen. "He can get him to do anything with a command."

Griff raised a disbelieving eyebrow. Jackson grinned at the challenge.

"Lay down, Eddie," Jackson said, and Eddie immediately dropped to the floor. Griff blinked, surprised.

"Sit."

Eddie plopped his backside onto the tile.

"Now come here."

Without a complaint, Eddie got to his feet and walked over to Jackson. Lydia had to follow him, the leash still coiled in her hand.

"He can stay, right?" Autumn said, looking at Griff.

He shrugged. "Yeah, I guess. But not in the nursery, okay?"

"Of course." Lydia caught Jackson's eye. "He'll be on his best behavior."

"You'd better be on your best behavior, too," Griff told his friend. "No getting dirty with Autumn's sister while I'm out."

Autumn gave Griff a pointed look. "Ignore him," she told

Jackson. "He's just anxious about leaving Skyler." Her expression softened when she mentioned her daughter. "Talking of the baby, I've made a list of everything you might need. It's on the kitchen counter. She shouldn't need feeding, but if she cries too much there's a bottle in the refrigerator."

"It's breast milk," Griff said, his eyes crinkling. "So don't go tasting it to see if it's warm enough."

Jackson shrugged. "I drink milk from cow's breasts. I can handle human ones."

Autumn covered her mouth, but her laugh still escaped. The smile slipped from Griff's face.

"Don't be drinking my fiancée's breast milk. That's not a request."

Jackson winked at Lydia, and she bit down a grin. "Don't worry," she promised. "Autumn's boob milk is safe with us."

"If we could all stop talking about my breasts, maybe we could get out of here." Autumn lifted Skyler from Griff's arms and passed her to Lydia. "Bedtime at eight. And we should be home by eleven. But make sure you call if there are any problems."

"We will," Lydia agreed. "I promise."

"And maybe send me a photo or something. Just so I know she's alive."

To Lydia's surprise, Jackson took Autumn's hands in his own. "We'll take care of her," he said softly. "I promise. You'll come home to her asleep and hopefully you'll both get a good night's rest, too."

Autumn leaned forward to kiss his cheek. "You're a good man, Jackson Lewis."

His lips curled as he whispered against her skin. "But it's our secret, right?"

She stepped back and smiled at him. "It's not a secret. We all know it. Now have a good evening, you two lovebirds. And don't do anything I wouldn't do." Autumn kissed the top of

Skyler's head and grabbed her purse from the counter, reaching out for Griff's hand. "And thank you both. We're grateful for the break, aren't we, honey? With all the planning for Skyler's celebration, I feel exhausted as soon as I wake up."

"Yeah, I guess we're grateful." Griff managed a smile. "I'll see you later." He glanced at Jackson then back at Lydia. "Good luck with the babysitting."

"Go!" Lydia said, laughing. "Before we change our minds."

❧ 16 ❧

"She's asleep," Lydia said an hour later. They'd divided the work between them, with Lydia reading a bedtime story to Skyler while Jackson warmed up the food he'd brought, then played with Eddie in the yard. The dog was curled up in a sweaty heap in the middle of the grass, snoring loudly. Throwing the ball for him about a hundred times had finally tired him out. Mission accomplished.

Jackson looked up from where he was standing on the deck, drinking her in with his gaze. She was wearing jeans today, with a white silky shell on top, her tanned arms glowing in the light of the setting sun.

"Come here," he said, his voice low. She bit down a smile, her green eyes meeting his as she slowly sashayed to where he was standing.

He cupped her face with his warm palms. "You look beautiful tonight," he told her, brushing her temple with his lips. "I've been thinking about you all day. I had to listen to thrash rock music to finally concentrate on my work."

Her gentle laugh rippled through the evening air. "I was

thinking about you, too. When I woke up this morning and I realized I was alone it was so disappointing."

"Stay tonight," he urged. "Come with me when Autumn and Griff are back."

She nodded. "Yes, please."

Her easy acquiescence filled him with warmth. She reached for him, sliding her hands beneath his t-shirt, her palms caressing his back. Her nearness was overwhelming. He couldn't remember ever craving somebody like this. He pressed a tender kiss against her lips, desire flooding through his body the same way it always did when she was near. Lydia sighed softly, her breath tickling his mouth. She kissed him back hard, arching her body into his as though he'd lit a fuse inside of her.

He was immediately hard. Emotions whirled and kicked inside him as he slid his hands down her sides, cupping her behind to pull her closer against him. When she felt the outline of his desire against her, she curled her arms around his neck, her tongue sweeping against his as they both gave in to the need they were feeling.

She was the first to pull back, her face flushed, her eyes wild.

"We need some ground rules," she said breathlessly. "Otherwise we're going to end up defiling Autumn and Griff's living room, and they'll never let us babysit again."

Jackson nodded. "Maybe we should pick a base," he suggested. "And make a pact to go no further." Until he got her back to his place, at least.

"First?" Lydia said, wrinkling her nose. "No, let's make it second. Any self-respecting babysitter would let her boyfriend get to second."

"Am I your boyfriend?" Jackson asked, wanting to know the answer.

"For the purposes of this discussion you are." She bit

down a smile. "Maybe we should pretend we're teenagers. You can be the football god and I'll be..." her voice trailed off as she thought through the options. "Definitely not the head cheerleader. That would be boring, and so predictable." Her eyes lit up. "I know, I'll be the nerd you're completely attracted to, but you only make out with me when none of your friends are around. I can be your dirty little secret."

The way she said dirty made the blood rush to parts he was trying to control. "We're playing make believe again?"

"It'll be fun," she told him. "Let me show you." She led him into the living room, and pushed him down onto an easy chair. "Jackson Lewis, the next time you want me to tutor you, maybe you could not touch me beneath the table."

He wanted to laugh. She looked so adorable as she tried to get into character. It made him wonder what she was really like when she was at school.

"Yeah, well if you'd stop staring at my dick every time I'm wearing my football pants, maybe I'd be able to concentrate." Hey, maybe this was easier than he'd thought. And yeah, he might be a thirty-three year old guy pretending to be a teenager, but if it made her happy, then why the hell not?

"You're an asshole, you know that?" Her eyes narrowed. "I hate you."

"I hate you, too." His mouth was dry with the need of her.

She let out a little scream of annoyance and leaned over him, her hands bracing herself against the wings of the chair. If he'd met her when he was a teenager, he'd have been toast. She would have overwhelmed him.

Who was he kidding? She was overwhelming him *now*.

His eyes dipped, taking in the smooth lines of her neck, the dip at the base of her throat, and the top that gaped open as she leaned. He could see the soft outline of her breasts, and his fingers curled with the need to touch her.

"Look at the eyes, not the tits, Lewis."

"Your tits are more interesting than your eyes."

"Yeah, well your dick is a hundred times more intelligent than your brain." She gave him a dirty look. "But we all have our crosses to bear."

"Come here," he told her.

"Why?" she asked coyly. Her half-smirk made his skin heat up.

"Because I want to try out a theory."

"What kind of theory?" she asked. "If it's got anything to do with my chest, it's a no."

"I won't touch your chest," he told her, his voice low. "Not until you beg me to. And you *will* beg me to."

"You're so full of yourself," she muttered. But she still climbed over him, her knees on either side of his legs, her body lifted so it didn't touch his. His dick was straining against his jeans.

"Kiss me," he told her.

"What? No." Her brow crinkled. "Why would I do that?"

"Because you think about it every time you look at me." He sat up until his face was inches from hers. He could feel her hot breath against his skin. "Because you've never been kissed, and if you're going to kiss anybody, you should do it with somebody who knows what they're doing."

"And that's you?" She quirked an eyebrow.

He smirked, and it made her eyes flash. She swallowed hard, her throat undulating. He watched her intently, waiting to see what she'd do.

"If you tell anybody, I'll cut your dick off," she muttered, leaning in to brush her lips against his.

He slid his hands around her behind, and she promptly reached around to lift them up, so he was cupping her hips. "First base only," she told him.

Taking control, he leaned forward and crushed his mouth to hers, sliding his tongue along her bottom lip until her mouth parted. Her arms curled around his neck as she kissed him back, hot and heavy, and that aching pulse in his dick intensified.

He wanted to grind against her. To make her purr with pleasure against his lips. Wanted to kiss his way down her neck, across her chest, then down to her breasts, to capture her nipples between his lips until she was calling out his name.

He dug his fingers into her hips, his mouth hot and needy as he plundered hers. But a loud cry cut through the silence.

Lydia leaned back, swallowing hard as her eyes met his. "The baby's crying," she said.

"I figured."

"I should go and..." she inclined her head.

"You want me to do it this time?"

Her lips pursed as she blew out a mouthful of air. "Do you mind? I'm feeling a little, um, flustered right now."

He grinned. Thankfully his body was calming down. Lifting her gently until she was standing, he caught her eye. "Hold that role play," he told her. "I was going to try for second base."

She laughed. "And I was going to fight you off. It would have been hot."

Skyler cried again, her sobs echoing down the hallway. "That's my cue," he told her, leaning forward to steal a kiss from her soft lips. "Wish me luck."

Lydia walked back in from the yard where she'd been petting Eddie, who was snoring on one of the old bean bags Autumn had put out. Jackson still wasn't back, though Skyler's cries had quieted at least ten minutes earlier. Maybe she was having her diaper changed. Lydia wrinkled her nose. She'd leave him to finish that before she went in.

He'd left his phone on the coffee table, next to his brown leather wallet. The screen was lit up, though no sound was coming out. Curious, she glanced at it.

Mom.

The screen faded as the call diverted to voicemail. Lydia picked the phone up and carried it into the hallway, quietly pushing open the nursery door so she could give it to Jackson.

He was in the rocking chair with Skyler. The baby was cradled against his chest, her tiny fingers clutching the thin fabric of his t-shirt, and the two of them were sound asleep.

Lydia's heart did a little leap at how adorable they looked.

There was a flicker in her memory – of the other night when Griff held Autumn sweetly as they both smiled at Skyler. But instead of Autumn and Griff, Lydia's mind replaced them with her and Jackson.

Her breath caught in her throat at the image of them cradling their own baby. Jackson would kiss her shoulder, and whisper dirty things in her ear to make her hurry up and get the baby to bed.

The thought was so sweet she could almost taste it. In another world, another life, that would all be hers.

Jackson cracked an eye open. "Hey."

She made herself smile, chasing the thoughts out of her mind. "Hey yourself," she whispered. "I don't know who is putting who to sleep here."

He looked down at Skyler and stroked her downy head with his hand, the baby so tiny in his big arms. Lydia swallowed hard. She might not need her ovaries right now, but she also didn't want them to explode.

"Holding her is like taking a sleeping pill," he murmured, his eyes soft as he pressed his lips to Skyler's cheek. "I don't understand why Griff moans about not getting enough rest. All he has to do is cuddle her."

Lydia chuckled. "You don't hear her in the middle of the night."

"This is true."

Standing, he carefully cradled the baby against his chest before he leaned to place her in her crib. Then he checked the wall thermometer, just as Autumn's detailed instructions had suggested he do. "One blanket," he said to himself, pulling the pink fluffy square over Skyler's sleeping body. "Sleep tight, sweet girl."

Walking quietly across the room, he took Lydia's hand. "Wanna go make out some more?" he asked her.

She glanced down at the phone in her other hand. "Yeah," she said, trying to ignore the melancholy feeling lying heavy on her shoulders. "But your mom called. You should call her back first."

He took the phone from her hand and slid it in his back pocket. "She can wait. Let's go back to the living room. I need you."

Lydia laughed. "You want me to pretend to hate you again?"

Tracing the outline of her lips with his finger, he slowly shook his head. "No," he told her. "As hot as that was, I want to kiss you. The real you. No pretend, no make believe, just you and me and nothing else."

She sighed, and the warm air rushed against his fingers. "You always know the right thing to say."

"It's the truth." And while he was being truly honest, the intensity scared him a little.

He wanted her to know who he was from the inside out. To kiss him because she wanted him, the true and honest version nobody else knew.

Rolling onto her tiptoes, she curled her arms around his neck, her warm eyes meeting his.

"Kiss me, Jackson," she whispered.

Sliding his hands beneath her behind, he carried her to the living room and did exactly what she'd asked.

And yeah, it was still hot as hell.

Lydia sighed and rolled over into Jackson's waiting arms. The bedcovers were a wrinkled mess at their feet, their clothes strewn all over Jackson's bedroom. They'd run upstairs as soon as Jackson had opened his front door and they'd both walked inside. She guessed that's what happened when you spent the whole evening only hitting second base.

Eventually, you were desperate for a home run.

"You okay?" Jackson murmured, pressing his lips to her head.

"More than okay." She smiled, nestling into his embrace. His skin was warm against hers.

"We should probably sleep. We don't want to be yawning tomorrow." He traced his finger down her spine. "People will talk."

"Are we that interesting?" she asked, wrinkling her nose as she looked up at him.

"This is Angel Sands. Somebody blowing their nose gets the gossips going. You and me, we're going to be the talk of the town."

She bit her lip. "Oh. I hadn't thought of that."

"Does it worry you?"

"Not really." She shook her head. "I was just thinking that my dad's flying in for Skyler's naming day on Saturday. I'm not really looking forward to seeing him."

"Why not?" Jackson frowned. "Don't you get along with him?"

She rolled onto her back and looked up at the ceiling. "I guess I just feel like I constantly disappoint him. I always have. Most of the time it doesn't bother me, but that's because I don't see him a whole lot."

"How could you disappoint him?" Jackson asked. "That's crazy."

"He wants me to be more like Autumn. He always did. I spent most of my childhood trying to hide my school progress reports from him, because he'd always look at them and sigh loudly."

"Your progress reports sound interesting." Jackson kissed her neck. "What exactly did they say?"

"Things like, Lydia needs to spend less time staring out of the window, and more time looking at the white board." Her lip curled at the memory. "Or variations on that theme. I was a dreamer. I didn't like learning the way they tried to teach me. And when I told him I didn't want to go to college..." She shook her head. "Let's just say he was lucky to come out of it with all his arteries intact."

"Why didn't you go to college?"

Running the tip of her tongue along her bottom lip, Lydia reached out to trace the swell of his bicep. "On my eighteenth birthday I got a letter from my mom. She'd written it for me before she died, and he'd kept it for all that time."

"What did it say?" Jackson asked, his voice thick with curiosity.

"She told me not to conform to what people wanted from me. That I was a free spirit and should follow my heart." Her lips curled at the memory. "And I realized that I'd never make my dad happy, but maybe my choices would have pleased my mom. So I booked a ticket to Paris the next day, using some of the money she'd left me in a trust. Dad was apoplectic."

"But you went anyway?"

"Yeah. And that was the start of a beautiful love story. Me and traveling," she said, her eyes dancing. "The perfect relationship."

"But your dad doesn't see it that way?"

"He thinks I'm flaky. For a while he blamed me for Autumn buying the pier and moving here. Thought I was a bad influence. But that was all her, nothing to do with me at all." She pressed her lips to Jackson's warm shoulder. "Though I still admire her for it."

"So now neither of you make your dad happy?"

"I think he's come to terms with Autumn's choices. She's still a business owner, and now she has a family. It might not be in New York, but at least she's still following a straight path. Mine zig zags everywhere."

"You own your own business, too."

She gave him a soft smile. "Yeah, I do."

"And you're good at it. Look at how in demand your services are. You're successful and doing exactly what you want. You're living the dream."

Her smile wavered. "Am I?" she asked. She wanted to tell him that's what she'd thought. What she was still trying to believe in. But lying here in his arms, she was wondering if she was missing something, too.

Missing somebody to share it all with. Yeah, she had friends all over the world. She loved spending time with them. But when she went home, she went alone.

And maybe that wasn't what she wanted for the rest of her life.

"Yeah," he said, his expression serious. "You are. And you know something else?"

"What?" she breathed.

"You impress me. Every part of me." He kissed her with

hot lips, his mouth demanding. Curling into him, she felt him harden against her hip.

"I thought we needed to sleep," she murmured, as he kissed his way down her throat. "We aren't supposed to yawn tomorrow, remember?"

He cupped her breasts. "You look beautiful when you yawn."

She chuckled, and kissed him again, all thoughts of tomorrow forgotten.

They had tonight. And right now, that was all she cared about.

❧ 17 ❧

It was just before six in the morning. Any minute now, Eddie would be scratching at the kitchen door, ready for his morning bathroom run out in the yard followed by a bowlful of kibble and raw chicken. But for now, the house was silent, save for Lydia's soft rhythmic breath as she lay in the bed next to him, her naked body curled up beneath his crisp white sheets.

Griff had been uncharacteristically silent when Jackson had picked Lydia up to stay for a second night. Jackson had expected a few sarcastic grunts, at least, but there'd been nothing. Instead he'd walked into the kitchen, grabbed himself a beer, and gone out to sit on the deck.

There was something wrong with him. It wasn't just the grumpiness that had manifested itself when Griff discovered Jackson and Lydia were a thing. That was understandable. Lydia was Autumn's little sister, and Griff cared about her a lot. She was a strange combination of completely independent and sweetly vulnerable. Jackson felt the same way about her – he wanted to protect her, but he also knew you couldn't keep something so untamed safe for long.

He glanced at the clock again. Only two minutes had passed since the last time. He wished he could curl up next to her, pull her into his arms, and hold her tight. But once Eddie was awake he'd need a walk. And then Lisa was picking him up for the day, because it was Skyler's naming day, and they were due at the pier at twelve for the ceremony.

Lydia murmured in her sleep, turning onto her side so he could see the rippled line of her spine. He'd kissed his way down it last night, until he'd ended up at her butterfly tattoo. In fact, he'd devoured every inch he could find of her, determined to memorize every rise and dip, loving the way his touch sent her crazy.

Soon she'd be gone. He blew out a mouthful of air at the thought. It was for the best, really. He was shit at relationships, and Lydia was serious about her job. There was no point in trying to think about the future.

So much better to have this short, sweet time together and still be friends.

He rolled onto his back, lifting his arms above his head as he thought about her leaving. She'd be gone for months.

He hadn't asked her about keeping in touch. He wasn't sure he wanted to. Talking to her without being able to see her, to touch her, felt like it would be more painful than no contact at all. He didn't want to know if she was having a good time without him – or even worse, with a guy that wasn't him. He just wanted life to be the same way it had always been. Work, friends, surfing, and sleep. He knew where he was with those.

Rolling to his side, he climbed out of bed. No point in wallowing in this funk that had come over him. It was going to be a long day, and he needed to be on form. This ceremony was important to Griff and Autumn. It would be important to Skyler, too, he guessed. She'd be his god daughter. His responsibility if anything ever happened to his friends. It wasn't a promise you made lightly.

In the kitchen, Eddie was already awake, pacing the floor impatiently and glancing out of the back door. Jackson opened it for him and he ran out, heading for his favorite spot in the corner of the yard. When he'd done what he needed to do, Jackson poured his breakfast into a bowl, and Eddie practically jumped on him before he could put it down on the mat.

"Hungry, huh?"

Eddie rolled his eyes and buried his snout in his food. Jackson flipped the coffee machine on, and fed a pod into it, grabbing a carton of milk from the refrigerator to fill the frothing jug.

The sun was rising over the mountains, casting a long shadow in the outline of Jackson's house across his grassy yard. Mist had risen up from the ocean, and lay across the lawn like a blanket, not yet chased away by the heat of the sun's rays.

As coffee sputtered from the machine, Jackson glanced out of the door. Through the mist he could see a tall figure walking along the cliff edge. Whoever it was got closer, enough for him to make out it was Griff, with Skyler tied to his front in some kind of papoose.

He stopped at the end of Jackson's backyard, and stared into the kitchen. Jackson lifted his hand in greeting, and Griff nodded back.

Opening the gate, Griff walked down the path, Skyler's head bobbing against his chest.

Jackson opened the door. "Coffee?" he asked, holding up a second mug.

"That'd be good." Griff sat down on one of the basket weave chairs, crossing his long legs at the ankle as he held

Skyler securely against him with his hands. Pouring a second mug, Jackson topped them both up with hot steamy milk and carried them out of the kitchen.

"You're up early," he said, passing the mug to Griff and sitting in the chair next to him.

"Couldn't sleep."

Taking a sip of coffee, Jackson studied him over the rim of his mug. "You know, Lydia's still here. Just in case you were planning on making a scene."

Griff sighed. "I'm not going to make a scene. I just wanted to..." he trailed off and shook his head. "I don't know. I guess I just wanted to see my friend."

"Is that what we are?" Jackson asked. "You haven't seemed so sure this week."

"I know. I've been an asshole, I'm sorry." Skyler lifted her head, blinking at the daylight. "Don't tell your mom I swore," Griff told her. "Our secret."

"Is it the naming day?" Jackson tipped his head, scanning Griff's face. "Are you worried about it?"

"No." Griff sounded almost incredulous. "It's going to be a good day."

"So what's got you walking five miles at the crack of dawn then?"

"I got a lot on my mind." Griff put his cup down on the table. "I guess I have for a while. Thought a walk might help. And Autumn needs some sleep. She's running on fumes right now. This way she'll be nice and rested for this afternoon."

"What's niggling you?"

"I dunno. I keep feeling this..." Griff screwed his face up. "Pressure, I guess. I look at Skyler and think how damn precious she is and how I'd hurt anybody who came near her. And then I remember my parents and how they treated me, and I just can't understand it." His voice was low. Thick.

"How do you abandon your kid? Ignore them because you have better things to do?"

Jackson ran his tongue along his bottom lip, thinking of all those times his mom walked away.

"I don't know. I guess it's not about us. They're messed up. Your parents, my mom. They look inward when they should be looking out."

"I'm scared I'm gonna fuck this up the same way they did," Griff mumbled. "I'm going to let her down."

"You're not going to mess this up," Jackson said firmly. "You're a great dad. Look at you, sitting there with a baby tied to your chest. That's not what bad parents do. You love her, man. I can see it in everything you do. If you mess up, it'll be because we all make mistakes. But unlike our parents, you'll make it right."

"I don't know what it means to be a good parent. I never had one."

"Yeah you did." Jackson looked him in the eye. "They might not have been related to you by blood, but you had my dad, as well as Lucas's parents taking care of you. If you use them as your guide, you won't go wrong."

Griff gave him the briefest of smiles and kissed his daughter's downy head. "I'm sorry I've been an asshole to you this week."

"You were just practicing for when Skyler dates." Jackson shrugged. "And I've been an asshole to you before. It's what friends do. If you can't take your worries out on them, what's the point?"

"I appreciate you, man. You know that, right? Choosing you to be Skyler's godfather wasn't something we did lightly."

"I'm not taking it lightly," Jackson told him, meeting his gaze with a confident stare. "I'm going to be there for her, the same way all our folks were there for you. Except she won't need me to be a surrogate parent, because she already has the best parents in the world."

Eddie ambled out of the kitchen and onto the deck, drunk with all the food he'd just eaten. Taking an interested look at Griff, he curled up in front of Jackson's feet, resting his chin on them the same way he always did.

"You look good with a dog," Griff said. "How's it going with him?"

"Pretty well. He's been here for a week and it's like I've always had him." Jackson petted Eddie's head. "It's nice having someone else in the house."

"And now you have two somebody elses." Griff glanced over his shoulder at the kitchen door. "So, you and Lydia, huh?"

Jackson swallowed, thinking about her all warm and soft in his bed. "Yeah. That's happening."

"Autumn thinks you two like each other."

"We do."

"As in *really* like each other." Griff lifted an eyebrow.

A shaft of sunlight moved across the grass. "She's special," Jackson said softly. "We're good together."

Griff nodded, as though he could read the subtext in Jackson's words. "What are you gonna do when she leaves?"

Jackson drank the last of his coffee, letting the bitter liquid play on his tongue. "I'm going to let her go."

Griff gave him a strange look. "You are? Why?"

Exhaling heavily, Jackson put his cup on the table. "People like me and Lydia... we don't do relationships. We don't settle down. She's got a life and so do I. This is like a vacation romance, except it happened in my home town, and I'm good with that. I don't want a long distance relationship. Heck, I'm bad enough at short distance ones. I'd rather let her go and remember the good times."

"That's really sad, man."

Jackson shrugged. "It is what it is." He leaned forward to gather the cups from the table, and Eddie fussed at the interruption of his nap. "You want another coffee?"

"Nah, we should get going. Lots to do before the party begins."

"I could give you a ride?"

Griff stroked Skyler's head. "You haven't got a car seat. And I parked at the bottom of the hill. It's only a mile and the walk will do me good." He smiled at Jackson. "Thanks for talking, I feel a little better."

That was good, because Jackson felt worse. The things he'd thought but hadn't vocalized were now out there, reminding him that this thing he had with Lydia was on a time limit.

Less than a week and she'd be gone.

"I'll see you at the pier," Jackson said, as Griff started walking toward the gate.

"Yep, I'll see you there."

———

Lydia softly closed the kitchen door and padded back up the stairs, not wanting Jackson to come in and see her listening to his conversation. She'd woken suddenly and looked around for him, checking in the bathroom and the guest room before walking down to see him sitting in the backyard with Griff.

Their voices were low, and from the expressions she could make out on the profile of their faces, whatever they were discussing was serious. She should have turned around and walked back up the stairs.

People have always said no good ever came from eavesdropping. And they were right.

I don't want a long distance relationship. Heck, I'm bad enough at short distance ones. I'd rather let her go and remember the good times.

He was right, she knew he was. And yet it hurt anyway. Because there was a piece of her heart that wanted more, no matter how stupid she knew it was. Maybe it was in the human DNA. The need for a white picket fence and children running around the yard. Nature's way of forcing you to do her work no matter how hard you've tried to resist it.

After they made love last night, he'd cradled her face in his strong hands, and she'd felt this overwhelming sensation of falling. His warm brown eyes had held hers, but ever other part of her was anchorless. Belonging nowhere but there in that moment, with him.

She sat down on the edge of the bed, clutching the covers in her hands. The last time she'd felt anything like this was when she was reading her mom's letter for the first time. But then, it was the sensation of everything falling into place. Of knowing exactly who she was supposed to be.

And now? She had no idea who Lydia Paxton is at all.

Jackson opened the bedroom door, his eyes crinkling when he saw her sitting there. "You're awake," he said, his smile warm. "Would you like some coffee? Breakfast?"

She forced a smile onto her face. There was no way she was spending her time in Angel Sands moping about things she'd never wanted. She'd do what Jackson said. Treat this like the vacation romance it was. Have fun, make love, and say goodbye before she left for the airport. Exactly the way it was supposed to be.

"I'm not hungry," she told him, her voice teasing. "Not for food anyway."

His smile deepened. "What are you hungry for?" he asked softly, walking toward her.

"You," she told him. "Always you."

He lifted his t-shirt over his head and climbed out of his

sweats, leaving them in a puddle on the floor. Then he walked over to her, falling to his knees in front of her, and gently pushing her back on the bed before taking her thighs in his hands.

"I'm hungrier," he murmured, burying his face between her thighs. "But I think this is a breakfast we can both enjoy."

❧ 18 ❧

Lydia smiled as she walked onto the pier. It was beautifully decorated for Skyler's naming day. The spring sun was beating down on the ocean, reflecting on the waves as they danced into shore. The pier was decked with flowers of varying ivory and baby pink hues, and at the end of the long wooden edifice, just before where Griff's ship was moored, was a covered trellis.

Lydia had left Jackson's house shortly after they'd gotten up for the second time. Jackson had given her a ride home, and kissed her hotly before she left his car, promising to catch up with her at the pier.

And now she was here early, because she wanted to give Autumn as much support as she could. She knew her sister worried about making everything perfect, even though she'd been hosting events like this on the pier for almost a year now.

"Dad's on his way," Autumn told her, as she rushed from her office with a wad of paper in her hands. "He's cutting it close, but he should make it for the ceremony." She was jittery as hell. "Can you help me with him? Make sure he's on his best behavior."

"Dad's never on his best behavior," Lydia pointed out. "He says what he thinks, whether you want to hear it or not."

"I'd still appreciate it if you could take care of him," Autumn said, her voice imploring.

Lydia gave her hand a squeeze. "Of course I will. And if he makes any cutting remarks, I'll gag him with whatever designer tie he's wearing."

Autumn chuckled. "Maybe you should introduce him to Jackson. Since you two are a thing and all."

"We're not a thing." Lydia shrugged, remembering his words from earlier that morning. "Not a long term thing, anyway. No point in getting Dad excited when I'm taking off soon." Her words sounded like a strange echo of Jackson's conversation with Griff earlier. Maybe if she said them enough times, they wouldn't hurt.

Autumn blinked. "So that's it? You're just having a fling and leaving?"

"Did you think it was something more?" Lydia really wanted to hear her sister's thoughts.

"I don't know. I just think you two have something special."

So did she. But she also knew Jackson was right. "Yeah, but we all know long distance relationships don't work. I'm going to be away for months, and Jackson's feet are planted firmly here in Angel Sands. There's no future for us, so we're going to enjoy the time we have together then go our separate ways."

Autumn stared at her for a moment, her lips parted as though there was something she wanted to say. But she closed them again, as footsteps echoed against the wooden planks behind Lydia.

"Meghan!" Autumn said, shooting Lydia a look that told

her this conversation was postponed, not canceled. "How are you?"

Lydia turned to see the new owner of the ice cream parlor approaching them, her hand held by a little girl with flaming red hair. "Hey," Meghan said, giving Autumn and Lydia a shy smile. "How are the preparations going?"

"Great." Autumn's smile was wide. "Hey Isla, how are you settling in?"

Isla shrugged, and nestled into her mom. "We're getting there," Meghan told them. "Most of our boxes in the apartment are unpacked, and business at Angel Ices is booming. Speaking of which, I thought you should try this," she said, holding out a waffle cone topped with white and pink swirled ice cream to Autumn. "We mixed it especially for today. If you think it works, we can serve it for dessert."

It was typical of Autumn to include Meghan as one of the suppliers for Skyler's naming day. She loved using local businesses where she could. Delmonico's on the Pier was providing a buffet for their guests, and Angel Ices would be setting up a cart and serving ice cream to all who wanted them.

"This is delicious," Autumn said, taking a lick of the ice cream. "What's in it?"

"Vanilla bean cream, with minted raspberries," Meghan said. "We've decided to call it the Skyler."

"I love it!" Autumn took another lick. "You're so talented. This is going to go down well this afternoon. It'll be perfect with champagne."

"Did somebody say champagne?" Ally Sutton grinned as she joined their little group. "I swear, all you have to do is say that word and my whole body goes on alert." She hugged all three of them, and ruffled Isla's hair. "Hey sweetie," she said. "I love your dress."

Isla was in pink and white to match the décor and the ice cream. "Thank you," she said shyly.

"We should go," Meghan told them. "I want to get everything ready before the ceremony begins. That way we can watch it with you all." She smiled gratefully at Autumn. "I really appreciate you inviting us, especially when we're so new around here."

"You're part of the community now," Autumn told her. "I'm so glad you can join us."

"Hey, next time we have a girls' night, you should come along," Ally suggested. Meghan nodded with a smile, and headed back down the pier.

"Speaking of girls' night, did either of you have the hangover from hell on Wednesday?" Ally asked Lydia and Autumn. "I swear my head was pounding all day. I blame the margaritas."

"I was in a world of pain," Autumn agreed. "Not Lydia, though."

"I have a large capacity for alcohol." Lydia grinned at them.

"That sounds like a challenge. We should have another get together soon." Ally nodded, her eyes sparkling. "Not this week, though. I need at least fourteen days recovery time."

Lydia smiled sadly. "We'll have to take a rain check. I'm flying out to Spain next week."

Ally's face fell. "So soon? But you just got here."

"I have a job waiting for me there."

"But you'll be back soon, won't you?" Ally glanced to her side and leaned forward. "Because between you and me, there's a certain guy who seems to be a hell of a lot happier when you're around." She lifted her eyebrows. "Jackson was all smiles when he came in to grab a coffee this morning. I hardly recognized him. And according to Ember, Lucas said the same thing. You're good for him, honey."

Lydia felt warmth rush through her. "It's a casual thing," she lied.

"I wish you could stay longer."

Lydia tried to ignore the way her chest tightened at Ally's words. There was a part of her that wished exactly the same thing.

The same part that wished Jackson would want this thing between them to be more than a short fling.

Autumn's phone buzzed, and she pulled it from her pocket. "That's Dad," she said, her eyes catching Lydia's. "He's parking now."

"I guess that's my cue to leave," Lydia said, giving her sister a rueful smile. "Wish me luck."

"Good luck," Autumn said emphatically. "And thank you, I owe you one."

"Did I tell you how proud I am of you?" Ryan asked, as he and Jackson headed up the pier. They were both wearing suits. Jackson's was grey, and tailored perfectly to his body. His dad's, on the other hand, was more flamboyant, with pleated, baggy pants and a matching jacket in a pale cream wool, that wouldn't have looked out of place in an old episode of *Miami Vice*.

"Yeah, you tell me all the time," Jackson said, smiling at his old man. He'd picked him up after leaving Eddie with Lisa, and the two of them had headed straight here.

"Well I'm telling you again. You're doing a good thing here, being godfather to Skyler. Griff and Autumn must think a lot of you."

Jackson's thoughts drifted to his conversation with Griff this morning. He felt easier with his friend than he had in days, thanks to their clearing the air. "Yeah, well I feel pretty blessed to be asked."

Ryan eyed him carefully. "Have I told you how proud I am of you?"

This time Jackson laughed. "You're a broken record." A good one, though. And it did make him feel better to hear his dad say that.

The pier was a hive of activity. Early guests were arriving and sitting in the chairs Autumn had set up, chattering among themselves as the ocean gently lapped at the struts beneath them. Ryan spotted Frank Megassey and Lorne Daniels and headed over to sit with them while Jackson looked around for Lydia.

She was walking along the other side of the pier with a man in a sharply tailored suit, his hair brushed back from his face and greying at the temples. Her eyes were uncharacteristically cast down. They looked almost sad. And it was crazy, but it made him want to walk over and make her smile.

He knew he could do it.

"Hey." Lucas slapped him on the back. "All ready for the big day?"

"It's not *my* big day," Jackson pointed out. "But yeah, I'm ready for it."

"I'm glad you two are here," Griff said, joining them. "I need to move a couple of stereo speakers after the ceremony. Autumn wants them closer to the food, so we can play music through them. You guys up for it?"

"Sure," Jackson agreed. "Is that Lydia's dad?" he asked, looking over at the man leaning in to whisper something in Lydia's ear.

Griff grimaced. "Yep, that's him."

Jackson watched as her dad dusted something from Lydia's shoulder and shook his head.

"You don't sound that excited to have him here," Jackson

murmured. He didn't like the way Lydia had her lips pressed together. She looked the opposite of relaxed. The opposite of how she was when they were together, their bodies touching, their legs entwined.

He thought back to their conversation last night, and a spark of anger lit inside him. How the hell could he not see that Lydia was amazing?

Griff lifted an eyebrow. "Let's just say I wasn't his favorite at first."

"I should go say hi," Jackson said, his gaze still stuck on her. If she was upset, he wanted to be there. To comfort her. Not standing here like a gawking spectator.

"Yeah, sure." Griff nodded. "He's mellowed a little since I first met him, but I have to warn you, talking to him is still kind of like listening to nails scrape against chalkboard. Except more painful."

Jackson laughed and walked over to where Lydia and her father were talking. When she looked up, her eyes widened when she realized he was making a beeline for them. Her dad was too busy talking to even notice her change in demeanor.

"Hey," Jackson said softly. He stopped a couple of feet away from her. "Everything okay?"

"Have we been introduced?" Lydia's dad tipped his head to the side. Jackson felt a rush of irritation wash through him. This man was annoying Lydia, and by extension, annoying him.

"Jackson Lewis." He extended his hand. Lydia's dad reluctantly took it, giving him the briefest of shakes.

"Richard Paxton."

"Jackson runs his own cyber security business here in Angel Sands," Lydia told her dad.

A flicker of interest appeared in Richard's eyes. "You do? What's it called?"

"Lewis Security Systems," Lydia replied, shooting Jackson a half smile. "It's very successful."

"I don't imagine you have a lot of customers here. You should think about moving to New York. The possibilities are endless there," Richard said. He glanced at Lydia. "Now if you'll excuse us, I need to finish my conversation with my daughter."

"This conversation is over," Lydia told him. "You asked, I said it isn't possible."

"No, you said you had better things to do." Richard's voice was full of disdain. "But I need you at the board meeting. Your vote is important. It could swing it."

Lydia sighed. "I can't. I already told you, I'll be in Spain. I made a commitment, Dad, and I need to keep it."

"A commitment to fun?" Richard gave a nasty laugh. "As if traveling is more important than *my* business." He lowered his voice. "Which, incidentally, is very profitable to you. Who do you think funds all these flights you take?"

Lydia's shoulders dropped, and it pissed Jackson off. "Dad, *I* pay for those," she told him. "I save the money I get from dividends. I don't use any of it for traveling. All my trips are funded by my work. None of that comes out of my savings or the trust fund mom left me. It hasn't in a long time."

"Work?" Richard rolled his eyes. "Is that what you call it?"

"I do a job and get paid. Just like you and Autumn."

"Hardly."

Jackson stepped forward so he was between Lydia and her dad. "Wait a minute," he said, his eyes catching Richard's. "Lydia's extremely good at what she does. And highly sought after, too. Did you know she has a waiting list of people who want to hire her? Or that she charges more per hour than any business consultant I know?" The muscle in his jaw twitched. "If she says she needs to be somewhere, then she needs to be somewhere. Her job is just as important as yours is."

A dazed look washed over Richard's face. "What's this got to do with you?" he asked. His voice was softer now, less sure.

Jackson looked over his shoulder at Lydia. She looked as shocked as Richard at Jackson's sudden outburst.

He brought his gaze back to Richard. "I'm her friend. But more than that, I'm her biggest damn supporter. She's amazing, don't you see that? She's created a business from nothing, doing something she loves. She gets paid to travel the world, for god's sake. Who wouldn't be impressed by that?"

Behind his back, he felt Lydia curl her fingers around his. He flexed them to let her know he was there.

"Yes, well." Richard shook his head. "I should go and take a seat. I'm sure the ceremony will be starting soon."

Jackson kept hold of Lydia's hand, rubbing his thumb across her knuckles. "Okay then," he said, his voice low. "I guess we'll see you later."

Richard raised an eyebrow at Jackson's use of *we* but said nothing. Giving Lydia a nod, he turned on his heel and walked along the pier to where people were beginning to sit down.

Jackson followed him with narrowed eyes and turned back to look at Lydia. "You okay?" he asked her.

She nodded, her teeth digging into her plump bottom lip. "Yeah," she breathed. "Or I will be once I get over the shock of somebody standing up to my dad."

Jackson's brows furrowed. "Maybe more people should stand up to him. And I didn't say anything that wasn't true."

She tugged him toward her, inclining her head to look at him, as their bodies pressed together. "That was pretty damn hot," she told him, tracing his lips with her forefinger. "Remind me to show you how hot when we get back to your place."

He swallowed hard. "How long will that be, exactly?"

For the first time since he'd seen her talking to her dad,

Lydia smiled. "How long can a naming ceremony last?" she said softly. "If we make our speeches really quick, then stuff some food down our necks for sustenance, I figure we can be back at your place in a couple of hours."

He dropped his brow against hers. "I have to pick up Eddie, though at least my dad's catching a ride home with Frank."

"Two and a half," she said, smiling widely.

"Don't you want to spend time with Autumn and Griff?" he whispered, brushing her lips with his. "And Skyler, too."

"Three?" she asked, as though she was bargaining.

"Three." He nodded and kissed her hard, curling his hand around her neck.

She kissed him back, her soft body pressed against his. "It's a deal."

❦ 19 ❦

Jackson cleared his throat and unfolded his reading glasses, sliding them onto the bridge of his nose. Taking a folded piece of paper from his pocket, he slowly opened it up, and put it on the podium in front of him. Lydia watched as he looked out at the throng of people, a shy smile on his face.

Damn, he was hot. Every time she looked at him she felt her heart thumping against her ribcage. It wasn't just that he was good looking – though of course he was. All close cropped hair and strong nose, with a jaw she'd be dreaming about for months to come. It was what lay underneath those looks that made her breath catch in her throat every time their eyes met.

Getting to know Jackson Lewis was like finding an untouched viewpoint on the top of a mountain. She got to see something nobody else could. The gentleness and softness that lay beneath his jokey exterior. And the kindness, damn, that was hot, too.

Griff placed Skyler into Jackson's arms, and he cradled her

against his dark grey jacket, not caring that she was blowing spit bubbles as she stared up at him.

"Skyler," Jackson said, his lips curling as he looked down at her wide blue eyes. "It's an honor to be your godparent. From the moment you came into the world, you've lit it up. For your mom and dad." He raised an eyebrow at Griff and Autumn. "For your family." He winked at Lydia. "And for all your friends who are so happy you're part of their lives. As your godfather, I promise to take care of you. To be there when you need somebody to talk to." He lowered his voice. "Especially when you're a teenager and your dad's being a big pain in the ass."

Autumn laughed loudly at that one.

"Don't swear in front of my daughter," Griff grumbled.

"Sorry." Jackson smirked. "I meant big pain in the patootie."

"Not much better."

Ignoring him, Jackson looked down at Skyler's interested face again. "I don't profess to know what it takes to be a parent," he told her. "But I know that every child needs a safe haven. An escape. Somebody who can be their brick wall when everything else is tumbling down. And I'll be that for you, Skyler. Wherever you are, and whatever you're doing, if you call I'll be there." He pressed his lips to her brow, and it felt like every woman in the place sighed audibly.

Autumn's eyes were shining as she took her daughter back from him. Griff wiped his own eyes with the back of his hand, and clapped Jackson on the back.

Jackson walked back to where Lydia was standing, and slid his hand into hers.

"That was beautiful," Lydia whispered. Her heart felt congested. Like it was too big for her chest.

"Thanks." Jackson looked shy again. For some reason she

really liked that side of him. It made her want to pull his glasses off and kiss him like crazy.

"Now we have a speech from Lydia Paxton, Skyler's godmother," the emcee announced. Lydia raised an eyebrow. "Wish me luck," she murmured. There was no way she could top Jackson's sweet words. He had an unfair advantage of looking so damn attractive with a baby in his arms. Still, she walked over and held her hands out, smiling as Autumn slid Skyler into them.

"Hey sweetie," Lydia said, pressing a kiss to Skyler's nose. It made her giggle loudly, and the audience laughed, too.

From the corner of her eye, she could see Jackson staring right at her. What was he thinking? She wasn't sure, but she thought she could see the same heat in his gaze as she felt in the pit of her stomach.

She took a deep breath and faced the people. "I haven't prepared a speech," she told them, smiling when she saw Autumn laugh. "Those of you who've met me before know that I tend to do things a little differently. I like spontaneity and flying through life by the seat of my pants. And if I can teach Skyler anything, it's that life isn't about surviving or enduring, or all those other things that we sometimes think it is." She smiled down at her niece, warmth washing through her as Skyler smiled back. "Skyler Lambert, life is for the living. I want you to eat it up like it's your favorite piece of cake. And by the way, I know you haven't tried cake yet, but when you do, it's the best thing ever. And I don't want you to ever think you shouldn't eat the cake. Because you always should. Cake tastes so much better than being skinny feels."

All the women in the audience laughed.

"As your godmother, it's my job to show you the world. To show you how to live, how to love, how to look at the sun setting over the bay of Naples and realize that whatever you do, it's going to rise back up again. There's no problem so insurmountable that it can't be solved. And if it can't be solved, then there's cake. That solves everything."

She took a deep breath, tracing Skyler's brow with her finger. "You have the best mom and dad in the world, so you don't need me to show you how to grow up and be a fantastic adult. But I can show you how to have fun, how to experience life, and how to see the world with fresh eyes."

"And how to make cake," somebody shouted out.

Lydia looked up. "Hey, I don't make the cake, I just eat it." She wrinkled her nose at Skyler, making her giggle again. "Being your godmother is the biggest privilege I've ever been given. And I promise not to mess it up." She looked over at Autumn and Griff. "Is that okay?"

Autumn nodded, her lips smashed together. "It's beautiful," she managed to choke out. Lydia passed Skyler back to her, and Autumn pressed a kiss to her cheek. Griff hugged Lydia tightly. "Thank you," he whispered. "That was wonderful."

"Thank you to Lydia and Jackson," the emcee called out. "And now we invite all of you to come up and formally introduce yourself to Skyler."

"Until she starts crying," Griff warned. "And then you'd better back off."

A wave of emotion passed over Lydia as she watched Griff and Autumn's friends surround them with love. Her sister was truly happy, you could tell that from her shining face.

She had her home, her beloved fiancé, and the family she hadn't dared to dream about.

"You did good," Jackson whispered, sliding his hand around Lydia's waist and kissing the top of her head. She leaned into him, not caring what anybody else thought. If they only had one week left together, she was determined to make every moment count.

Somebody cleared their throat. Her dad raised his

eyebrows and forced out a smile. "That was a very good speech," he told her. "From both of you."

Jackson squeezed her waist. She liked the way he kept hold of her in front of her dad. As though he had no fear at all.

"Thank you," Lydia said softly. "I appreciate that."

"I have to head to the airport," he told them. "My flight to Hawaii leaves in two hours."

Lydia nodded. "It was good to see you."

"You, too. Will you be coming back to New York soon?"

"I don't think so." She squinted her eyes, trying to remember her itinerary. "Not before summer at least."

"Well, maybe you can let me know. It would be good to see you." He caught her eye. "And, um, I hope your job goes well."

Lydia blinked back her surprise. "Thank you."

He turned to Jackson, their gazes meeting. "Jackson," he said, giving him a nod.

"Sir." Jackson nodded back, his voice strong.

"It was good to meet you." Her dad held out his hand, and Jackson shook it. "What you said about Lydia, you were right. I'm very proud of her."

"Maybe you should tell her that," Jackson suggested. Lydia's heart clenched at his protective tone.

Richard inhaled sharply, then looked at her again. "Sweetheart, you're doing a wonderful job."

Her throat felt scratchy. "Thank you, Daddy. I hope your vote goes well."

He waved his hand. "It doesn't matter. I'll get a majority somehow."

She didn't doubt it. What Richard Paxton wanted, he always got. Well, *almost* always. Pulling out of Jackson's hold, she leaned forward to hug her father. "Have a safe journey," she whispered against his chest.

Richard patted her hair. "You, too, sweetheart."

As he walked away, she lifted her eyes to Jackson. He was smiling softly at her, his eyes holding promises only she could understand.

"You okay?" he murmured.

"Yeah. I am now." Life was for the living, wasn't that the essence of her promise to Skyler? And now she was ready to eat Jackson up like her favorite piece of cake.

"Tell me about your trip to Spain," Jackson asked as they walked along the ocean's edge at twilight. Eddie was running in and out of the water, yelping with happiness every time Jackson threw a ball for him.

The naming day had been perfect. They'd stayed until people started to say their goodbyes, then helped Autumn and Griff clear up the pier. On their way home, Jackson had picked Eddie up from Lisa's house, promising her a day off very soon to repay her for dog-sitting.

Of course, Lisa had shooed him away. "I like Eddie. You can just buy me lunch some time."

And then he and Lydia had spent the next two hours in bed, touching every inch of each other like they were trying to commit it to memory. And it had felt so damn good to have her in his arms. Even knowing that this thing between them couldn't last.

Lydia looked up at him, the setting sun casting a pink and orange glow on her skin. "Well, I'm flying into Barcelona and meeting with a family who're traveling their way through Europe. I've told them to do the usual stuff before I get there. The Sagrada Familia, Las Ramblas, and maybe Monserrat."

"Sagrada Familia?"

"It's probably the most amazing basilica in Spain. Gaudi designed it a hundred and forty years ago, and it still isn't finished." She laughed. "They do things at a much slower pace in Europe."

"I guess time seems different there," Jackson mused. "They have so much history, they don't need to rush."

"The Spanish are so laid back," Lydia agreed. "It's one of the reasons I love the country so much. When they say *mañana* it means that whatever you've asked for might happen tomorrow or not until next week or next year. But it doesn't matter, because there's so much to enjoy in the meantime."

"Where will you take the family?"

Lydia took the ball from Eddie's panting mouth, throwing it for him again. "They're a couple with teenage kids. When I met them to plan their itinerary, they seemed kind of frazzled, you know? So I'm going to take them into the hills. I have some friends who run a beautiful vineyard, and the parents will do wine tasting and get a lesson in making authentic paella. That evening they'll go to a local flamenco show. The next morning, if they're a little rested, we'll head back into Barcelona itself and I'll take them to all the little places the tourists don't know about."

"What about the kids?" Jackson asked. "Will they do the same thing?"

"Not on the first day." Lydia smiled. "The family we're staying with have two college age sons, and I'm employing them to show the kids around so they can get an authentic teenage experience of the area. There's a lot of sports and ziplines and stuff around there. And hopefully, they'll be ready to spend some quality time with their parents in Barcelona for the next few days."

They were strolling slowly, shoes in hand as their feet padded through the breaking waves.

"You're going to be busy," he said softly. There was a

strange twisting in his chest at the thought of her working around Europe. "I hope you get some down time, too."

"I'll have Paris," she said brightly. "And after I spend some of June in Brazil, I should have a week or two free. I'm not sure where I'll go though."

It was on the tip of his tongue to ask her to come back here, to spend time with him, but he chased the thought away. He didn't want to be another man who thought her job was disposable. She'd heard enough of that from her father.

If she had the choice between time in South America or a week in Angel Sands, it was no contest.

Eddie splashed through the water toward them, and dropped something in the sand. Whatever it was, it stank to high heaven. Jackson leaned down, and realized it was half of a damn jellyfish.

Eddie started to prod at it with his paw.

"No," Jackson told him. "Leave it. Where's your ball?"

Eddie gave a little whine and looked at the jellyfish, then hopefully up at Jackson.

"Get your ball," Jackson repeated firmly. Realizing he was fighting a losing battle, Eddie turned and headed back into the water.

"Will you keep him, if nobody claims him?" Lydia asked, watching Eddie splash through the ocean.

Eddie found the ball bobbing in the shallows. Jackson could swear he saw the dog smile before he scooped it up in his jaws.

"Yeah, I guess I will. I'm getting used to having him around. And he's not too much of a hassle. He sleeps in the office as well as he sleeps at home."

"And you have your dad and Lisa to help," Lydia added.

Jackson nodded. "Brooke mentioned that she knows a good dog sitter, too. If I need one." If, for example, he ever got the urge to fly to Spain or Brazil between working twelve hours a day, six days a week.

"I'm glad you're keeping him," Lydia told him, sliding her hand into his. "I hate to think of him all alone in one of those shelters, looking up hopefully whenever somebody walks in, and letting out a whimper when he realizes it's not you."

"I'm glad, too." Jackson's voice was thick. He couldn't stand the thought of a shelter any more than Lydia could. He hadn't lied, he was getting used to having Eddie around. And if Lydia was leaving – which, let's face it, she was – having Eddie around would make him feel a little less lonely.

And give him a connection to her, even if she was far away.

A breeze danced in from the ocean, lifting Lydia's hair as it tangled around her face. He tenderly brushed it away, leaning in until his lips covered hers. She wrapped her arms around his waist, pulling him closer until her soft body molded to his lean contours, deepening the kiss and making them both breathless.

Without taking his eyes from hers, Jackson lifted his hand and called for Eddie. "Walk's over, boy," he said, as Eddie ran toward them. "It's time for bed."

Lydia awoke to the sound of somebody coughing. Blinking the sleep from her eyes, she looked at Jackson, whose eyes were tightly closed, his arm slung over his head.

The noise cut through the silence again. Three wheezing coughs coming from somewhere downstairs. Immediately alert, she sat up, looking around Jackson's bedroom in the moonlight to try to find something to protect them both.

There had to be an intruder down there. It didn't sound like a noise Jackson's dad would make, and she knew for a fact he was the only person other than Jackson to have a key. Her heart rate switched to overdrive as she swung her legs out of the bed and stood.

Jackson mumbled something and turned on his side, cranking open half an eyelid. "Whassup?"

There were four hacking coughs this time. "Did you hear that?" Lydia whispered.

"What?" He frowned.

"Somebody's broken into the house. I can hear them downstairs.

"It's probably Eddie." Jackson's eye shut again.

"It sounds like a person," Lydia told him. "Not a dog."

This time when the coughs came, Jackson sat straight up. "There's somebody here," he said, scooting out of bed onto his knees. When he stood, he was holding a baseball bat he must have retrieved from beneath the divan. "Stay here," he told Lydia. "Be ready to call the police."

"I'm not staying. I'm coming with you," she told him, following him out of his bedroom and down the stairs. She was wearing one of his t-shirts with *I translate coffee into code* printed across her chest in black writing.

Jackson was in his shorts, and she really tried not to notice the way his back muscles knotted and tightened as he lifted the bat up and kicked the kitchen door open.

Almost immediately, he dropped it and ran into the room. "Jesus, Eddie," he said, scooting down next to the dog. "You stink, boy."

Instead of wagging his tail the way he always did when he saw Jackson or Lydia, Eddie whimpered and started hacking again. A mass of brown sludge escaped from his mouth and onto the tiled floor, joining five piles he'd already made.

Along with piles of something else that Lydia didn't even want to acknowledge, because she knew *those* hadn't come from his mouth.

When he'd finished vomiting, Eddie collapsed to the floor, his body shaking. "What should we do?" Lydia asked urgently, tiptoeing through the minefield of excrement until she reached Jackson's side. He was cradling Eddie's head and telling him softly it was going to be okay.

"Call the emergency vet," Jackson said. "We need to take him in."

❦ 20 ❦

"We're giving Eddie fluids through an IV drip," Max Jenkins, the on-call vet, said, walking out into the waiting room. Jackson and Lydia were the only people there. "The vomiting has stopped for now, but his airways are swollen, so we've given him some anti-histamine. Do you know if he's eaten anything unusual in the past twenty-four hours?"

"No." Jackson shook his head. "He's had his usual food. He was watched by a friend this afternoon, but she would have told me if she'd given him anything."

"Maybe best to check anyway," Max suggested, his grey eyebrows knitting together. "What about last night? Did you take him anywhere he doesn't usually go?"

"We took him to the beach the way we always do." Lydia curled her fingers around Jackson's hand. She wasn't sure who was more shook up over Eddie's horrible sickness. While they'd waited for the vet to examine him, Jackson had sat staring at the floor, his elbows on his hard thighs, his hands raked in his hair. "He was in the water and played catch a lot. He seemed happy, you know?"

196

"Maybe there was something in the water," Max mused. He'd taken his cap and gloves off, but was still wearing the plastic gown he'd put on as soon as Eddie had arrived. "Though I'd have expected to see more animals come in if there was. Half of Angel Sands walk their dogs on that beach."

Lydia looked up, her eyes widening. "What about the jellyfish?" she asked Jackson, before turning to Max. "Eddie brought half a jellyfish to us. We made him drop it, but I didn't think about the other half. Could that have caused a reaction?"

"Damn," Jackson swore softly. "I hadn't thought about that. Jellyfish can be poisonous, can't they?"

"They can certainly cause extreme reactions if they're eaten," Max agreed. "Depending on what type. I don't suppose you got a good look at it?"

"Not really. I was too busy making Eddie drop it." Jackson looked like he wanted to kick himself. "Will he be okay?"

Lydia held her breath until the vet nodded. "If it's just half a jellyfish, he should be fine. I'd like to keep him in for a few hours to make sure the anti-histamine is working, and I'll call you when you can take him home." He checked his watch. "It's still early. You should go home and get some sleep. You'll need to watch Eddie carefully for the next day or so until he's back on his feet."

"We can stay," Lydia offered. "In case he needs us."

"We'll take good care of him," the vet reassured her. "There's no point in sitting around here. I've been told many times that the chairs here are uncomfortable." He gave them a rueful smile. "And when you come back in, our receptionist will be here. She can take all your insurance details in the morning."

"I don't have insurance," Jackson told him. "I'll pay by card. Whatever it costs to make him well."

Lydia squeezed his hand harder.

"You really should think about pet insurance," the vet told him. "Dogs like Eddie love to eat things they shouldn't. This time he should be okay, but if he'd needed surgery it could be very costly."

"He's not my dog. I'm just taking care of him," Jackson informed him.

"We found him by the side of the road. Brooke looked over him and promised to keep an eye out for his owners, but they haven't been found yet," Lydia added.

"That's a shame." Max frowned. "I'll ask Brooke to do some more digging. You shouldn't have to pay for his care when you don't own him."

"I'm happy to pay," Jackson insisted. "Eddie got sick on my watch."

"We'll see. In the meantime, I'm going to head back and check on Eddie, and see if there's anything else he needs to get the jellyfish out of his system."

Jackson shook his hand. "Thank you for seeing us so quickly."

Max gave a half smile. "You won't thank me so much when you get your bill. But you're welcome, anyway. We'll call you some time after nine and give you an update. And hopefully you can take him home soon after that."

"You're shaking," Lydia murmured, as Jackson steered his car into the driveway. His hands were tightly gripping the wheel, yet she could still see them trembling.

"Yeah." Jackson let out a sigh. "I really thought it was bad. That we might lose him."

"I was scared, too," Lydia whispered. "I've never seen a dog throw up that much before."

"Hopefully we'll never see it again." Turning off the ignition, Jackson faced her. "You doing okay?"

She nodded.

"I'm glad you were here with me," he told her, taking her hand between his. "I wouldn't have wanted to go through that alone."

"If it wasn't for me you wouldn't be going through it at all," Lydia reminded him. He turned her hand over and traced circles in her palms. It made her shiver in the best kind of way. "I'm the one who found Eddie."

Jackson lifted his gaze. "And I'm glad you did. I don't like to think about what could have happened if we hadn't found him. He could have run into the road and gotten hit by a car. Or starved." He cleared his throat. "Or worse."

He lifted Lydia's hand to his mouth and kissed her wrist. She squirmed in her seat. "Maybe you were always meant to find him. You need each other."

His lips curled against her skin. "Yeah, I think we probably do. Now let's go inside. I need to show you how much I need *you* right now."

Oh! She'd been wondering if it was wrong to feel this sudden need for him when Eddie was still at the vet. But from the way he was kissing her neck, he felt exactly the same. She'd once read that scary circumstances could increase desire. As though people needed the distraction from reality, and the reminder they were still alive.

"Oh yeah?" she said, the corner of her lip curling. "How are you going to show me that?"

Tugging at her hand, he pulled her until she was leaning across the console. There was a neediness in his gaze that sent desire through her body.

"First I'm going to kiss you," he murmured, brushing his lips against hers. "And then I'm going to strip every item of clothing off you, throw you on the bed, and give you exactly what you need."

"More sleep?" she said, arching an eyebrow.

He grinned. "Yeah, more sleep. Just as soon as I've made you scream my name."

———

Somebody needed to stop that screeching noise. Jackson blinked open one eyelid and reached out for his phone, his hand patting the bedside table in a futile attempt to find it.

Then he remembered about Eddie, and sat up ramrod straight. Was it the vet calling? He finally located his phone in his jeans pocket, where he'd hastily shoved it before they'd headed to the emergency vet. Pulling it out, he frowned when he saw the dark screen.

Another screech. It was coming from Lydia's side of the bed. Shaking his head wryly at himself, because it wasn't Lydia's side, both of them were his, he reached across her still sleeping body to shut the noise off.

He could feel the heat of her skin against him as he leaned across. "What's that?" she asked, her eyes still closed.

"It's okay. Keep sleeping, it's your phone buzzing."

Grabbing it, he tried to turn it off, but instead the screen lit up.

'*Your flight is ready for check in*' the banner on the screen announced. He stared at it for a moment, then turned down the volume and replaced her phone on the table next to the bed.

Flopping back on the mattress, he could feel a frown pull at his lips. It was stupid, because he knew she was leaving soon. He'd known it from the start. And yet seeing those words had put him in the worst kind of mood.

The kind that left a bad taste in his mouth.

Grabbing his own phone, he checked on the time. It was seven a.m. Usually, he'd have been up for at least an hour. Even on the weekends he rarely slept in late. Not because he liked getting up, but because there was always something to do. But right now all he wanted to do was look at Lydia as she half-slept, her blonde hair spread across the pillow in a crazy mess, her cheek red from where she'd been sleeping on it. And her lips pink and so damn kissable, something he knew from a lot of experience.

Less than a week, and he wouldn't wake up next to her again.

The thought of it made his stomach feel tight. It was crazy, because they'd only been sleeping with each other for a few days, but it felt like so much longer. Since she'd arrived, he'd fostered a dog, become a godparent, and had the best damn sex he could ever remember, and all of those things had changed him.

But it was Lydia who had changed him the most. Every time he looked at her he felt contradictory emotions. He wanted to bundle her up and protect her, to make sure her sunny nature wasn't taken advantage of, but like a bird he wanted her to fly free.

He couldn't imagine her being anything but that wild, intrepid explorer who flew from country to country the same way other people commuted to work. And he couldn't ask her to change. Not for him.

In another world, maybe he'd go with her. Give up his job and his house and follow the sun the same way she did. But in his heart, he knew he couldn't do it. He had a business to run. Staff to take care of. And his dad needed him, too.

Not to mention Eddie.

The fact was, Lydia traveled alone and made friends as she went. He was just another friend. Yeah, one with benefits they both enjoyed, but in a few weeks she'd probably have moved on.

He gritted his teeth at the thought of her with somebody else. The thought of it made him want to curl up his fists and hit something.

There was another buzz, this time from his phone. He didn't recognize the number that flashed across the screen, but he opened the message.

Hi, it's Brooke. I just got into work and found out that Eddie has been sick. In case you're worried, I checked on him and he's sleeping happily. I think he's dreaming of food, because he keeps chewing the air! Give the office a call when you're awake and we'll arrange for you to pick him up!

It was stupid how happy that message made him. He pushed down the dark thoughts that had been swirling around in his brain. He'd wake Lydia up and they'd go pick Eddie up, then spend the day spoiling him so he knew that they cared. And he'd persuade her to spend the night again, so he could wake up and see her beautiful face lying next to his.

That was enough. It had to be, because he wasn't getting any more than that.

"We have two pieces of good news," Brooke told them as she led Jackson and Lydia into the kennels. Eddie was laying on a blanket in a pen. As soon as he saw Jackson, he scrambled to his feet, his tail wagging wildly as he pressed his wet nose to the Plexiglas door. "First of all, Eddie's managed to eat something and keep it down. Just boiled rice, but it's a great sign. We'd advise you to keep his diet bland for the rest of today and tomorrow, but after that you can start trying kibble again."

"He'll be better that quickly? I thought food poisoning could take weeks to get over," Jackson said. There was a smile on his face that Lydia found infectious. She loved the way his face lit up as Brooke opened the door.

"Dogs tend to recover a lot faster than humans." Brooke hooked Eddie's leash on, and passed it to Jackson. "They're like children. They want to be running around and having fun, so they tend to recuperate fast."

"What's the second piece of good news?" Lydia asked, as Jackson scooted to his haunches and ruffled Eddie's fur. Eddie put his front paws on Jackson's shoulders, and licked him all over his face. Jackson laughed, and tickled beneath his chin.

"We think we might have found his owner."

Jackson looked up, his hands stilling. "You have?"

"Yeah. Doctor Grant has a friend who works in a veterinary office on Golden Ridge. We sent them a photo of Eddie, and they think they know the owners. They're going to make a phone call today." Brooke lifted her eyebrows. "So you may be free before you know it."

Lydia sneaked another glance at Jackson. He was stroking Eddie again, but his expression was distracted. "How will we know if they're the real owners?" he asked. "And not some people who want a free dog."

Brooke laughed. "No dog is free. After you pay our bill you'll know that. But the vet up in Golden Ridge should have details that match Eddie's. And of course, Eddie'll recognize his owners if he sees them."

Jackson nodded, his expression impassive. "Okay. Keep us updated once you speak to them, please."

"We will." She patted Eddie's head. "You're good to go. If you stop at the front desk you can pick up Eddie's medicines."

When they'd signed Eddie out of the veterinary office, Jackson glanced at Lydia. "It looks like I'm going to be stuck in the house for the day with him. You should go spend some time with Autumn. I feel like I've taken up all your time while you've been here."

Lydia pulled her bottom lip between her teeth. "I can come keep you company."

He gave her a smile that didn't quite reach his eyes. "I have a lot of work to catch up with anyway. I'll get Eddie's bed out and work on the deck. There is one thing you could do for me though."

"Sure." Lydia nodded. "Just say the word."

"Could you dog sit for me tomorrow? I have to go into the office to meet a potential new employee and I can't give Eddie my full attention while I'm there."

She nodded. "Of course, I'll be happy to."

"That's if his owners don't pick him up in the meantime." Jackson's voice was low. She glanced up at him, but she couldn't read his expression.

"Maybe they're not his owners," she said, trying to find a way to make him feel better.

He set his jaw, and opened the car door, helping Eddie into the backseat. "I hope they are," he told her. "It'll be so much easier if I'm not having to take care of him when I should be working."

Her smile wavered. "But you'll miss him, won't you?"

He shrugged. "It's been fun having him around. But it was never meant to be permanent."

She wanted to remind him of what he said that morning – that he and Eddie needed each other – but the words died in her throat. Maybe it was better this way. If Eddie's owners really had been located, the dog would be going with them, whether Jackson liked it or not.

"Are you sure you don't want me to hang around today?" she asked. "I can be quiet and keep an eye on Eddie."

A ghost of a smile passed his lips. "It's okay. I got this. You go home and have some fun with your sister. I'll see you tomorrow."

So he didn't want her to come over tonight? Lydia swallowed hard, trying to hide the hurt from her face. "Sure. I'll be over by seven. I know you like to leave early for the office." Rolling onto her toes, she pressed her lips to his. He kissed her back, but didn't deepen it.

"Thanks," he murmured, walking around to the driver's seat and climbing inside the car. "Hop in, I'll give you a ride home."

Autumn walked into the living room later that evening, carrying a bottle of red wine and two glasses. "Skyler's asleep and Griff is in the garage working on his surf board," she said to Lydia, who was moping on the black leather sofa. "So I figured we'd open a bottle of cabernet sauvignon and you can tell me why you've been walking around all day with a face like thunder."

"Do I really have a face like thunder?" Lydia asked.

Autumn put the glasses down and filled them both generously. "Kind of. I guess it's more like a hurricane. Which isn't how somebody should be looking after they've spent the night with Angel Sands' hottest bachelor."

"I spent most of the night watching a dog vomit from both ends," Lydia reminded her, as Autumn passed her one of the glasses. "I'm sorry. We're supposed to be spending quality time together and I'm bringing us both down."

"Did Jackson do something wrong?" Autumn asked. "Because the last time I saw the two of you, you couldn't keep your hands off each other. The way he looked at you when you were giving your speech, whew!" She fanned herself. "It made me sweat like a Manhattan summer."

Lydia swallowed a mouthful of wine, and put her glass on the table. "He's a bit hot and cold," she admitted. "One minute he's all over me, the next he's talking about having to work and giving me the distinct impression I'm not wanted."

Autumn shot her a sympathetic glance. "He does work hard. Maybe he was just being honest."

Lydia sighed. "Maybe. But it didn't feel right. He didn't mention me coming over tonight, or whether he'd even call."

"So that's it? You're left hanging?"

"Well, I'm going over to dog sit tomorrow so he can go to the office. I guess I'll see him then." She curled her feet beneath her, laying her head back on the sofa. "It's just that I have so little time. I really want to spend it with him."

Running the pad of her finger around her wine glass, Autumn looked up at her sister. "Maybe he's finding this whole last week thing difficult," she said, giving Lydia a soft smile. "It's easier to be the one leaving sometimes. You have something new to look forward to, things to distract you. But the one who stays, that's tough. There's an emptiness where things were once full."

Lydia shook her head. "No. I'm just a distraction for him. A bit of fun, I guess. He said as much to Griff."

"What exactly did he say?" Autumn leaned forward.

"I wasn't supposed to be listening," Lydia admitted. "But I overheard him tell Griff that he was bad at relationships and this was just a vacation fling."

"Oh, honey." Autumn pressed her lips together in sympathy.

"Please don't feel sorry for me. He's right. I guess I just wanted... I don't know. Something other than this."

"Would you stay if he asked you?" Autumn asked, her brows pulling together.

"I can't," Lydia whispered. "I have my job. And I know how much you love living like this, but I don't know if I can. Traveling is who I am. It's what I do. I don't know anything else."

Griff walked into the living room, took one look at Autumn and Lydia leaning in and speaking softly, and went to walk out.

"Where are you going?" Autumn asked him, as he turned his back.

"I thought you were having girl talk." Griff shrugged. "I'll go sit out on the deck."

"Sit here," Autumn said, patting the empty seat next to her. "You might be able to give us some insight."

"Into what?"

"Into Jackson, of course."

Griff's eyes widened. He held his hands up as though to ward them off. "Hell, no. That kind of talk will only end in tears. Probably mine."

"I'm not asking you to betray any confidences," Autumn said, shaking her head at his mock-horror. "Just give us a male point of view."

He sighed, but sat down. "Okay, hit me with it."

"Why do guys blow so hot and cold? One minute they're all over you, the next they don't want to know you." Autumn glanced at Lydia from the corners of her eyes.

"So we're talking hypothetically and not about Jackson, right?" Griff lifted a brow.

Autumn sniggered. "Yup."

Blowing out a mouthful of air, Griff raked his hands through his thick hair. "Well, let's say this *hypothetical* guy had some heartbreak with women before. He got dicked over by the woman he loved, after he saw his dad go through exactly the same thing when he was a kid. And he's learned that the only way not to feel hurt is to wear some armor over his heart. To protect himself. So every time he gets close, there's this little warning bell that goes off in his head. Telling him there's danger everywhere. He retreats and armors his heart all over again, because he's too afraid to do anything else."

When he'd finished, both Lydia and Autumn were staring at him, their mouths open.

"What?" he asked.

"I've never heard you speak for that long before," Lydia said, biting down a smile.

"Wow," Autumn agreed. "You really know this stuff, don't you?"

His lip quirked up. "Yeah, well it wasn't so long ago that I was living it, too. Remember how I tried to keep things between us casual?" he asked Autumn.

"I remember." Her eyes were soft. "We both thought we were so clever. Pretending we were friends when there was so much more going on. I swear all of Angel Sands knew we were in love before we did."

"It's hard to gauge the strength of the storm when you're in the eye of it," Griff told them. "And since we're still talking hypothetically about this guy who doesn't exist, he's tried everything. He's been a player, he's sworn off relationships, and then this woman comes along who knocks his socks off. In another world, she'd be perfect for him. But she's leaving and he knows it, and the only way he can deal with it is to brazen it out."

Autumn wiped a tear from the corner of her eye. "This is so sad. They're like star crossed lovers."

Griff caught Lydia's gaze. "Go easy on him," he urged gently. "I know I was against you two being together, but that's when I thought he wasn't invested. When I spoke to him the other day, I could see how he felt. He looked exactly like I did when I fell for Autumn. Shell shocked and so damn happy."

"Are we still talking hypothetically?" Lydia asked.

Griff shrugged. "Whatever floats your boat."

She wasn't sure what floated it. Her mind was a whirlwind of thoughts. Did he really care? And did it matter? One thing was for sure – very soon, she'd be stepping on a plane and leaving them all behind.

And maybe she'd be leaving her heart behind, too.

Skyler let out a loud wail from the nursery, and Griff immediately stood. "Saved by the scream." He glanced at Autumn. "I'll settle her down and head back to the garage. Let you two finish your wine."

"You sure you don't want some?" Lydia asked. "I can grab another glass."

"Nah. You two look like you need some sister time." He kissed Autumn's cheek as Skyler wailed again. "I'll see you both in a while."

Jackson reached down to stroke Eddie, who growled softly and wagged his tail. "You okay, boy?"

Eddie lifted open an eyelid. "It's okay," Jackson told him. "You can go back to sleep." Brooke had been right, Eddie's recovery was fast. He wasn't himself yet, but he'd eaten more boiled rice for dinner, and had walked for ten minutes on his leash that evening. He was like a different dog to the one who'd woken them up this morning deep in the throes of food poisoning.

Taking off his glasses, Jackson ran his hand through his hair and sighed. Eddie might be feeling better, but he was still feeling bad. He had been ever since Brooke told him that Eddie's owners might have been found.

This afternoon she'd called again to tell him that they'd be home in two days, and asked permission to give them his address. Of course he'd permitted it. He wasn't an asshole.

Okay, so he *was* an asshole, but he wasn't *that* bad.

You were an asshole to Lydia, the little voice in his head reminded him.

Was he? He'd just needed some space to think. And he knew that she'd want to spend time with her sister. He'd monopolized her time for the past few days, after all.

Liar.

He shook his head, trying to ignore the voice. But the words echoed in his mind.

Liar.

Damn it. He stood and poured himself a glass of water, swallowing it down as though it would wash the dark thoughts away. But it didn't. Because they were the truth. He was *lying* – to himself. He didn't tell Lydia to go home because he thought she should spend time with Autumn.

He sent her home because he wanted to wallow. And maybe protect himself from getting hurt.

In his mind, he'd somehow consoled himself that though Lydia was leaving, at least he'd have Eddie. A reminder of her. A connection, even. And when she came home to visit Autumn, she'd want to visit Eddie as well.

The same way your mom visited you and saw your dad. Yeah, great one.

Damn it, this wasn't the same. Lydia wasn't his mom and he wasn't his dad. She was different. Stronger, kinder.

Yeah, so why are you pushing her away?

Leaning on the kitchen counter, he blew out a mouthful of air. Pushing her away was definitely an asshole move. Right out of the player playbook. And he wasn't a player, goddammit.

So show her.

He blinked, tipping his head to the side. He had two choices. He could wallow and be angry and push her away even more. Or he could throw caution to the wind and enjoy the time they had left.

One way led to regrets and misery. The other? He'd probably still be miserable, but at least he'd have better memories.

And no regrets.

He picked up his phone and glanced at the screen. It was later than he'd thought. Nearly midnight. For a moment he considered putting his phone down, but then he unlocked it, bringing up Lydia's contact detail, and pressing the call button.

She was leaving, he had no control over that. But she was here for a few more days.

And he was determined to make the most of them.

———————

Lydia climbed into bed, a nice buzz rushing thought her veins thanks to the bottle of Cabernet she and Autumn had shared. Pulling the covers over her, she wriggled and turned, trying to find a comfortable position, annoyed because she prided herself on sleeping like a baby in the worst of conditions.

Her sister's guest bed in the beautiful town of Angel Sands definitely *wasn't* the worst of conditions.

Sighing, she threw one of her pillows on the floor. A minute later, she picked it back up again, pummeling it to make a cozy dip for her head. Just as she was about to give up the fight and grab a book from the shelves in Autumn's hallway, her phone started to buzz.

She lifted it to her ear. "Jackson? How's Eddie?"

"He's doing good. Slept most of the day curled up at my feet. But he ate some rice this evening, and we sat out in the yard and he ran around a bit. Hopefully within a few days he'll be back to his normal self."

"And how about his owners? Have they been found?"

"Not yet. Apparently, they're away on vacation. Left the dog with a friend who lost him out on a walk. They arrive back in a couple of days and I've arranged to meet them."

"I'm so sorry," she told him. "I know how much you love Eddie."

He cleared his throat. "It's good. He deserves to be with his family. They must love him, too."

"Well, I'm glad he's okay. And that you are. Did you get much work done?"

"Yeah, I did. Managed to solve a couple of snafus my

coders have been having. And I also moved some things around in my schedule. I still have to go into the office tomorrow, but after that I'm taking a few days off." He paused before adding, "I was wondering if you'd like to spend them with me."

"Are you sure you can spare the time? You seemed pretty stressed this morning," Lydia said, letting her head fall back on the pillow.

"I'm sorry about that. I took it out on you and I shouldn't have done that." She could hear his soft breaths echo through the phone line. "I was worried about Eddie, and it all built up in my mind. I didn't mean to make you feel bad." His voice lowered. "Let me make it up to you."

His words sent a shiver down her spine. "How are you going to do that?"

"By making your last few days here the best they can be. I want to take you out, have fun, and show you that Southern California can be just as amazing as all those places you've visited."

It already was in her mind, because *he* lived here. She didn't need to be wowed by the scenery when she had Jackson Lewis to look at. "I don't care what we do," she admitted. "I just want to spend some time with you."

"I want that, too." His voice was firm. "So what do you say?"

She couldn't stop the smile from bursting out on her face. "It's a deal."

❦ 22 ❦

"You're taking *how* many days off?" Lisa asked, as Jackson leaned on the corner of her desk. They'd just finished their meeting with her preferred candidate, and offered him the job. Lisa was writing the email as she spoke. "Did hell freeze over, too? Because that's more likely than Jackson Lewis using some vacation time."

"I own the business," Jackson pointed out. "I don't get vacation time."

She stopped typing and turned to look at him. "Damn right you don't. I swear the last time you took any days off George Bush was still president."

His brows knitted. "Which one?"

"Walker. You were a little kid peeing in your diapers when his dad was president." Lisa ran her finger across her chin. "Though come to think of it, I bet you were an overachiever as a kid. Were you out of diapers before any of your friends?"

"I don't know." Jackson wrinkled his nose. "And can we not talk about diapers? I had a run in with one of Skyler's a few days ago. I'm still working on repressing the memory."

Putting her chin in her hands, Lisa smiled up at him. "So

what are you gonna do with your time off? You should take a real vacation for once."

Jackson shrugged. "I'm staying here in Angel Sands."

Her eyes were wide. "A stay-cation? Oh my. Won't that be a bit boring? You'll be dog-free, won't you? When are the owners picking Eddie up?"

"Tomorrow." Jackson's stomach dropped at the thought. "And I want to stay around here. There's so much to see and do."

"Does this have anything to do with a certain blonde you were spotted kissing on the pier?" Lisa asked.

"You heard about that?"

She laughed. "The whole damn town heard about it." Her warm eyes met his. "She must be something special for you to be taking time away from the business."

Jackson glanced at his watch. "Actually, you'll meet her in a bit. She's bringing Eddie in to say goodbye to the office."

"She is?" Lisa's face lit up. "I wasn't sure I'd get to see him again. I'm gonna miss seeing his face around here."

"He's only been with us for a week."

Lisa sighed. "I know, but he made a big impression. I got used to having him around. His gorgeous face kind of lit up this office."

"Some people have that effect." Jackson thought of Lydia, his sunshine girl with a smile that lit everything up. "But he has a family. He belongs with them. It wouldn't be fair to keep him."

"Well at least we got to have fun with him while he was here." She shot Jackson a sympathetic smile and clicked her mouse. "The contract is sent. He said he'd be available to start next week, so I'll start talking to him about the other candidates then. Before you know it, you'll be able to take more time off. Not like that will actually happen."

Jackson caught her gaze. "I've been listening to you. I

need to stop getting so deep in the weeds that I can't see the sunlight." Jackson shrugged. "We need a bigger team so I can start working on strategy. And maybe work less than an eighty hour week."

Lisa grinned. "Just think of all that free time you'll have. No dog, no eighteen hour work days. What will you do to fill it?"

"Sleep," he told her deadpan. "And the occasional surf."

A month ago that would have sounded perfect. Now it felt lame. And a little empty, too. It was ironic that he'd spent the last few years of his life complaining about having no free time, but now that it was a possibility it made his gut clench hard.

Shaking his head at himself, he walked back to his desk and sat down heavily on his office chair, swinging it around until he was facing the big screens on his desk. He might be facing a future of free time, but right now he still had a load of work to do, and only a few hours to get it finished.

Lydia wrapped Eddie's leash around her wrist and balanced the cardboard tray filled with coffee cups and bagels in her hands, using her butt to push open the office door. She and Eddie had dropped into Déjà Brew to see Ally and Nate so the dog could say goodbye to them, before she picked up her lunchtime order and went to Jackson's office. Eddie had sniffed the bagels with interest – his appetite was definitely returning.

Maybe animals had the right idea. They didn't let little things like food poisoning ruin their week. They got over it and picked themselves up so they could go back to whatever it was that interested them.

She wondered if she'd be able to get over heartache as easily as Eddie got over his stomach pain.

As soon as Jackson saw her walk through the door, he was out of his seat and heading toward her, his expression warm and soft. Such a difference to yesterday and the hard, blank look he'd had on his face when they'd left the vet's office.

"I bought lunch," she told him. "For you and Lisa. And the third one's mine. I'll take it back with me and Eddie."

Jackson didn't reply for a minute. He was too busy looking at her, his eyes filled with tenderness, and something darker that made her shiver.

"You didn't need to buy me lunch," he told her, his gaze holding hers. "I should be buying it for you. To say thank you for looking after the dog."

"I wanted to," she admitted. "Mondays are always such dull days. Everybody should get bagels on Mondays."

"Amen to that," Lisa agreed, giving her a grin. "And thank you. How's Eddie doing?"

Jackson put the tray on the table and dropped to stroke Eddie. The dog stared at him adoringly, his tongue lolling with pleasure as Jackson tickled behind his ears.

"He's got a lot more energy. When we went to the coffee shop he wagged his tail so hard he almost knocked down one of their displays."

"They let dogs in the coffee shop?" Lisa asked.

Lydia laughed. "Only Eddie. He's special."

"Thank you," Jackson said again, his thigh muscles flexing as he stood. "Lisa, can you keep an eye on Eddie for a moment? I want to talk to Lydia in the meeting room really quick."

"It'd be a pleasure." Lisa stood and grabbed Eddie's leash. "In fact, I think I'll go eat my lunch outside. It's such a beautiful day. Eddie can come with me." She pulled at his leash, grabbing her purse and her phone. "Come on, Eddie."

"Don't forget your bagel and coffee," Lydia said, passing them to her. Lisa somehow managed to fit the bagel in her purse, and grabbed the Styrofoam cup with her free hand, making a hasty retreat, and leaving the two of them alone in the office.

The silence danced around them, as he stared at Lydia, drinking her in. Her head was lifted, her skin tight over her throat, and she swallowed hard, as though she could feel the tension in the moment.

"Hey," he said softly, closing the gap between them. "I'm so sorry for being an ass yesterday."

"I didn't know what to do," she admitted. "You just closed off from me. It... hurt."

Her words felt like a knife to his chest. Hurting Lydia was the last thing he wanted to do. She was too good for him to so casually bat away. "I know," he told her. "And I'm sorry. The last thing I wanted to do was hurt you. I just got spooked knowing Eddie's leaving tomorrow. And you'll be going soon after that. I've had the best few days with you two, and I don't want it to end."

"Jackson, I..."

He cupped her face with his warm hands, his breath soft against her skin as he brushed the corner of her mouth with his lips. "You brought me lunch," he murmured again. "That's the nicest thing anybody's done for me."

"It's just a bagel," she murmured, before he pressed his lips against hers and swallowed her words. Her arms wrapped around him, her body pressing against his as he deepened the kiss. For a moment all words and coherent thought disappeared.

"Sorry," he said, when they parted, breathless. "I needed to kiss you."

Her eyes twinkled with amusement. "No need to apologize for that. And I'm glad you're okay. I missed you." It was her turn to initiate the kiss this time, rolling onto the balls of her feet as she inclined her face toward his. Her lips were sweet, soft, and sent a thrill of pleasure right through him. He ran the tip of his tongue along the seam of her mouth, his body aching as she opened up for him, letting him in the way she always did. Sliding his hand down to the small of her back, he hitched her against him, leaving her in no doubt how damn needy she made him with one simple kiss.

"Stay with me tonight," he murmured, tracing circles against her spine.

"Yes," she gasped into his lips.

"And tomorrow night."

Her mouth curled against his. "You want me for two nights in a row?"

"I want you every night until you leave," he said, his voice certain. "I know you want to spend time with Autumn and Skyler, and we'll make that happen. But I need you in my bed. It felt empty without you last night."

"I didn't sleep well without you," she admitted. "I kept reaching out and hitting my hand against the wall instead of your warm ass."

He slid his lips along the delicate skin of her throat. "I promise to make up for lost time tonight."

"Just don't shut me out again," she requested, her voice soft. "Not when we don't have much time left."

"I won't." He kissed her jaw, her cheek, the thin skin on her eyelids. "I'll be an open book. You can ask me anything and I'll answer." And he meant it. Wanted it, even. Wanted to share everything with this woman. Yesterday, alone with a sick dog, he'd felt like he was at rock bottom. He didn't want to feel that way again.

At least not until she left. He pushed that thought away, because it was a grey cloud that threatened to settle over them both.

Sliding his hand beneath the hem of her t-shirt, he curled his fingers around her waist, pressing into her warm flesh.

"God I've missed you." He kissed her again. It wasn't soft this time. Instead, it was full of hunger for her, so deep he wasn't sure he could ever satisfy it. "You smell so good," he murmured, pulling her closer. She arched her body against his, the pressure making him harder than ever. He slid his other hand beneath her top and softly stroked her skin. Her breath shortened against his mouth, her cheeks flushing as he moved his hands upward. When he brushed his thumb over her nipple, she let out a gasp.

He was going to take her in his office. There was no choice. He couldn't wait until tonight. That was for sure. The need for her throbbed through his veins, making his thoughts fuzzy and his movements sure. Sliding his hand down her thigh, he hitched her leg around his hip, grinding against her until her hips were moving with a rhythm of their own.

"What are you doing to me?" he murmured. She didn't answer, she didn't have to. They both knew what they were doing, after all. Kissing at lunchtime in his office, their bodies full of need, the bagels and coffee she'd brought for them both long since forgotten.

With her eyes on his, Lydia pulled out of his hold. For a moment, he felt bereft. She took his hand and looked up at him, her expression full of mischief.

"Why don't you show me your meeting room? I have an agenda I need you to fill."

———

The words were barely out of her mouth before Jackson was pulling her across the office, his hand tight around hers as he kicked open the door to the meeting room, tugging her inside.

The door banged closed as he pushed her until the back of her thighs hit the thick oak table. His hands curled around her waist and he lifted her up until her backside was firmly against the surface.

Something about him had changed. She couldn't quite put her finger on it, but he was different. More certain. The closed off Jackson of yesterday had been replaced by this dark-eyed, masculine sex god, who was setting her whole body on fire with just a brush of his fingertips against her thighs.

She sent a prayer of thanks to the pleasure gods that she'd worn a skirt today. Jackson's hands were firm as he pulled her legs apart. He stepped into the space they'd left, deftly pulling her t-shirt over her head and exposing her skin to the cool air.

She glanced at the door to make sure it was shut. His lip curled as he followed her eye movements. "Are you worried about us being disturbed?"

She shook her head. "Not in that way. I just don't want you to start something you can't finish."

Flashing her a wicked grin, he dropped to his knees and pulled her panties down, pressing his lips against her inner thigh. "Lisa takes an hour for lunch," he told her, kissing his way up to the crease at the top of her legs. "I can probably make you come five times before then."

"Promises...oh!" He slid his finger along the neediest part of her, making her whole body contract with need. Tiny pinpricks of pleasure danced through her abdomen, her thighs, and right down to her feet. He dropped his head until his lips were against her, moving his tongue in a long, languid lick.

Her head dropped back, a sigh escaping her lips as he licked her again, this time circling her nerve center in the most delicious of ways. Her hips gyrated on the table as the pleasure built up inside of her with every lick of his tongue and every suck of his mouth.

"Jackson, I..."

"Hush," he murmured against her, sucking and licking until stars were bursting behind her eyelids. "Relax."

She was trying, she really was. But it was impossible to relax when a Californian god was kneeling between her legs, pushing two teasing fingers inside her. The movement intensified everything, making her toes curl tightly, as she felt the pleasure coil and whip at the bottom of her belly.

He curled his fingers inside her, and everything exploded, her sweet moans filling the air as he coaxed the pleasure from her. Her body contracted around him, and she reached for him, raking her fingers through his hair as he slowly brought her down from the peak.

"Come here," she told him, her voice thick and low. "I need you inside me." Reaching for his belt, she fumbled with the buckle, finally releasing it and unzipping his pants. He was warm and hard, so hard, as her fingers coiled around him, sliding her palm up and down until it was his turn to gasp.

He leaned down to give her a wet, lazy kiss. She could taste herself on him, and was amazed at how warm it made her. "Condom," she murmured.

He stilled in her hand. "Fuck."

Her eyes widened. "No condom?"

"Nope." He shook his head. "I don't have a stash of them in the office."

Her body ached for him. She let out a ragged breath. "I've got an IUD."

His eyes met hers. Dark and needy. "You sure?"

Yeah, she was. So damn sure. "Just get inside me," she told him, running her thumb along him until he gasped again. "I need you."

His jaw twitched as he slid his hands along her thighs, pulling her forward on the table until she could feel his tip press against her. He swallowed hard, as though he felt the significance of the lack of barrier between them. She felt it, too. It was like they were removing the last obstacle between them. Opening themselves up in a way neither of them ever had before.

And as he slid inside, she felt him everywhere. But most of all in her heart, that was beating like crazy, and aching as if she'd just finished a fifteen mile race.

"So good," he muttered. "So warm and tight." He rocked against her, and her body quivered. "I don't know if I can keep going like this for long." Reaching down between them, he circled his finger against her, making her tighten around him as he buried himself deep inside her. She grasped onto the fabric of his shirt as he captured her mouth with his, the rhythm of his movements setting her on fire all over again.

This time the spasms wracked through her whole body, making her jerk against him as she let out a loud shout. He dug his fingers into her hips, pumping against her until she was soft and pliant in his arms, his movements stilling as he let out a low, needy moan.

When he lifted his head, their gazes connecting, she could feel the electricity connecting them, sizzling and sparking as they panted out their breaths. Could he feel it, too? This thing that was making her want things she'd never believed in before.

As he gave her a lazy smile, she found herself hoping he did.

❧ 23 ❧

J ackson leaned in the doorway of his kitchen, watching
Lydia as she sat cross-legged on the tiled floor, Eddie
curled happily on her lap. It was early in the morning,
the dawning sunlight catching the waves as they danced in
the ocean and softly reflected into the kitchen as the sun
lazily made her way above the mountains.

True to her word, Lydia had spent last night at his place,
their bodies entwined in his bed, as he'd made good on his
promise and gave her another three orgasms to make up for
the ones he'd missed earlier.

After that, they'd talked about Eddie. Whether he knew
that he'd be leaving soon. The dog had been back to his usual
self by the evening, though they still hadn't taken him down
to the beach, just in case. Instead they'd played with him in
the yard, throwing balls for him. Jackson had grabbed her for
kisses in between Eddie's catches, the two of them laughing
as Eddie had tried to nudge them apart with his nose.

It had been a good night. Carefree and light, even though
they knew Eddie would be gone in the morning. And now
that morning was here, his breath was catching in his throat

as he watched Lydia gently tickle Eddie's ears the way he liked it, her voice so soft that Jackson had to lean in to hear her words.

"It's going to be okay," she murmured softly in his ear. "You're so loved. There will always be somebody to take care of you. Your family, of course, but if you need him, Jackson will be there. You know where to find him." She buried her face in Eddie's fur. "And he knows where to find me, if you need me."

Jackson's throat tightened, but he said nothing, standing still as he watched them.

"I love you," she told Eddie, her voice muffled by his coat. "So much. We were meant to find you. You know that, right? I remember glimpsing this flash of fur and just knowing that we needed to stop that car." She sighed. "I'm going to miss you, baby."

Jackson listened to her words, his jaw tight. There was an ache in his chest that he couldn't shake off. Not just because Eddie was leaving, though that was hard enough, but because she was saying the words that Jackson wanted her to say to him.

He wanted her to tell him she'd miss him. That she didn't want to leave. That she loved him so much.

Because he'd already fallen for her.

Lydia looked up, a smile curling her lips when she saw him standing there. "Hey," she said, stroking Eddie's ears. "I was just telling him how much we love him."

Jackson walked into the kitchen and dropped down behind her, his legs surrounding hers as he pulled her against his chest. He pressed a kiss to her hair as he cradled her the same way she was cradling Eddie. "Yeah, we do," he agreed.

For a moment, the three of them sat there in silence, holding each other as the sun slowly rose high enough to cast her rays across the yard. They inhaled and exhaled in unison, their three heartbeats pounding sure and strong against their chests.

He wanted to take a picture of this with his mind. Not just a 2-D image of the three of them curled up on his kitchen floor. But a full 4-D experience, with sounds, touches, smells, and most of all the emotions that were coursing through him. A memory that would carry him through the days without this perfect woman who'd changed his life, and the dog who'd made him realize he had more than coding to give the world.

Lydia rested her head against his chest, inclining it until her lips brushed his. "We have two hours before his owners come," she said, stroking Eddie's velvety ears between her fingers. "Let's take him for a walk on the beach. Finish watching the sun rise over the mountains."

"Yeah," Jackson agreed. "I'd like that. And so would Eddie."

And it would be another moment he could add to his library of memories with Lydia.

Maybe that would be enough.

The knock on the door came at ten o'clock that morning. Jackson stood and blew out a mouthful of air, walking to the front door to open it. Eddie was lying next to Lydia on the sofa – and he lifted his head at the sound of movement, a muted growl rumbling from his throat as he looked over at the door.

"Simba!" a high voice cried out. A boy – aged maybe nine or ten – ran in, sliding onto his knees and throwing his arms around Eddie's neck. Eddie's tail started wagging so hard it was whipping Lydia's legs as he licked the boy's face.

"You bad boy. We were worried about you," he said, his voice muffled by Eddie's fur.

"This is John and Alice Maxwell," Jackson said. Lydia looked up to see a couple follow him into the living room. They were well dressed, in expensive jeans and polo shirts, maybe in their early forties. "This is Lydia. She's the one who spotted Eddie... I mean, Simba, in the bushes."

"Thank you so much." Alice walked forward, giving Lydia a smile. "I'm so grateful to you. We left Simba with a friend while we went to New York for a couple of weeks. She didn't even tell us he was lost." She lifted an eyebrow. "Said she didn't want to ruin our break. Not that it would have mattered. We would've come home right away if we'd known."

"We won't be leaving Simba with her again," the man – John – added grimly. "And of course we'll pay you for the cost of having him." He pulled a wad of bills from his wallet, and started sorting through them. "Damn dogs aren't cheap."

Jackson gave him a faint smile. "We don't need your money. Simba was a pleasure to take care of."

It was strange hearing his real name. Lydia wasn't sure she liked it. Eddie didn't look like a Simba at all. But he did wag his tail every time somebody said it, like he knew they were talking about him.

"He smells funny," the boy said, wrinkling his nose as he looked up.

"He's had a few baths," Lydia told him. "He got sick from eating a jellyfish and we needed to clean him up. That's probably what you can smell."

"I heard you paid the vet bill," John said, looking at Jackson. "At least let us reimburse you for that."

Jackson shook his head. "It's fine. He wouldn't have needed the vet if he hadn't eaten that jellyfish while we were walking him. That one definitely wasn't your fault."

"But he's okay now, right?" the boy asked. "He's not gonna get sick and die or anything?"

"The vet said he should be back to normal very soon," Lydia reassured him. "He might need a lot of extra cuddles for the next few days, but I have a feeling you'll be good at those."

"Oh yeah." The boy smiled, nodding rapidly. "I'm an ace at hugs."

John glanced at his watch. "We should go. We got in late last night and haven't unpacked yet." He reached his hand out to shake Jackson's. "Thanks again for taking care of him."

Jackson nodded, his face impassive. "No problem. I've got his leash in the hallway. You can take that." He glanced at Eddie's bed, and his toys. "Maybe you'd like these too," he said, pointing at them. "I won't need them anymore."

There was a catch in his voice that made Lydia's heart ache.

"It's okay," Alice said, glancing at her husband. "We have way too much stuff for Simba as it is."

As Jackson went to the hallway to grab the leash, Lydia leaned forward to stroke Eddie's fur. "Be good," she whispered. "We're gonna miss you."

Eddie licked her hand, his eyes wide and warm. He nuzzled against her as though he knew it was goodbye. She tickled him above his neckerchief, and his tongue lolled out.

"Come on, Simba," Alice called out, shaking his leash. "Let's go."

The dog lazily climbed to his feet and jumped off the sofa, trotting obediently over to where she was waiting. Clipping the leash onto his collar, she beckoned to her son, who joined them.

Jackson's face was pale. Lydia saw him swallow hard, his Adam's apple bobbing in his throat. He scooted down to stroke Eddie with both hands, ruffling his fur as Eddie nudged him with his muzzle.

"Be good," Jackson murmured to him. "And don't run away again. We might not be there to save you next time."

"He won't be going anywhere for a while," John promised. "Next time we go away, he comes with us."

As they walked down the steps toward their waiting car, Lydia stood behind Jackson, sliding her hand into his. "He looks happy," she whispered, as John opened the car door and Eddie readily jumped into the backseat, letting out a bark of joy when the little boy climbed in after him.

"Yeah, he does." Jackson nodded. "But that name."

She laughed. "It doesn't suit him, does it?"

"Nope. He's definitely an Eddie. At first I thought it was a weird name, but it's *him*, you know. He's laid back and relaxed, but will always try and get one over on you."

"That's it exactly," Lydia agreed. "He's an Eddie for sure."

John climbed into the driver's seat, starting the engine.

"Do you think he'll be okay without us?" Jackson asked her. There was still an edge to his voice that sent a shiver down her spine.

"Yeah. That kid obviously loves him. And he seemed happy to go with the mom. I think they'll take good care of him."

Jackson nodded again, leaning against the doorjamb as the car reversed. The back windows were open, and Eddie stuck his face out, letting out a bark of joy when he spotted Lydia and Jackson standing at the door. The car pulled away, and he was gone, leaving the two of them and the empty house.

"I'm gonna miss him," Jackson said, swallowing hard.

She slid her arms around his waist. "Me, too."

Kicking the door closed, Jackson turned and wrapped his arms around her, burying his head in her hair and breathing her in. Sliding his hands beneath her shirt, his fingers traced along the line of her tattoo on her hip, warm and teasing as they reached the hem of her shorts.

"You know what?" he said. "Let's get out of here. Go and do something before I start staring at the empty dog bed and get all crazy and miserable."

"Okay." She smiled. "Where should we go?"

He winked. "It's a surprise."

❧ 24 ❧

"You sure you don't want to practice your driving?" Jackson asked, as he drove along the cliff top road. The sun's rays were dancing and sparkling on the tips of the waves as they undulated into the shore. They had the windows down, and the spring breeze lifted the tips of Lydia's hair and made them tickle her shoulders.

He hadn't mentioned Eddie once since they'd left the house. He also hadn't told her where they were going – in spite of her insistence. All she knew was that he'd made a quick phone call as she was climbing into his car, and she'd heard him promise to head straight over to wherever it was he was driving.

"I don't think so. You've probably had enough trauma today," she said lightly.

"Do you think you'll keep practicing while you're away? That's what you need to do if you want to get your license."

"I don't know. I don't really have access to any cars abroad." She shot him a grin. "Not everybody is as laid back as you when it comes to driving. Plus there are all those rules of the road that I don't understand. You ever tried driving around a roundabout in the middle of Paris?"

"You mean a traffic circle?"

"Yeah, those big round things with all the roads leading off them. They make a four way stop feel like a walk in the park." She shuddered. "Nah, I think I'll just keep using public transport."

He opened his mouth to say something, but closed it again. His unspoken words seemed to linger in the air anyway. Was he going to suggest he teach her again when she was back here to visit Autumn?

They drove past the Silver Sands Resort, and Jackson turned the car left, toward a strip mall on the other side of the road, parking outside a shop with tinted windows, and the words *Beyond Ink* in gold lettering on a dark background.

Lydia turned to him, excitement fluttering in her belly. "A tattoo parlor?" she asked, her eyes lighting up. "Are we going in?"

He nodded, eyeing her carefully. "Only if you want to. They have time to do something small for us. Clay's a friend and he has a couple of hours free this morning."

"Hell yeah I want to." She gave him a wide grin. "What shall we have done? Do you have any ideas?"

"Yeah, a couple. But Clay can help." He climbed out of the car and walked around, opening Lydia's door and taking her hand. She slid her fingers between his and squeezed them.

"This is perfect," she told him, as they walked inside the shop. The floor was lined with alternate grey and black tiles, the color theme extending to the walls and the furniture – with five sleek black leather chairs and shiny chrome and black tables that were covered with magazines and equipment.

On the walls were framed photographs of intricately drawn tattoos. Lydia breathed in, the sterile aroma of cleaning products filling her nostrils, as a man walked out from the door at the back of the shop, his face splitting into a grin when he saw Jackson standing there.

"You must have gunned it to get here so fast," he said, shaking Jackson's hand.

"The roads were empty," Jackson told him. "And I didn't want to miss our slot. This is Lydia." He glanced at her. "This is Clay, he owns this place."

"It's a pleasure to meet you," Clay said, taking her hand in his. "Any friend of Jackson's is a friend of mine."

"How do you two know each other?" Lydia asked, amused at how different they were. Clay's body was like a canvas, covered in beautiful tattoos up to his neck. His ears were pierced in multiple places, and his head was fully shaved.

"Our website got hacked, and Jackson got it back online within an hour," Clay told her. "After that, he had a customer for life. He's a genius."

He looked genuinely impressed by Jackson, and her heart gave a leap. "So are you," she told Clay, looking at the framed tattoos on the walls. "Are these all yours?"

"They sure are. Did that dragon a couple of weeks ago. It took four visits. Twelve hours in total. But it came out great." He brought his gaze back to them. "Speaking of which, do you have any idea what you want? We have a two hour window, so we probably need to crack on." He looked up at Jackson. "You talked about a compass over the phone. You still up for that? I have a few I can show you."

Jackson nodded. Lydia looked at him from the corner of her eyes, interested in his choice. "A compass?" she asked. "Why?"

He shrugged. "I thought it would be cool."

"How about you?" Clay asked Lydia.

She sighed. "I'm still trying to decide."

"You can take a look through the portfolio while I work

on Jackson. That should give you some ideas." He pointed at the black leather easy chairs. The coffee table in front of them was covered in different colored folders. "The red one's where you can start."

"Great."

"And if you want a water or soda, help yourself," he said, pointing at the glass door of the refrigerator, next to the front desk. "Okay man, let's get started with you." He walked with Jackson to the desk, where he pointed at some sheets. "This one's cool," he said, as he slid his finger across a design, "but kind of boring. Personally, I like this one. We can do it in black today, and if you want to add color we can do that in the future, or even extend it into a more detailed design."

"Yeah. I'll take that one," Jackson agreed.

"On your chest?"

"Yep."

Clay nodded. "Okay. Take your shirt off, and get on the tattoo chair behind the screen, and I'll go wash up and get everything ready. Lydia can come along with if you'd like."

Carrying the portfolio, Lydia followed Jackson into the private area. Jackson pulled his shirt over his head, and Lydia tried really hard not to ogle his chest as he dropped onto the chair and stretched his long, jean-clad legs out in front of him. Clay walked out of the backroom with the template, grabbing a wheeled stool and his cart, pulling them next to Jackson. After preparing his needles and ink, he sterilized his hands and put on some black vinyl gloves, shaving Jackson's chest, and dabbing alcohol cleaner all over the area he was going to tattoo.

When he put the transfer of the tattoo on Jackson's chest, he asked him to check that it was how he wanted it.

Jackson looked down. "Yeah, that's good." He glanced over at Lydia. "What do you think?"

It looked hot. That's what she thought. "It's great."

Clay winked at her. "Okay then."

She was supposed to be flipping through the portfolio while he tattooed Jackson's chest, but she found herself too entranced by the process to look at the folder on her lap. She had an idea of what she wanted anyway. If Jackson's tattoo was going to be about travel, she wanted hers to be the opposite.

To represent home.

"Am I hurting you, man?" Clay asked, as he moved the needle across Jackson's skin.

"It feels like a scratch," Jackson said, smiling over at Lydia. She smiled back, and her heart ached, because she wanted this moment to last forever. To have his smile imprinted on her memory, the way the compass would be imprinted on his skin.

"If you didn't have such tight muscles, it would hurt less."

"I like his muscles," Lydia protested. "Don't listen to him, Jackson."

Clay chuckled. "I like her. Where did you two meet again?"

"I picked her up at the airport," Jackson told him, his gaze dark as it slid over her.

Lydia bit down a smile. "He's a friend of my future brother-in-law."

"The whaleboat captain?" Clay asked, lifting a brow. "The big guy, right?"

"That's Griff." Lydia nodded. "And he wasn't too happy about us getting together. Nor was Jackson. It took all of my womanly wiles to persuade him I was worth it."

"You are worth it." Jackson's voice was low. "Completely."

His words stole her breath away. "So are you."

"You guys are so damn sweet I'm going to need a dentist," Clay complained with a laugh. "Where are you from, Lydia? Do you live in Angel Sands?"

She shook her head. "I'm just visiting. I'm not really from anywhere. I travel a lot. I guess if you pushed me, I'd say New York, but that doesn't really feel like home anymore."

"What do you do that you travel so much?" Clay questioned her, lifting the needle and glancing her way.

"I'm a travel consultant. I arrange personalized trips and accompany the travelers around various countries."

"That's seriously cool. Where are you going next?"

"Spain. Then to France and Italy." The thought made her stomach contract. "After that, I'm heading to South America."

Clay's eyes widened. "Whoa. You weren't kidding. That's a lot of traveling. Do you like it? You must like it, right? You wouldn't do it otherwise."

"I don't know how to do anything else," she admitted. "I'm really good at finding places nobody else knows about, and I enjoy getting to know my clients and discovering what they're looking for. I'm not sure I'd be cut out for any other job."

He glanced at Jackson. "So what, you guys gonna do the long distance thing or something?"

Lydia froze for a moment. She couldn't bring herself to look at Jackson. Didn't want to see the truth in his eyes. Taking a deep breath, she plastered a smile on her lips. "I think we're going to be great friends," she told him. Pulling her lip between her teeth, she looked down at the red folder on her lap. "I guess I should get to choosing my tattoo, right?"

"Yeah, I've got about twenty minutes left on this one, then it's over to you," Clay said, using his foot to move his chair to give him a better angle.

Lydia nodded, but didn't look up, flipping through the plastic sleeves until she saw exactly what she was looking for.

Great friends. That was enough. It had to be, because he

wasn't offering anything else. Even if he was, it wouldn't work because their lifestyles were totally incompatible.

All she knew was that getting on that plane was going to be the hardest thing she'd ever done.

"You want to stop for coffee?" he asked, as they headed back to Angel Sands. Lydia twisted in her seat to rub her fingers along the back of her hip. Jackson tried not to look. The memory of her lying face down on the tattoo chair with her back exposed as Clay meticulously traced her design was hot enough. He didn't need to see the real thing as well.

Not if he wanted to keep this car on the road.

"Coffee would be good," she agreed, her brow creasing as she rubbed again.

"Try not to scratch it. Remember what Clay said?"

"Yeah, but it's itchy." Her pout was damn adorable. "Now I know how Eddie felt whenever he tried to scratch his face with a paw."

His chest tightened at the mention of Eddie. Or Simba, as he should probably think of him now. Leaving the house shortly after the dog did had been the right thing to do, and a great idea to head to Clay's tattoo parlor. It had taken both of their minds off the emptiness of the kitchen, and the fact they wouldn't see the dog again.

For a while, it had even made him forget about Lydia's impending departure. Even if he'd always have the memory of her tattooed on his skin. He'd lied through his teeth when he'd told her he'd chosen a compass because it was cool. The truth was, he'd chosen it as a reminder of her. That she was always traveling, and wherever she was, north, south, east, or west, the compass would be pointing toward her.

It was saccharine as hell, but once it came into his mind it was impossible to push out.

Yeah, she was going. But they'd always have the tattoos connecting them.

When they parked, Lydia was still rubbing at her back. "Come here," Jackson murmured, leaning across the console, "let me check it for you."

Gently, he pulled the tape from the dip in her lower back, opening a gap between the plastic and her skin. He swallowed hard as he looked at the design. The outline of two wings and a halo etched into the warmth of her flesh. An angel.

"Because I want to remember my time here," she'd told Clay when he'd asked. "I've had such a great experience. And wherever I am, the angel will always point me home."

Her eyes had met Jackson's, as she turned her head until her cheek was resting against the back of the tattoo chair, her gaze soft as she stared at him. He'd swallowed hard, painfully aware that she'd been more honest about her choice of tattoo than he was.

He felt like an asshole, but then Clay had pressed the needle gun against her back and she'd cried out with pain, reaching her hand out to clutch Jackson's, and the moment had passed.

"It's a little red from where you've touched it, but everything looks fine," he told her, taping the plastic wrap back down again. "Let's go and grab a coffee and go home. You can put some more ointment on it."

"Sounds good."

Déjà Brew was busy as they pushed open the door, tables filled with groups of friends and school kids, along with a few familiar faces. Frank Megassey and Lorne Daniels waved at them from the corner booth, and at the counter Autumn and Ally were talking with Deenie Russell, as Nate stood behind the espresso machine making their orders.

"Hey!" Ally said, spotting them over Autumn's shoulder. "We were just talking about you."

Deenie grinned when she saw Jackson and Lydia together, his hand firmly holding hers. "So you really did take the day off?"

He grinned at her. "Word gets around fast."

"It always does when hell freezes over." Deenie grinned at him.

Autumn's expression was soft as the two of them reached the counter. "How did it go with Eddie?" she asked them.

"Fine." Jackson nodded. Lydia squeezed his hand tighter. "They seem like a nice family."

"That's good, because otherwise I was going to plot a ninja escape plan for him," Ally said, leaning across the counter. "I have a black cat suit somewhere. I've always wanted a reason to wear it."

"You can stand down with the cat suit," Jackson said, his voice deadpan. "Anyway, Eddie doesn't like cats."

"Did you know his real name is Simba?" Lydia said to Autumn. "That's weird, right?"

"It's kind of cute." Autumn shrugged. "*The Lion King* is a good movie."

"Yeah, but he doesn't look like a lion at all. He's too dark and his fur is too short."

Deenie smiled at them all. "He's definitely an Eddie."

"So, we were all talking about you leaving and we came up with an idea," Autumn said, as Nate handed her and Deenie their orders. Skyler was fast asleep in her stroller, and Lydia dropped down to gently kiss her cheek while Jackson asked for two flat whites and two Danish pastries to go.

"What kind of idea?" Lydia asked. "I hope it's not too outlandish. I have to pack at some point."

Autumn looked from Lydia to Jackson. "We thought we might have an old fashioned cook out on the beach to say goodbye. That's if you two are okay with it. If you'd rather spend time alone, that's fine with us." She blew at the steam from her coffee and took a sip.

"A cook out sounds good." Jackson nodded. He knew Lydia would want to spend her last night with her sister. She was the one she'd come to visit, after all. "You want me to talk to Griff and the guys and organize it?"

"I've already got Griff and Lucas on the case," Autumn told him. "They have it covered."

"Will there be s'mores?" Lydia asked, the itch in her tattoo forgotten. "I love s'mores."

Autumn's reply was drowned out by the shrill sound of Jackson's phone ringing. Normally he would've ignored it, but he'd promised Lisa he'd answer in case of any problems. But when he pulled it out, he frowned, because it wasn't Lisa calling. It was his mom.

He went to reject the call, but he stopped himself. She'd only call his dad, and that would piss him off more than actually speaking to her. "I'll take this outside," he said, passing a ten to Ally. Turning to Lydia, he asked, "You okay to pick up our drinks?"

"Sure," she said happily. "I'll meet you out there."

He lifted the phone to his ear as he walked toward the open glass doors that led to the deck. "Mom?" he said, heading down the steps to the beach. "Is everything okay?"

"I really need your help with my car," she said. "Can you drive up and see me?"

"You want me to drive up to Sacramento today?" His brows dipped. "You're five hundred miles away. I can't head up at the drop of a hat."

"But I need you, honey." She sighed. "There's a part that needs looking at. Maybe I should call your dad. He could help."

"No." His voice was sharp. "Don't call Dad." She needed to start leaving the poor guy alone.

He sighed, sitting down on the edge of the boardwalk and raking his hand through his hair. He was so sick of dealing with her every time she called. Of her slinking beneath a rock for a couple of weeks before she surfaced again, needing money or attention, or god knew what else.

"Listen, I'm busy until the weekend," he told her. "I can't do anything until then. How about we talk then and you can tell me what's going on?"

"You want me to wait until Saturday?" Her voice rose up.

"The car can wait," he said firmly. He only had a couple of days left with Lydia, and there was no way he intended on spending them driving up to Sacramento. "If you call Dad, you'll get nothing from either of us. It's the weekend or bust. Take it or leave it."

She sighed loudly. "Well if they find my dead body in a ditch somewhere, it'll be your fault."

From the corner of his eye, he saw Lydia walk out of the coffee shop, two Styrofoam cups in her hand and a paper bag wedged between her arm and her body. She smiled at him, and he nodded back.

"I need to go," he told his mom. "I'll speak to you in a few days." And he'd be firm that her car wasn't his problem – or his dad's. He'd spent way too many hours trying to help her. She was a grown woman, and it was time she started acting that way.

"Okay," she mumbled. "I guess it can wait."

"All right then." He stood, dusting the sand from his jeans. "Take it easy."

"Bye, Jackson." She sniffed. "You know, even fifty dollars would help."

"No." His voice was firm. "Goodbye, Mom."

Sliding his phone into his back pocket, he headed to

where Lydia was waiting for him, taking the coffee cups from her hands and pressing his lips to hers. "Sorry about that," he said.

"Work problems?" she asked, sliding her hand into the crook of his elbow as they walked back to his car.

"Yeah. Something like that."

❦ 25 ❦

"**D**o you think you'll regret this tattoo the way you regret the eagle?" Lydia asked him, pressing her lips against his chest and breathing him in. He smelled of warm spice and Jackson Lewis, a lethal combination.

"No." His voice was sure. "I was sober when I got this one." He ran his hands through her silky hair and curled them around the base of her head, lifting her up for a kiss. His mouth moved against hers, hot and needy, as their tongues slid together, sending a shot of desire through her veins.

"Can I tell you something?" he murmured, his fingers drawing circles on the base of her neck.

"Yeah," she breathed. "As long as you keep doing that."

He did as she instructed, tracing patterns with his tips. "I lied when I said the compass didn't have a meaning."

Lifting her head up, her eyes met his. "You did?" she asked, bemused. "Why?"

"Because I thought you might think I was... I don't know." He sighed. "Weird or something."

She grinned. "I already know you're weird." She pressed

her lips against his warm shoulder. "I *like* your weird. It turns me on. So what does the tattoo mean?"

"It means I'll always remember this time we've had together. When you showed me that life doesn't have to be about standing still. It's about opening up to all the possibilities."

His words took the breath from her lungs. For a moment, she had no idea what to say. Jackson wasn't one for talking, especially not deeply. In the days she'd spent with him, she'd learned more from his silences than his sentences.

"That's beautiful." Her voice cracked. "I guess that's what my mom taught me. Never to settle for anything less than what your soul needs."

The glance he shot her was dark, making her body ache. Her soul needed him, she knew that now. It needed his smile, his voice, his touch. Needed to know he cared about her as much as she cared about him.

But she couldn't have that. And that hurt.

"What does your soul need?" he asked her, his finger tracing her cherry blossom tattoo.

You.

She didn't say it, though. And that made her feel like a fraud. But there was no possibility of having him. Not when she had to travel and he had to stay here.

"It needs air, and people, and laughter. To hear the ocean crash against the shore and birds chirping in the trees. It wants happiness, not just mine but everybody's." She smiled as he hooked his hand around her upper thigh and pulled it over his. "I guess it needs to see the good in the world." Lydia blew out a mouthful of air. "What does yours need?" she asked softly.

His brows dipped as he thought about her words. "I guess it needs security," he told her. "The knowledge that everything is going to be okay. That I'm not the little kid who sat and stared at the door, waiting for his mom to come see him." He swallowed hard, as though the words were making him ache. "I just want things to be easy, you know? For people to be happy, and not to get hurt." A ghost of a smile crossed his lips. "I guess it's pretty far away from what *your* soul needs."

"Not really." She shook her head. "You want happiness the same way I do. But I guess I go out and seek it in other places, while you're trying to create it here." She felt like he was showing her a part of himself nobody else could see. A secret that they'd always share, no matter where they were in the world. And it touched her soul.

"Tell me about your mom," she said, her voice low. "How old were you when she left?"

Jackson pulled her against his chest, his biceps flexing against her upper arms. She could feel the tension in his body at the mention of his mom. Damn, that woman must have done a number on him.

Pressing his lips against her hair, Jackson took a deep breath. "She left when I was ten. I guess I should have seen it coming. She was never the kind of mom who baked cookies or helped out in class. Dad and her, they argued like crazy all the time. But I guess I thought it was normal. That everybody's parents threw things at each other and screamed like animals on a Saturday night when they'd drunk too much. But that wasn't all she was. She was fun, too. She'd wake me up in the middle of the night and drive us to look out point because the moon was full and looking pretty. Or she'd turn up at school and take me out for the afternoon, telling my teacher I had a doctor's appointment when really we'd go to the movies or a theme park, just because she was bored."

"Those trips must have been fun," Lydia said, lifting her head to look at him.

He raised an eyebrow. "Yeah, but when we'd get home she and dad would have a massive argument about taking me out of school, or disappearing without telling him. Once she took me camping for three days without notice and he was on the verge of calling the police."

Lydia ran her tongue across her lips. "Why did she leave?"

He kissed her shoulder, sending a delicious shiver through her. "I don't know. I guess she'd gotten bored of being a wife and mom. It never really suited her. She's a free spirit. Never likes staying anywhere, or with anybody, for too long. If she hadn't had me, I don't think she and dad would have lasted very long"

"Did you see her much after she left?"

A ghost of a smile passed his lips. "Not really. She'd drop in on a whim and ask to see me, then drive Dad crazy because I'd miss school or scouts or something else that was important to him. She'd make promises about taking me to Disney Land and never show. I think those were the worst days." His eyes were cloudy as he looked at her. "I'd sit and wait at the door with my bag, positive she'd turn up. Looking back, it must have killed my dad to watch me with so much hope in my heart."

"I'm so sorry."

He nodded. "Thank you, but you don't need to be. It isn't your fault."

Didn't stop her from feeling bad. Wasn't she the same as his mom, flying in and out of his life, leaving a trail of devastation in her wake?

"Was it her who called you today?" she asked him, curious about the so called work conversation he'd had out on the beach. When she'd carried the coffees out to him, he'd had the same expression on his face as the time his mom had called when they were at the mall. A mixture of little-boy-lost and grown-man-angry.

"Yeah. She needs help with her car. God knows what's wrong with it. I told her we could discuss it over the weekend." He sighed. "There's always something. Last week it was her water heater, this week her car. Next week it'll be something else. Then she'll disappear for a while until she needs something again."

"Why do you still talk to her if she drives you crazy?"

He pulled his lip between his teeth. "I don't know. I guess because she's my mom. And if I don't talk to her, she calls my dad and I hate the way he always gives in to her. It's like he's still in love with her after all this time." He sounded almost lost.

"That's sad." Lydia gave him a soft smile. "But it's not your problem."

"It doesn't always feel that way."

There was one question still lingering on her tongue. Somehow she found the guts to ask it. "I heard a few people talk about Hayley and your engagement ending. That must have hurt."

His hold on her tightened. "I guess it did at the time. But now I'm older and wiser and so glad it ended." He pressed his lips to the top of her head. "I wouldn't be here now if it hadn't. And there's nowhere else I want to be."

Her heart cracked open a little more at his words. How did his friends not see this side of him? This sensitive, caring man who loved his parents despite their faults. Who was still paying the price for his mom's choices, and his dad's obsession with her? The same man who'd once been engaged to a woman who'd broken him again, leaving shards of what he used to be in his wake.

He amazed and astounded her. And the thought of leaving him made her heart hurt.

Tracing her finger up the line of his chest, she touched his jaw, his lips, his eyelids. "I think you're beautiful," she whispered. "Inside and out."

He curled his fingers around her wrist, pulling it down to press a kiss to her pulse point. "Show me," he said, his voice so low it made her muscles tighten and release.

And she did. With her mouth, her hands, and her body. Until they were both sweaty and breathless, their bodies glowing with satisfaction when they finally parted.

And her soul? It felt complete. As though it had finally found what it was searching for.

"So where are we going?" Jackson asked her the next day, as he started the car and the engine rumbled to life. It was her last day here, and he wanted to spend every moment of it with her, the same way they'd spent half of last night with their bodies wrapped around each other.

And the other half of it with him inside her.

"I told you, it's a secret. You surprised me with the tattoo parlor yesterday, I get to surprise you today."

He bit down a smile. "Yeah, but you need to tell me where to drive, otherwise we'll be sitting here for hours."

"Good point." Amusement danced in her eyes. "Okay, so you need to head into town, past the boardwalk, then take a right."

"Toward the grocery store?" Jackson shrugged and shifted the car into reverse. "Are we going shopping?"

"Yes, Jackson," she said, deadpan. "I thought our last day together should be spent deep in the freezer aisle. It's practical *and* romantic." She leaned over to press her lips to his neck, and his foot slipped onto the brake. The car juddered into a halt. "Oh damn, sorry."

"S'okay. I kind of like living on the edge with you." He

pulled out of the driveway and onto the road, following her directions.

Lydia sat back. "In that case, you'll love what I can do with a frozen zucchini."

He coughed out a laugh. She was his kind of wild.

It only took five minutes to get into town. The shops were open, and people were walking in the streets wearing jeans and t-shirts, the sun warming their skin as they crossed the roads. Jackson followed the rest of Lydia's directions, parking in a lot at the back of a long white stuccoed building. "What is this place again?" He was trying to remember exactly what the building housed. He'd passed it enough times, but never paid attention.

"Before we go in, there's no pressure, okay?" Lydia told him, in a strange echo of his words outside the tattoo parlor. "This is just for fun."

He flashed her a confused grin. "Okay…"

When he'd locked the car, she slid her hand into his, and they walked around to the front of the building. They were a few blocks from the ocean front, but he could still smell the hint of salt and ozone in the air, as he looked up at the lettering over the top of the main entrance.

Angel Sands Pet Rescue.

Of course it was. He glanced at Lydia, bemused.

"I just thought we could see what kind of dogs they have," she said. "I know you're missing Eddie like crazy, and that's completely understandable." She gave him a soft smile. "But I called yesterday and they told me they have at least eight dogs that need a loving home. Maybe one of them is the one you're looking for."

Jackson blinked, saying nothing. This wasn't what he'd expected at all.

"Is this a stupid idea?" Lydia asked him. "It is, isn't it?" She tugged at his hand. "Come on, we don't have to go in. We can go and grab a coffee and do something else."

She shifted her feet, but he didn't follow her. Instead he looked up at the sign again, blowing out a mouthful of air.

"We can go in," he told her.

"Are you sure? It doesn't mean you're committing to anything. We can take a look around and come right back out."

Strangely, he was sure. All those years he'd spent living alone in his house, and he hadn't realized just how empty it was until Lydia and Eddie came along. He'd enjoyed having a reason to go home every night, to walk along the ocean's edge and throw balls into the water.

He'd even enjoyed waking up early to open the door so Eddie could go and do his business.

"Yeah, I'm sure," he said in answer to her question. "Let's see what they've got."

They walked into the main reception area, stopping at the front desk that was teeming with leaflets and papers.

"Hi," the woman behind the counter looked up. "Can I help you?"

"I called yesterday," Lydia told her. "This is Jackson Lewis. We've come to talk about your rescue dogs."

The woman nodded, tucking a strand of grey hair behind her ear as she reached for a clipboard. "Oh yes, that's right. Hi, and welcome to Angel Sands Rescue. I'm Sarah, and I volunteer here. Can I ask you to fill this out?" she asked Jackson, handing him a chewed down pen. "Am I right in thinking you live alone? No kids?"

"Yeah, that's right."

"It makes things easier. A lot of our dogs have been through trauma. We don't like homing them with young children if it can be avoided." She leaned over the form that Jackson was completing. "You have your own business?" she asked. "Does that mean you'll be out of the house a lot?"

"Yeah, but I own the office, so the dog could come with me." Jackson blinked, surprised at his answer. Was he really considering this?

"So you'll need a calm dog if you're bringing him to work with you. We have a lovely bulldog that came in last week. Sadly, her owner passed on, and the owner's daughter lives in an apartment that doesn't allow pets. We've called her Bella, though of course whoever adopts her could rename her." She gave Jackson a quick smile. "Would you like to see her?"

"Yeah. I'd like that a lot."

They followed Sarah through a set of double doors, down a corridor filled on both sides with glass pens. There were animals of every size in them, from Great Danes to tiny kittens. Nearly all of them came up to the glass as Lydia and Jackson walked past, looking up with interest.

"How long do you keep them here?" Jackson asked. He hated to think of these beautiful animals being cooped up.

"We try to rehome them as quickly as possible. Most are only here for a week or two," Sarah promised him. "And we take them out daily for exercise and fresh air. If you look on the right, there are some empty pens. One of our volunteers has taken them for a walk."

They reached the far end of the room, and Sarah pointed to the glass. "This is Bella's pen."

Jackson could feel his heart start to hammer against his chest as he turned to look at the dog walking toward them. She was white with brown patches, her tongue lolling out as she waddled toward them, little pants escaping from her open mouth. When she reached the glass door, she looked up at them, her soulful eyes wide as she took them in.

"Hey, Bella," Sarah cooed. "I brought you some visitors."

Bella's tail wagged as though she could understand. She

pressed her nose against the glass, her breath misting it, as her paws scrabbled at the barrier.

"She's excited to see you," Sarah told them. "I'm going to open the door, okay?" She unlocked the door and opened it, and Jackson and Lydia walked inside, both immediately dropping to their haunches to pet Bella.

She let out a happy bark and started to lick Jackson's face as he ruffled the folds in her fur. "She likes you," Lydia told him. "Look at her. She can't take her eyes off you."

Jackson laughed. "Maybe I still smell of boy dog."

Truth was, it felt good to be stroking her. Beneath Bella's fur, he could feel the tightness of her muscles, and the layer of fat that characterized her breed. He pulled his hand away for a moment, but she nudged it, encouraging him to stroke her again.

That earned him another face lick. This dog sure was demonstrative.

"Should I feel jealous?" Lydia whispered. "I thought I was the only one who got to lick your face."

Jackson laughed. "You're gonna want to stay a away from my face until I wash it again."

Lydia ruffled Bella's fur. "Ah, I'm okay to share you with this beauty."

They spent ten minutes in the pen with her, playing with her toys and letting her barrel them over and climb on them. Bella's tail didn't stop wagging the whole time. She was clearly in love with Jackson, though she gave Lydia some attention, too.

"What do you think?" Sarah asked, as they reluctantly left Bella and walked back to the reception.

"She's beautiful," Lydia said. "And so funny."

"She's got a lovely character. Playful but calm," Sarah agreed. "And she liked you," she added, looking at Jackson. "Have you owned many dogs before?"

He shook his head. "I fostered a dog recently, but I've never had one before that."

"Really? You're a natural. You seem so at home here." Sarah smiled. "It's good you've had some experience, though. It makes things much easier." She put her clipboard down on the reception desk. "So what do you think? Are you interested in her?"

"Yeah," he found himself saying. "I'm definitely interested."

Lydia looked up at him, a ghost of a smile playing at her lips.

"That's wonderful," Sarah said. "The next step would be for you to come back for a second visit. This way you can spend more time with her, and take her for a walk in our grounds. Just to be certain you know what you're letting yourself in for."

"After that, if you want to adopt her, we'll need to run a security check on you. And we'd bring Bella for a visit to your home. That's our way to make sure she'd be happy there, and that it's safe for her. And it gives us a chance to talk through everything you'll need to get to make her feel at home." Sarah smiled. "How does that sound?"

It felt a little like being run over by a soft, furry steamroller. Pleasant, but life changing. "That sounds good." He smiled at Lydia, who squeezed his hand. It was crazy, because this morning all he had ahead of him was Lydia leaving and the silence in his house. And now in one easy move, his future was shifting and changing all over again.

Thanks to Lydia.

She'd changed him in every way. In the space of less than two weeks, he'd gone from being a workaholic to somebody who'd fallen in love with two dogs.

And for the woman who'd introduced them to him.

Damn, he was going to miss her. His chest tightened at the thought of her leaving.

One more night. That's all they had left. Life would go on without her, he knew that. Making an appointment to see Bella again the following week was testament to that fact. But it wasn't the life that his soul was searching for.

He knew that for certain.

❧ 26 ❧

Lydia placed the final piece of clothing into her suitcase and zipped it up, hauling it off the guest bed and onto the floor. She'd pack her overnight bag in the morning. She still had things she needed tonight. But in fifteen hours she'd be heading back to the airport and onward to Spain, leaving Angel Sands behind her like a sweet, distant memory.

Leaving Jackson behind, too. She tried to ignore the pang that caused in her chest, because tonight was supposed to be fun. Autumn and Griff and all their friends had thrown themselves into organizing a huge party on the beach, and she was determined to enjoy it for their sake.

"Are you ready?" Autumn asked, popping her head around the guest bedroom door. "The babysitter's here and Skyler's fast asleep thanks to the bath you gave her. We should head down to the beach."

Griff had left an hour earlier to help Lucas and their friends set up while Autumn and Lydia waited for the babysitter. If she stood very quietly, Lydia swore she could hear the steady beat of the music coming up from the shore.

"I'm ready," she said, taking another glance at her case.

"And all packed up."

Autumn stepped forward and hugged her tight, pressing her lips to Lydia's cheek. "I'm going to miss you so much. It feels like you just got here."

"I'm not leaving until tomorrow," Lydia said, though she felt her throat tighten at the thought of leaving her sister. They never spent enough time together. With her job taking her around the world, and Autumn settling with her family here in Angel Sands, they were lucky to spend more than twice a year in each other's company.

"I know," Autumn said, her voice quiet. "But tomorrow morning's going to be crazy. I assume you're staying at Jackson's tonight, so you'll have to hurry back here and we'll drive you to the airport first thing."

"Is it okay if Jackson comes to the airport, too?"

Autumn smiled. "Of course it is. That's so sweet. He really likes you."

Lydia couldn't get the tightness out of her chest. It had been there since Jackson had dropped her off at Autumn and Griff's house earlier that evening. It was all feeling real now. Her leaving, his staying. She wasn't sure she'd be able to make it through the evening without crying.

Or begging him to come with her.

"It's a shame you have to be away for so long," Autumn said as they headed out of the house and toward her car. "Have you and Jackson talked about when you'll see each other again?"

Lydia shook her head. "It isn't like that. We both know our lifestyles are incompatible. He's here and I'm not." It sounded so simple when she said it.

"Maybe you could cut down on the travel." Autumn opened the car and they climbed inside. "Change your business model a little so that you can work from the US a little more."

"Travel's what I do," Lydia said. "It always has been. I don't know who I'd be if I stayed in one place for very long. And anyway, Jackson hasn't asked me to stay. So it would look a little crazy if I hung around like a bad smell."

"So that's it? You leave and this thing between you is over? Won't that be awkward the next time you come and visit us?"

"I'm always friends with my exes," Lydia said. "And I promised you from the start I wouldn't make it awkward. I like Jackson." Like was way too weak a word, but she didn't want to alarm her sister. "He'll always be special to me."

"Oh, honey. You're in love with him. Anybody can see that when they look at the two of you. And it's killing me that neither of you will admit it."

"What good would it do to admit it?" Lydia asked. "It won't change anything. It would only make it hurt even more than it already does."

Autumn drove them toward the boardwalk, parking in the lot beside the coffee shop. Déjà Brew's doors were open, people standing on the deck and spilling onto the beach. Griff had set up a music system on the deck and the sounds were pumping out into the evening air. The aroma of burgers and hot dogs wafted up from the sand where Lucas and his friend, Breck, were cooking on two oversize grills.

The beach was full of familiar faces, all lighting up as she greeted them. She hugged Ally and Brooke, and chatted with Harper and Ember about their children, before heading over to a group of older folk who were calling out her name.

"Look at this," Deenie Russell said, pulling her phone from her pocket. "I took ten new photographs today for my Instagram. One of them has sixty comments."

Lydia smiled at her as she took her phone, flipping through the photos. "You're a natural," she told Deenie. "Give it a couple of months and you'll be an influencer."

"What's that?" Lorne Daniels asked. He wrinkled his face. "It sounds dangerous."

"Do you think you can set me up on Instagram the next time you visit?" Frank Megassey asked. "I'd love to drum up some business for the hardware store."

"Of course. We could have a lot of fun with that," Lydia agreed. "I'll be sure to come in just as soon as I'm back."

"Don't forget to come see me at the surf shop, too," Lorne said. "I might need a refresher course by then."

"It's a date. For sure," Lydia told him.

"Who's asking you out on a date?" Jackson asked, sliding his arms around Lydia's waist and pressing his lips to her cheek. "Don't they know that you're taken tonight?"

She leaned her head against his chest, smiling up at him. "I was just about to tell them."

"You two are too cute for words," Deenie told them. "You look good together."

"Well thank you." Jackson gave her a grin. "Now if you guys don't mind, I'd like to dance with this beautiful woman before she skips town."

"Be our guest," Frank said. "But I might be over to steal a dance later."

Jackson blew Frank a kiss. "I'll dance with you any time, Frank."

Lydia burst into laughter at Frank's expression as Jackson led her down to the beach. His warm hand was tight on hers.

"I missed you," Jackson murmured, as he slid his hands around her waist and pulled her body to his, moving his hips to the rhythm of the slow music Griff was playing.

"It's only been a couple of hours." Lydia leaned her head against his chest, letting him take the lead. She loved dancing. Loved even more that Jackson could dance and didn't have to be dragged onto the beach to hold her. He actually wanted to be here, swaying softly to the beat.

"Three hours and forty minutes," he told her. "I think I counted every second."

"Well you have me now." Her eyes sparkled. "What are you going to do with me?"

He brushed his lips against her forehead. "I have a few ideas."

"I like them already," she said, looping her arms around his neck, and pressing her body against his. "Especially if they involve dancing."

"I'll dance with you all night if you want." He brushed her lips with his.

"We can stop for refreshments," she said, nodding seriously. "But yes please." Being in his arms felt so good.

So did looking at him. The sun was setting, casting a soft orange glow across his skin, making him look warm and sweet and everything she knew she was going to miss.

She pushed that thought down. They still had tonight. Somehow that would have to be enough.

"So she's going tomorrow." Lucas handed Jackson a beer. Frank Megassey had finally walked onto the beach to claim his dance from Lydia, and Jackson had gallantly left them to it. He and Lucas were sitting on the edge of the boardwalk, overlooking the ocean, and watching as the sun finally hit the dappled surface. In a few minutes the ball of fire would slide beneath, and the sky would be dark, the beach illuminated only by the shops that lined the boardwalk and the strings of lights that hung from lamppost to lamppost.

"Yep." Jackson nodded. "She's catching a flight in the early afternoon."

"And you're okay with that?"

Jackson took a mouthful of beer. "I don't think I get a

choice."

Lucas tipped his head to the side. "There's always a choice. Have you two thought about long distance dating? She'll have to come back here at some point, right? You'll see her again. And maybe you can even dust off your passport and travel to her."

Jackson ran his finger around the rim of his bottle, considering Lucas' words. They weren't anything he hadn't thought of himself. "I don't think I can do the long distance thing," he admitted. "I don't want to be like my dad, begging her to come home and waiting at the door every time she might visit. It made him a shadow of the man he used to be." The thought of her leaving tomorrow was painful enough. Having to go through this every couple of months would probably kill him. "And she hasn't mentioned it, even if I was interested. She's leaving. It's time to let her go."

Lucas sighed. "Look, I don't know if you want to hear this or not, but I was in the same position as you. I thought Ember didn't want anything serious. She'd just gotten out of a long term relationship, and I was supposed to move back to White City. There didn't seem to be a future for us. But then I realized that nothing – not my career, or my fear of rejection – was worth losing her for. Sometimes you just have to take that leap in the dark."

"That was different," Jackson pointed out. "Ember had a steady job, and she loved living here in Angel Sands. All you had to do was get a job and move back here, plus White City isn't that far. Lydia's..." He blew out a mouthful of air. "She's like some kind of exotic bird. She has to use her wings. The same way my dad couldn't clip my mom's wings, I can't clip Lydia's. Some relationships just aren't supposed to last long term." Damn, it hurt to admit it out loud. He inhaled sharply, trying to ignore the constant ache in his chest.

"You're in love with her." It wasn't a question.

"Yeah, I guess I am." A ghost of a smile passed his lips. "It's kind of ironic, isn't it? The player played."

"Lydia hasn't played you."

Jackson looked over to where she was talking with Autumn and the new owner of the ice cream parlor – Meghan or Maggie, or something. The three of them were bathed in moonlight, their faces shining with amusement as Lydia made some kind of joke.

"No, she hasn't." She'd woken something inside of him. Something that had been dormant for longer than he could remember. And now he wanted things he'd never imagined could be his. "And yeah, I've fallen for her. Who wouldn't? She's perfect."

"So tell her," Lucas urged. "I don't want us to be sitting here in a few weeks' time with you feeling lower than ever because you missed your chance. What's the worst that can happen?"

Jackson opened his mouth to reply, but his phone started to ring. He pulled it from his pocket, frowning when he saw the unknown number. "I should take this," he said. "It could be something to do with work."

"Go ahead. I'll go check on the food."

Jackson swiped to accept the call, walking along the beach to where the music wasn't so loud. "Jackson Lewis," he said, pressing the phone against his jaw.

"Mr. Lewis? Are you the next of kin for Ms. Jennifer Marks? Date of birth, February third nineteen sixty-four?" a female voice asked.

His stomach clenched. "Yeah I am. Who's asking?"

"My name is Rita Martin. I work at Saint Agnes hospital in Anaheim. Your mother was admitted an hour ago after a traffic accident. We have you listed as the next of kin."

He frowned. "Is she okay?"

"She has suspected fractures in her ribs, and multiple

contusions to her face from the impact. The doctors also think her nose may be broken. She may need surgery, but the swelling on her face will need to reduce first. Do you know if your mom has any medical insurance?"

"I...ah... don't know. Sorry." He looked over at the party. At his friends. They were dancing and laughing. And Lydia was hugging her sister tightly, a huge smile on her face. "I'm in Angel Sands. About an hour and a half away from you. I'll leave now."

"That would be great. I'll let your mom know you're on your way. She might be moved from the ER by the time you get here, but if you come into reception I'll be able to direct you."

"Thank you." He ended the call, sliding his phone into his back pocket. He closed his eyes, trying to work out what the hell just happened, and why his mom was driving near Anaheim, when she lived in Sacramento.

When he opened them, he turned to seek out the one person who'd understand. Who'd be able to help him when his head was completely messed up, yet again, by the woman who always let him down.

His dad.

"I'll come with you," Lydia said, reaching for his hand. The music was still playing, she had to shout to hear herself over it.

"No." Jackson shook his head. "You won't get back in time for your flight. Dad's driving. He hasn't been drinking tonight." Unlike Jackson. "But we need to leave now."

He looked so lost, standing in the moonlight, and all she wanted to do was wrap her arms around him. Tell him it was all going to be fine. But he could barely even look at her. It was as though he was completely wrapped up in his thoughts, his fingers drumming a rhythm against his jeans as he explained that he had to leave, and he wouldn't be seeing her for a while.

"Will you let me know how she is?" Lydia asked.

"It'll be after one by the time we get there. You'll be asleep. I'll message in the morning when we have more news." He looked to his left, his eyes wary. "Dad's waiting in the car. I should go. I...ah...guess this is goodbye."

She tried to smile, but her muscles weren't playing ball. She couldn't believe this was it. There was so much more she wanted to say, but now there was no time to say it. "I guess it is," she said, her voice low.

His eyes softened. "I've had an amazing time with you. I'm sorry it has to end this way. I was hoping to say goodbye at the airport."

"Maybe this is better. I'm really bad at goodbyes." Finally the smile curled her lips, though it was fighting with the tears pooling in her eyes. "I really enjoyed spending time with you, Jackson. I'm going to miss you like crazy."

His throat undulated as he swallowed. "I'm going to miss you, too." His voice was thick. Graveled. "I just wish..."

She put her finger on his lips, silencing him. "I know," she whispered. "I know." But she didn't want to hear it. Whatever he wished for, she wished for it harder.

That things were different. That she wasn't leaving in the morning. That he wasn't leaving now.

It didn't matter, though, did it? Because they couldn't change anything. All they had was this moment and goodbye, and then he'd be gone.

"I hope your mom is okay." It didn't matter how fractious his relationship was with his mom. Because she was still his mother. And she knew how much it hurt to lose somebody you loved. Even if you barely knew them.

"Yeah, I hope so, too." The car engine revved from across the parking lot. "I'm sorry for leaving like this."

"It's not your fault. None of this is." And it wasn't hers, either. It was life and it sucked sweaty balls sometimes. From the corner of her eye, she saw Ryan climb out of the car, his expression as concerned as Jackson's as he looked over at them.

"You really should go." She pulled her lips between her teeth. "But can I have a hug first?" The thought of him leaving without touching her was too unbearable.

"Yeah." He wrapped his arms around her, pulling her close, dropping his face to her hair the way he always did. And for a moment it was just them, standing between the beach and the parking lot. She lifted her head and he kissed her. Not demanding, the way he did when they were alone in his house. This kiss was soft and sweet and made her heart want things it couldn't have.

"Goodbye, Lydia," he murmured. "Be safe."

She swallowed her sob. "You be safe, too."

He turned and walked to the car, and she watched him, her lips trembling as she inhaled a ragged breath. His dad climbed into the driver's seat of Jackson's car, and a moment later Jackson sat in the passenger seat, closing the door behind him. Her eyes blurred with tears as they drove out of the parking lot, and out of her line of sight, leaving an emptiness inside her she wasn't sure she could ever fill.

"Was that Jackson's car?" Autumn asked, sliding her arm through Lydia's. "Where's he going?"

"He isn't going," Lydia whispered. "He's gone." And that's when the tears started to spill out of her eyes, trailing in hot rivulets down her cheeks, and pooling at her chin.

"Oh honey. Come here." Autumn folded her arms around her sister. "It's okay. Everything's going to be okay."

❧ 27 ❧

Hospitals at night were an entirely different animal to their daytime bustling activity. Voices were hushed, people sitting in waiting rooms slept, even the staff seemed different, their focus on the patients razor sharp. Jackson and his dad walked up to the desk in the ER, feeling heavy with fatigue, and gave their names to the receptionist, who immediately turned to her computer.

"Jennifer Marks. Yep, we've moved her to a ward. She's on the second floor." The receptionist pointed to the elevator. "Visiting times are over, but I'll call ahead and they'll let you in. Husband and son, right?"

"Yeah." Jackson nodded. No point in trying to explain his fractured family to her. It wouldn't make a difference anyway. He was going to see his mom no matter what, and he knew that wild horses couldn't keep his dad away.

The ward was as quiet as the rest of the hospital. Their footsteps echoed through the sanitized hallway as the night shift nurse led them to his mom's room. "She looks worse than she actually is," the nurse told them. "Her ribs will take some time to heal, but the rest of her injuries are superficial.

The doctor wants to see her in the morning, but after that she'll be able to go home."

"What about her nose?" Jackson asked.

"We'll take an x-ray in the morning, but it isn't as bad as the ER doctors first suspected. Mostly swelling, but the x-ray will tell us for certain." She pushed the door open. "Ms. Marks, you have some visitors." She nodded at the chairs next to the hospital bed. "You can stay as long as you'd like."

Jackson looked at his mom as she lay on the hospital bed. One of her eyes was black, and there was a bandage across her nose. But what shocked him more than anything was how swollen her face was. Her eyes looked like little buttons in the center of her flesh. There was no sign of the high cheekbones that had always been her defining feature. Just a mess of cuts and bruises, along with a long suture down the left side of her face.

"Jenny." His dad shook his head and walked over to the bed, taking her hand in his. "Look at you, sweetheart."

Jackson followed him, walking around to the other side. "How are you feeling?"

She turned her head from father to son. "I'm sorry," she said. "I didn't mean for this to happen."

"Hush," his dad said. "We know. Are you feeling okay? Does it hurt anywhere?"

"They gave me the good stuff. Nothing hurts." She tried to smile. "Except when I laugh."

"Got it." Ryan winked at her. "No laughing." He sat, his hand still holding hers. Jackson did the same, swallowing hard when he looked at his parents. How many times had he wished to see them together like this when he was a kid? How many times had he dreamed of his dad and mom being together again?

And now they were, for one night at least, and all he could

think of was Lydia and how she was leaving tomorrow. Without him being able to say a proper goodbye.

"The nurse said you should be able to leave in the morning," Ryan said, his voice upbeat.

"Yeah. I have two fractured ribs, but they don't need surgery. Just lots of rest and recuperation. Hopefully my nose will be okay once the swelling goes down. They'll check on that before they discharge me."

"What happened?" Jackson asked her. "What are you doing in Anaheim?"

"I was driving down to see you." She cleared her throat. "I thought it would save some time. I guess I did that, huh?"

"I told you I would call, you didn't need to come." He raised an eyebrow. "You need to start taking care of yourself rather than expecting us to do it."

"I know." She sniffed. "I'm so sorry, Jackson. I really am."

He hated the way she always made him feel. Fury mixed with relief as he looked at her, taking in all the injuries she had. It could have been so much worse. She could have died, or hurt somebody else. The fact that she didn't was more due to luck than intent.

"We'll talk about your car in the morning," his dad said, shooting Jackson a look. "You should rest now, that's the only way to feel better."

"I do feel sleepy," she agreed, closing her eyes as her head rested on the pillow.

Strange, because Jackson felt completely wide awake. Maybe because his mind was a hundred miles south of here, thinking about a girl whose hand he already missed holding.

"I'm sorry," Lydia said, wiping her eyes with a tissue. "I don't know why I can't stop crying. It's not like I didn't know I was leaving. We were going to say goodbye tomorrow, so why am I so upset it happened a few hours early?"

"Because it's a shock," Autumn murmured, stroking her hair. They'd left the party almost an hour after Jackson and his dad had driven away. Lydia had helped them clean up, thinking the work might take her mind off things, but it hadn't worked. And now they were back at Autumn and Griff's house, sitting on the sofa, Lydia's head resting against Autumn's shoulder as she tried to console her. "Shock always makes me cry. I don't know why, but it does. Remember when the pier caught on fire? I was almost comatose."

"I remember," Griff murmured, from the easy chair on the other side of the coffee table. "I thought you'd end up in the hospital."

A fresh trail of tears ran down Lydia's cheeks. "Do you think his mom is okay?" she asked. She'd considered calling him, but he'd been adamant she should get some rest and he'd call her in the morning.

"I don't know, honey," Autumn murmured. "I guess we'll find out soon enough. In the meantime, you should get some sleep. You've got a long journey ahead of you."

"I don't want to go," Lydia admitted, crumpling the tissue in her hand. Her eyes met Autumn's. "I want to stay here and make sure that he's okay. But I can't because I'm due to meet my clients at the airport on Monday afternoon. If I leave any later, I'll miss them."

"Jackson understands," Autumn reassured her. "It's not like he didn't know you were leaving. Out of anybody I know, he gets that business has to come first. Your reputation is everything. You can't let your clients down." Her smile was soft. "Jackson will be okay. He has all of us to take care of him. I'm more worried about you."

"I'll be okay. I always am." Lydia gave her sister a watery smile. "I just need to get on that plane. I always feel better when I'm traveling." But she'd never left half of her heart behind before.

Another sob escaped from her lips, and Autumn frowned, hugging her again. "Sweetheart, I'm worried about you. I've never seen you cry like this."

"I can't remember the last time I did," Lydia said honestly.

"Maybe you've never been in love before."

Lydia blinked away the tears and looked at her sister. "If this is what love feels like, it sucks."

"It only sucks when you're fighting it." Autumn looked over Lydia's shoulder at Griff, her expression softening. "But when you both admit it and let it guide you, it's the most amazing feeling in the world."

"But if I told Jackson I love him, nothing would change. I'd still have to leave and he'd have to stay, and we'd both be miserable."

"Maybe," Autumn said, nodding slowly. "But maybe if you'd admit it to each other, you'd find a way to make things work. It doesn't have to be all or nothing. You don't have to give up traveling and stay in one place for the rest of your life to be together. You two could find a way to compromise."

Lydia frowned. "But mom told me not to let myself be tied down. To travel and find what makes me happy."

"What?" Autumn blinked. "When did mom tell you that? You were a baby when she died."

"In the letter she left for me. The one I opened on my eighteenth birthday."

Autumn stared at her, running the tip of her tongue along her bottom lip. "What exactly did the letter say?"

"I've got it in my overnight bag," Lydia told her. "I carry it everywhere. I'll go get it."

A few minutes later, Autumn put the letter on the table after reading, and gave Lydia a soft look. "It's a beautiful letter," she told her. "Even more beautiful that you kept it with you all this time. Mom loved you so much. She loved both of us. But I don't understand why this is stopping you from being with Jackson."

"Because of this part," Lydia said, pointing to the fifth paragraph. "Where she tells me to travel and keep searching for what makes me happy. I've lived my life by that. I did exactly what she told me to. I've traveled and found happiness."

"I don't think that's what she was trying to say," Autumn said carefully. "She wrote this almost twenty-five years ago. I think she was telling you not to get tied down to the New York way of life. To see what else is out there that makes you happy. I don't think she meant that you have to travel forever otherwise you'll be sad."

Lydia stilled, staring at her sister. "She wanted me to change the world. How can I do that if I'm not traveling?"

Autumn took her hand. "Sweetie, you *have* changed the world. You change everybody you meet. Look at Deenie Russell, telling everybody how Instagram has improved her business. She wouldn't have done that if it wasn't for you. And then there's Eddie. You saved him and got him home to his owners." Autumn squeezed Lydia's palm. "And Jackson," she said softly. "You changed his life, too. You don't have to go far to make a difference. It's you who makes things better. Not the fact you travel."

"You think she'd want me to settle down?" Lydia asked, her voice low.

"I know she'd want you to be happy. In whatever form that takes. Doesn't matter if it means traveling or staying in one place. This letter is all about *you* being open to things. Maybe you should think about being open to love, no matter how it comes into your life."

Lydia opened her mouth and closed it again. All these

years that she'd traveled, she'd thought she'd found the one thing that made her happy. And for a long time, it did. But she hadn't found what she was looking for then. Hadn't found the thing that filled her soul.

It wasn't places that made her soul sing. It was people. The people she met. The ones who became her friends and she visited over and over again. Her family, her sister, her niece, and her sister's fiancé. Even her dad.

And now there was somebody else that made her whole body sing with delight. Who only had to smile at her to make her world feel full. Who knew how to touch her and kiss her in a way that made her toes curl with pleasure.

Happiness wasn't about searching. It was about accepting.

"I have to go to Barcelona," she whispered. "And then to France and Italy and South America." She had no choice. She had clients and a reputation to keep. And there was no way she could ruin their vacations. Especially after they'd paid her so much.

"I know." Autumn nodded. "And what happens after that?"

"After that?" Lydia repeated, pondering the words. "I choose happiness."

❧ 28 ❧

"I'll take her home with me," Ryan said at six a.m. the next morning. The two of them had slept fitfully in the hospital room. The nursing shift was changing, and they'd taken the opportunity to walk to the hospital cafeteria to grab a caffeine fix. "I don't want her on her own. Not the first few days. She can have my guest room. It's not like anybody else needs it."

That guest room used to be Jackson's bedroom, a hundred years ago before he moved out. Like everything else in Ryan's house — or his life for that matter — it was practically unchanged since Jackson was a kid. Sure it was clean, something he'd never managed to achieve in his eighteen years of living there, and the posters of surfers and bands had been taken off the wall. But the blue paint and the grey rug were the same, not to mention the single bed with a crochet bedspread.

"She's not your problem," Jackson told him, as they waited for the elevator. His back was aching from hunching over the bed, holding his mom's hand as she drifted off.

"Of course she is," Ryan said softly. "She's the mother of my child."

This conversation was so predictable. Jackson could probably say his father's lines for him. How many times had they talked about this? And yet he still answered, the same way he always did.

"Your child is a grown up. And you're divorced. The only reason I told you about mom is because I'd been drinking and couldn't drive myself. This has to stop at some point, Dad. You're enabling her. When are you going to stop pining after her and start living your life? It's been twenty years since you divorced. All that time and you haven't moved on."

Ryan shifted awkwardly on his feet. "Yeah, well some relationships don't stick to the rules, you know. Jenny will always be special to me. I'll always love her. You can't turn those feelings off, no matter how much you want to."

Jackson would have laughed, but it wasn't funny. He knew exactly what his dad meant. And for a moment, he saw himself in twenty years' time. Would he pine after Lydia the way his dad pined after his mom?

The thought felt like a punch to the gut. He couldn't live his life like that. He didn't want to be like his dad, always hoping she'd come back. Living his life around the hole she left. Christ, he loved her, but he couldn't keep saying goodbye.

This was killing him.

Anger surged up inside of him. At the situation he and Lydia had found themselves in. At his mom and her inability to be a grown-up, no matter how old she was. And for his dad and his refusal to move on from the love of his life.

"You need to let go," Jackson told him. "This thing you have for mom, it's unhealthy. Stop riding in like a knight in shining armor."

"I can't," his dad said quietly. "Believe me, I've tried."

Jackson gritted his teeth. "She walked away, Dad. She left us. Left you."

"No, she didn't."

Jackson froze. "What do you mean? Of course she did. I watched her leave." And the little kid inside of him still hurt over it.

"You saw what you wanted to see. She didn't leave, I kicked her out."

He blinked. That wasn't true. His mom was the one who walked out of their lives. She was the one who'd wanted a divorce, to be single and free. Not his dad.

"I don't understand," Jackson said, his brow creasing.

"It was the hardest thing I ever had to do, asking her to leave. But she was making our lives a misery. She'd take you out of school and I'd get calls from them telling me you'd disappeared or hadn't showed up at all and they had no idea where you were. Some days I'd come home and you'd both be in your pajamas. Other times you'd disappear for days, and come back wearing Mickey ears and telling me all about your great adventures." Ryan looked down at his hands. "And then there were the days when she'd go off on her own, and I'd come home and you'd be eating beans from a can. The house would be a dumpster. She'd fling things around and leave them everywhere, then walk out for a day or two without telling me. I begged her to see a doctor, or for us to go to counseling, but she refused. So I told her she needed to go."

Ryan looked up, his eyes full of sadness. "I didn't want to do it. But it was affecting you. You were confused and angry, and a lot of the time your school work was suffering. They started talking about keeping you back a year, and that's when I knew something had to give."

"You didn't tell me..." Jackson whispered. "Why didn't I know this?"

"Because you were a kid. You didn't need to be involved in

grown up stuff. I didn't want you to be. I wanted you to enjoy being a child."

Jackson shook his head, trying to make sense of his dad's words. "But all these years, you've still loved her?"

"Yeah. It's a strange mixture of love and guilt. Once she left, she really went off the rails. There was a year or two that I was terrified for her."

"So the money you give her, it's guilt money?"

Ryan's eyes met his. "It's money I have and that she needs. That's all it is."

Another thought captured Jackson's mind. "But you let me believe she was the one who left. All these years... I've blamed her. I've been mad at her." His muscles stiffened at the thought. "You should have told me." He raked his fingers through his hair. "You should have..."

"I know."

The elevator arrived, the doors opening with a ping. But Jackson couldn't get into it. Not when everything he knew was upside down. Couldn't go to the cafeteria like nothing had happened with the two people who'd made him what he was – good and bad. Their relationship was messed up, the same way his childhood was.

"I need some air," he said, turning on his heel to head for the stairs.

"Son, I—"

Jackson held up his hand. "Just let me be alone for a minute. I need to think."

His dad nodded, lips turned down. "Okay," he said softly.

The hospital was even quieter as Jackson walked down the stairs and through reception, heading out of the glass sliding doors to the parking lot. The air was cool as it hit his skin, and he took a deep breath, slumping against the wall of the hospital as he tried to make sense of his thoughts.

For as long as he could remember, he'd believed that his

275

mom had been the one to walk out. He'd thought that some people were never supposed to be tied down. He'd built defenses around his heart to make sure he'd never be like his dad, pining for somebody he could never have.

If he was truly honest, that's why his relationship with Hayley never worked out. Sure, he'd gotten engaged to her, but he'd never truly let her in. Never let himself be vulnerable to her. And when she'd met somebody else and gotten pregnant – he'd told himself that's just what women did.

After that, the shields he'd carefully built around his heart had gotten stronger. Harder. He'd told himself he was fine being alone. He had his business, his friends, and never wanted for female company.

Until Lydia.

He swallowed hard, remembering the way she'd looked before he walked away hours ago. Her eyes dark and full of clouds he knew he'd put there. Because he hadn't been honest. Not with himself and not with her. He'd walked away without telling her how he truly felt about her, because he'd been too damn scared she didn't feel the same way.

If he was truly honest, he was still scared. She'd found the tiniest chink in the armor of his heart, and burrowed her way in. And now that the barrier was breached he had no idea how to close it again. She was there, whether he wanted her to be or not. And when she left today, it would hurt like hell, because he'd let her in.

He stood there for ten minutes, but thoughts were still buzzing like flies in his head.

"I know you said you needed space, but I wanted to check if you were okay." His dad stood next to him, holding two Styrofoam cups of coffee. He offered one to Jackson, who took it silently, lifting it to his lips and taking a mouthful of the bitter drink.

"I just needed to get out of there."

"Most people feel that way about hospitals," his dad said.

Jackson laughed, and Ryan smiled at him.

"I'm sorry," his dad said quietly. "For messing you up with our relationship. I know things haven't been easy for you. Not with Hayley leaving you and all."

"That was years ago," Jackson told him. "And she did me a favor."

"I'd agree with that. To a point. She certainly wasn't good enough for you." Ryan sipped at his coffee. "But she also hurt you. Even if you pretended everything was fine. The same way me asking your mom to leave hurt you. It might have been for the greater good, but it doesn't make it any less painful."

"Yeah." Jackson leaned his head against the brick. "I guess it's like lancing a boil. It hurts, but you gotta get the pus out."

Ryan laughed. "Another good description of Hayley. But seriously, I'm sorry that we never had this conversation before. We should have. But I'm just not good at talking."

"Yeah, well there are a lot of things I should've said before. Like I hate the way you always give in to mom whenever she needs anything."

Ryan nodded. "I know. But she's different from us. She's not strong. And she's still your mom."

"She's an adult," Jackson pointed out. "There has to come a time when we stop bailing her out."

"You're right." Ryan sighed. "I'll tell her there are some conditions to me taking her home. First of all, she needs to agree to get some help. Proper counseling. And she needs to stop asking for money."

"And if she doesn't?"

Ryan caught Jackson's eye. "Then we learn to say no."

Jackson smiled. "Good."

Ryan eyed Jackson carefully. "And where are you?" he asked. "I don't mean the hospital, but where are you with life? I know you and Lydia got pretty close these past two weeks."

"I've fallen in love with her," Jackson admitted. "Every damn part of me aches when I think about her."

Ryan's eyes opened wide at his son's candor. "You love her?" he asked, a smile breaking out on his face. "That's great."

"She leaves today. And she has no idea how I feel." Jackson pulled at his hair, letting out a sigh. "I need to call her. Tell her."

"What time's her flight?"

Jackson glanced at his watch. "Twelve. She has to leave Angel Sands by eight to get there in time."

"You should drive to see her. You have enough time. Some things should be said face to face."

Jackson lifted his head. His dad was right. He couldn't let Lydia get on that airplane without telling her how he felt. Couldn't let her go without touching her, feeling her, seeing her.

"I need my car keys," he said, then shook his head. "How will you and mom get back?"

His dad smiled. "That's my problem." He pulled the keys from his pocket and passed them to Jackson. "Now go get your girl."

❊ 29 ❊

Could there be a worse time to hit complete gridlock? Only in the L.A. area could you get gridlock like this. They were bumper to bumper. Jackson gritted his teeth and looked out of the window. There was a cop car right next to him, idling in the middle lane as Jackson strummed his hands on the steering wheel, willing the car in front of him to move.

He'd been in such a rush to leave the hospital that he hadn't even turned the Bluetooth on his phone back on, having turned it off the previous night to save his damn battery. And though he'd sent a message to Lydia before he left, telling her he was coming to talk to her, there was no way he could pull his phone out of his pocket and start typing on it now.

Not when the cop kept looking over at him, as though he had *criminal intent* stamped on his forehead.

There was a chopper overhead, the blades twirling and reflecting the morning sun. It belonged to one of the local TV stations, and was no doubt giving a report to whatever news was causing the back up.

The car in front of him moved forward a yard. He gritted

his teeth and did the same. The clock on the dash told him it was almost eight. Lydia would be on her way to the airport soon. There was no way for him to make it to her in time.

After ten minutes of moving forward an inch at a time, he saw a ramp ahead, and quickly tapped the details of the airport into his GPS, breathing out a mouthful of air when he saw he could make it there by ten.

It took another fifteen minutes of waiting on the ramp before he was able to join the highway and press his foot down on the gas. There wasn't enough time to stop and call her, not if he wanted to make it to the airport before she left. He weighed the two options in his head, pressing a little harder with his sneaker. Face to face was the only way.

He wasn't ready to tell her he loved her over the phone. Though if he had to, he would.

Since he was a kid, he'd watched people walk in and out of his life, without asking them to stay. He'd watched his dad, believing him to be weak, when all along he'd been the strong one.

Now it was his time to be strong. To fight for what he wanted.

And the only thing he wanted was her.

"Any sign?" Autumn asked, as Lydia pressed her face against the window. She shook her head, remembering the text message she'd woken up to that morning.

I really want to see you before you leave. I'm going to head to Angel Sands now. Should be at Griff's before you head to the airport. I hope you're doing okay. J xx

. . .

There'd been no mention of his mom, or anything else. Just a few simple words that had set her heart on fire.

But despite his promise, there was no sign of him.

"If we want to make it to the airport on time, we need to leave now," Griff told her. Lydia's huge suitcase was in the hall, where it had been since she'd woken at six that morning.

"I'll call him again," she said. But like the other two times, it rang a few times then went to voicemail. Pulling the phone from her ear, she turned to look at her sister and Griff, who was cradling Skyler in his arms as she played with his hair. "He isn't answering," she said softly, and Autumn winced.

"What do you want to do?" Autumn asked her. "If we don't leave now you'll miss your flight."

Lydia blinked back the tears that had been threatening all morning, and took a deep breath. "I can't miss that flight. I have obligations," she said, ignoring the ache in her heart. "We should go," she said, though it only made her chest hurt more. "I'll just send Jackson a message to let him know we're leaving."

And pray to God he gets it before he shows up and we're gone.

"Okay then." Autumn stood and walked over to hug her. "It'll work out. I know it will."

She barely spoke on the drive to the airport. Her chest felt too full to form any coherent words. Instead, she stared out of the window, as she sat in the backseat next to Skyler, looking at the same scenery she'd seen on her way into town almost two weeks ago.

In Jackson's car.

Skyler was kicking her legs, laughing when her sock started to work its way down her feet.

"You're gonna lose them, you little monkey," Lydia told her, pulling them back up so that Skyler could do it all over again.

Every now and then she'd press her finger on her phone screen, just to make sure it was working. And every time the photograph of Skyler that was her wallpaper would come, with no mention of a message or missed call. Her heart felt like it it was breaking.

When they walked into the departure lounge, the bustle and the noise was overwhelming. Griff had stayed in the car with Skyler, leaving Autumn to walk with Lydia into the airport. She looked up at the screens lining the wall, and saw her flight listed.

"Desk thirty-eight," Lydia murmured, giving her sister a closed-lipped smile. "I guess this is where we say goodbye."

"I could stay," Autumn offered. "Walk you to security at least."

"No, it's okay." She kind of wanted to be alone with her misery. Her phone was still resolutely silent. Maybe once she was through security her heart would accept that she was really leaving without seeing Jackson again. "Thank you for everything." She hugged Autumn tightly. "Now go back to Griff and your adorable baby before he racks up a fortune in parking costs."

"Are you sure?"

"Yep. I'm sure."

Autumn sighed. "Okay. Let me know once you're through security. And call me when you land in Barcelona. I worry about you."

"Of course I will." Lydia glanced at her phone again before looking up.

Giving her a worried glance, Autumn nodded. "Maybe he'll call you when you get to Spain."

"Maybe." Lydia forced her shoulders to roll back, and lifted her cheeks to brighten her smile. "I love you. Now go."

Autumn laughed gently. "I love you, too. Safe journey. I'm going to miss you like crazy."

With her passport in hand, Lydia walked toward the check-in desk and stood in line, pressing her lips together as she checked her bags, before heading to security. She was three people from the front when her phone rang. She looked down, fully preparing herself for it to be Autumn, checking if she was through security yet.

But she saw his name, and her heart leapt.

"Jackson?"

"Hey. I'm sorry. You'll never believe how long it took me to get here. Where are you?" He sounded breathless. Like he'd been running.

"I'm at the airport."

"Have you gone through security?"

The man at the front was pointing her toward a scanner. "Not yet. But I'm just about to."

"Shit. Don't go. I'm almost there. I can see you, I think."

There was a man in a suit behind her. He seemed so desperate to get through security, his body was almost pressed against hers. "You should go first," she told him, her phone still at her ear. "You seem in a hurry."

"Lydia!"

The voice came in stereo, through her phone, but also echoing through the terminal. That's when she saw him, pushing his way around people, muttering apologies as he moved determinedly toward her.

She wasn't sure whether to laugh or cry. In the end she did both, tears stinging at her eyes as her lips curled into a grin. Ignoring the muttering behind her, she ducked under the tape barrier and ran toward him, clutching her phone in one hand, her passport and boarding pass in the other.

Jackson swept her into his arms, burying his face in her hair as he twirled her around. "Thank god," he murmured. "I thought I'd missed you."

"You nearly did." She was as breathless as he was. "How's your mom?"

"She's battered but okay. Dad's taking her home with him to recuperate."

"That's such good news." She was beaming up at him. "I can't believe you're here. I really thought that was it."

"If I didn't make it in time, I was already planning on booking a flight to Barcelona. There was no way I could let you go without seeing you."

But he was still letting her go. The hope in her chest died a little.

"I need to tell you something before you leave," he continued, his breath still coming fast. "It's something I should have already told you, but I was too damn chicken shit to admit it. But not anymore." He brushed the hair from her face, his expression soft. God, he was beautiful. She'd already forgotten how much he sent her heart spinning. And how tall he was, compared to her small stature – especially in the sneakers she was wearing for comfort. "And before I do, you need to know I don't expect anything in return. I just need you to know this before you get on the plane."

"What?" she asked, her brows knitting.

"I'm so damn in love with you it hurts," he told her, sliding his nose against hers until their lips connected in a soft, gentle kiss. "You're beautiful, funny, and you've changed me in every way. When I walked into the airport to pick you up I was somebody else. Somebody who didn't see the beauty in life. But when you're around, I see it, Lydia. All of it."

Her heart clenched. "I love you, too," she told him. "So much."

His smile was glorious. It sent a wave of warmth through her, from the tip of her head to the end of her toes.

"You don't know how happy I am to hear that."

She grinned back at him. "I can hazard a good guess."

Because she felt it too, this happiness that washed over her. "So what happens next?"

"First of all, we need to work out when we can see each other again. I have a new member of staff starting next week, and I'll need to train him. But I figure I can get away in a month."

"*Away?*"

"I want to fly out to see you. Wherever you'll be in a month. France, Spain, Italy, I don't care. I just want to be with you."

Her heart started to speed. "I'll be in France."

"Then that's perfect."

"Can you really afford the time off?" she asked, hope lighting her up inside.

"I imagine it'll give Lisa the shock of her life, but yeah. I'm owed about five years' worth of vacation." He stroked her face softly with his fingertips. "What's the point of owning your own company if you can't give yourself time off?"

"What about Bella?" she asked. "Does that mean you won't be adopting her?"

"I'm still adopting her," he said firmly. "But my dad will help take care of her when I'm not there."

"You've thought of everything," she said, her lips still curled.

"I had a lot of time to think when I was driving here. I was stuck in traffic for hours."

She pressed her hand against his, as he cupped her jaw. "I'd love to see you in France. That'll give me a chance to make some plans."

He gave her a questioning stare. "What kind of plans?"

"I've been thinking, too," she admitted. "And I kind of had a revelation." She didn't have time to tell him all the details about her talk with Autumn. That would have to wait. "All this time, I've been searching for what filled my soul. And here you were, all along, waiting patiently for me."

"I'll always wait for you," he told her, pressing his lips to hers. "You're worth waiting for."

"Well, now that I've found you, I want to be with you. So I figure I can travel a little less. Maybe only take on four jobs a year once I fulfill my outstanding commitments."

He looked surprised. And happy. "What will you do with the rest of the time?"

"I can still plan clients' vacations for them and charge a premium for that. I just won't always be there to show them around." Her eyes were bright. "And maybe I can diversify. Do some travel writing, or help people run their social media. Like I did with Deenie."

"You'd be amazing at that. Deenie's already singing your praises everywhere."

"Sometimes people just need a little nudge. I can run training sessions or something." She grinned. "And the rest of the time, there's this guy who needs to learn how to relax. I figure I can make that my life's work."

"I don't feel relaxed when I'm with you," he told her, his voice dipping as he kissed her again. "I feel alive."

An announcement came over the P.A. and Lydia looked at the line for security. It was getting longer by the minute. She turned back to Jackson, who was looking at the same thing.

"You need to go."

A sigh escaped her lips. "I don't want to."

"I know, sweetheart. But I'm only a few weeks behind you. Get on that plane to Barcelona, and give that family the best vacation they can have. And when you're done working, I'll meet you in Paris."

"Can we talk every day?" she asked him.

"I'm counting on it. We'll talk and message and video chat. The time will fly. I promise."

Her body relaxed. "Four weeks," she said softly. "I guess I can do that."

"Four weeks isn't long when it's compared to the rest of your life," he told her, pressing his hand to the small of her back as they walked to the end of the security line. "Will you wait for me?" he asked. She knew from his tone he wasn't only talking about the next few weeks. He was asking her to be his.

"Always," she promised. "I'll always wait for you."

He was right. A few weeks was nothing. She'd been waiting all her life for him, and just hadn't realized it.

He kissed her hard this time, and she kissed him back, memorizing each touch so that it could carry her through their separation.

"Will you wait for me, too?" she asked back when they parted, so aware that in a few moments she'd be walking through security.

"Lydia Paxton," he murmured, running his hands through her silky hair. "You're the best thing that's happened to me. And the only thing worth waiting for."

EPILOGUE

S *ix Months Later...*

Her flight had landed late, and her stupid damn luggage was the last to appear on the carousel, taunting her as it slowly made its way around to where Lydia was waiting impatiently. She grabbed her three suitcases and somehow maneuvered them through customs, waddling like a duck as she walked into the arrivals terminal.

The California sun was bright, shining through the glass wall of the airport, warming her skin as she rushed through the sliding doors.

And then she saw him. Well, them. Jackson and Bella, sitting in his car. And her heart did a little flip.

It had been two months since they'd last been together, the longest time they'd been apart since that fateful day at the airport when they'd declared themselves. These eight weeks had been the longest of her life, even though they'd managed to speak to each other every day. Even the days when she was up in the Pyrenees Mountains between France and Spain and had to walk for a mile to find reception.

Finally spotting her, Jackson's face lit up as he opened the driver's door and almost ran to where she was standing. Clearing the last few feet, he picked her up and swung her around, pressing his lips to hers with an impatient, hot kiss.

"You made it," he said, his voice low. "Damn, you look good."

"I look terrible. I've been traveling for twenty-four hours."

He shook his head. "Nope. You look amazing. You always do." With a final kiss, he put her back down on the sidewalk, and grabbed her bags. "You traveled light this time," he joked.

"I bought a few gifts," she admitted. "Some cute outfits for Skyler, and a matching scarf for you, me and Bella."

Hearing her name, Bella barked loudly, her tail wagging like crazy as Lydia leaned in to give her a hug. "I'm happy to see you, too, pumpkin," Lydia told her, as Bella licked her face all over. "She looks like she's grown," Lydia said, turning back to Jackson. Damn, it was so good to see him. She loved to travel, but she loved to be with him more.

Jackson shook his head. "I might have given her too many treats after the last time I came back. She's on a strict diet now." In the past six months, he'd visited her in France, Argentina, and most recently, Bali. Those had been her favorite locations, showing him all the places she loved, introducing him to her friends. She'd discovered he was an intrepid explorer. He had no fear, not when he was riding down a zip line over a deep gorge, nor when they climbed part of Mont Blanc with a tour guide.

And the nights when he held her close, after an evening of good food, wine, and dancing, were her favorites of all.

Once Jackson had put her cases into the trunk – though one had to go in the back seat next to Bella – he walked around to the passenger side and opened it up. Lydia went to follow him, but he put up his hand.

"You're driving," he told her, pointing at the other side of the car. "That's your seat."

"Seriously? I haven't driven for two months." Not since he'd given her intensive lessons the last time she came to Angel Sands, and somehow she'd managed to pass her test and obtain her license.

"It's like riding a bike, you have to practice. Use it or lose it, baby."

"It's your funeral." She shrugged with a smile. "Possibly literally."

"Get in and drive, woman." He winked. "We've got things to do."

It took her half an hour to warm up to the car. Thirty minutes of jolting stops, shuddering accelerations, and turns that were more like diversions, they were so far off the mark. But eventually she relaxed, right as she turned off the highway and they reached the hills and brush above Angel Sands.

"How's your dad?" she asked him, feeling more confident as the minutes past.

"He's good. He beat Frank Megassey in the Angel Sands Chess Tournament, so he's riding on a high from that."

Lydia grinned. She had such a soft spot for Ryan. He was already like a second father to her. "And your mom?"

"I spoke to her a couple of weeks ago. She has a job. Only part time, but it's a start." Jackson shrugged. "As long as she's paying her own way, I'm good."

She loved the way he looked so relaxed about his parents. He'd really taken his dad's words to heart, letting them sort out their own problems. Which was good, because right now she wanted him to concentrate on her.

They had a lot of catching up to do.

In front of her, the Pacific Ocean danced and sparkled, as though it was filled with a million tiny diamonds. She could feel the warmth of the sun on her face through the windshield, making her smile.

"The water looks so pretty today."

"Does it?" Jackson murmured. "I can't see past the view right here."

Her smile widened. "Hey, have you heard from Simba's family recently?"

"He and Bella had a play date on the beach last week," Jackson told her. "The two of them had a contest to see who could shake the most water off and get us drenched. We called it a tie."

"Can we arrange another play date soon? I've missed that guy."

Bella barked. "But not as much as I've missed you, pretty girl," Lydia crooned.

"Hey, stop!" Jackson called out. Without thinking, she pressed her foot to the brake.

"What is it?" she asked, as his car came to a juddering halt.

But he was out of the car, pulling Bella's door open and running into the shrubs. Was this the same spot that she'd found Eddie? Lydia frowned, it certainly looked like it. What were the chances he'd spotted *another* dog?

By the time she climbed out and chased after them, Jackson and Bella were at least thirty yards ahead. She ran, feeling breathless already, coming to a stop where they were both standing in front of a large brown rock.

"What is it?" she puffed. "Did you see an animal?"

Jackson shook his head. "No," he told her. "Not an animal." He pointed at something, and she leaned over the rock to get a better look. It was nestled in a crevice, glinting in the sun.

Slowly, she turned to look at Jackson. Her chest was already tight from her sprint across the grass, but now it was tighter still. "Is that...?"

Jackson picked the glinting gem from the rock and dropped to his knee, holding it out for her to see. It was a beautiful white gold ring, set with a square diamond at the center, bordered by more sparkling gems at the edges. Lydia swallowed hard, her eyes watering as Jackson smiled up at her.

"Yes!" she said, before he could open his mouth.

Jackson laughed and shook his head. "I have a speech planned. I practiced it on Bella last night."

Bella barked as if in agreement.

"Okay." Lydia nodded. "But I thought I'd take the tension out of it. The answer is definitely yes." She bit her lip. "Sorry, go ahead. I'm listening."

His lip quirked as he stared up at her, his eyes full of love. "Lydia Paxton, will you do the honor of being my wife? Not because I want you to be tied to me, but because I want us to fly together. To land together. To live together wherever we decide to call home. And I don't care where that is, because home isn't a place. Not anymore. Home is you, and wherever you go, that's where I'll be."

Her chest hitched. "I want home to be here," she whispered. "I want to be here with you." She'd been thinking about it for months. She'd always want to travel, to see new places and familiar friends. But Angel Sands was her anchor. She was drawn to it like a magnet. "You once told me I was like the sun, lighting everything up. But that's not true. You're the sun. I was a planet without an orbit until I met you. You made me want things I never knew I could have." A tear ran down her cheek. "And you taught me to drive, which makes you the bravest man I know."

He chuckled. "It was scarier than that zip line in Bali." He slid the ring onto her finger, and she held it up, her heart full of love and happiness.

He stood and kissed her, his lips warm and certain. She held onto him like she held onto the rocks when she climbed Mont Blanc. Like he was her lifeline.

Maybe he was.

"Come on," Jackson said when they parted, sliding his arm around her waist. "The whole town is waiting for us at Déjà Brew."

"They know about your proposal?"

He lifted an eyebrow. "You can't keep a secret in a small town. Blame Bella, she's a blabbermouth."

Lydia looked down at Bella. Her tail was wagging, her tongue lolling, and if she wasn't a dog, Lydia would swear she was grinning up at them.

He was right. Home wasn't a town or a city or any physical location. It was the thing that filled your soul. The place in your heart filled with the people you loved.

And she'd finally found it.

She rested her head on his shoulder as he led her back to the car, still holding her hand up to admire the ring.

"Okay then, handsome," she told him. "Take me home."

DEAR READER

Thank you so much for reading Jackson and Lydia's story. If you enjoyed it and you get a chance, I'd be so grateful if you can leave a review. And don't forget to keep an eye out for HEART AND SOUL the next book in the series, releasing in summer 2021

I can't wait to share more stories with you.

Yours,

Carrie xx

ABOUT THE AUTHOR

Carrie Elks writes contemporary romance with a sizzling edge. Her first book, *Fix You*, has been translated into eight languages and made a surprise appearance on *Big Brother* in Brazil. Luckily for her, it wasn't voted out.

Carrie lives with her husband, two lovely children and a larger-than-life black pug called Plato. When she isn't writing or reading, she can be found baking, drinking an occasional (!) glass of wine, or chatting on social media.

You can find Carrie in all these places
www.carrieelks.com
carrie.elks@mail.com

ALSO BY CARRIE ELKS

ANGEL SANDS SERIES

Let Me Burn

She's Like the Wind

Sweet Little Lies

Just A Kiss

Baby I'm Yours

Pieces Of Us

Chasing The Sun

Heart And Soul (Releases Summer 2021)

THE HEARTBREAK BROTHERS SERIES

Take Me Home

Still The One

A Better Man

Somebody Like You (Coming March 2021)

THE SHAKESPEARE SISTERS SERIES

Summer's Lease

A Winter's Tale

Absent in the Spring

By Virtue Fall

THE LOVE IN LONDON SERIES

Coming Down

Broken Chords

Canada Square

STANDALONE

Fix You

Made in the USA
Monee, IL
13 February 2021

60431592R00177